KING

Graham
Edwards

Talus
and the Frozen
King

SOLARIS

First published 2014 by Solaris
an imprint of Rebellion Publishing Ltd,
Riverside House, Osney Mead,
Oxford, OX2 0ES, UK

www.solarisbooks.com

ISBN: 978 1 78108 199 0

A CIP catalogue record for this book is available
from the British Library.

Designed & typeset by Rebellion Publishing

Printed in the US

For Helen

and in memory of Dot

CHAPTER ONE

SCREAMS RANG THROUGH the freezing night air.

Bran leaped up from where he'd been dozing by the fire. His worn moccasins scattered snow into the low flames, which hissed and spat in fury. He felt just as exhausted as when he'd settled down to sleep. He hadn't slept well for days; bad dreams about a wild ocean storm, and a sky full of fire, and a pale face framed with red hair.

Dreams about Keyli.

With his good hand, Bran grabbed the flint axe from his belt, then hurried to where Talus was standing on the cliff edge. Away from the fire, the air was bitter. Bran pulled his bearskin tight around him. His breath clouded briefly before freezing onto his beard. The screams came again, stronger now. His heart pounded against his ribs.

'What is it?' he said.

'Trouble,' Talus replied.

The wind whipped Talus's robe open, exposing his skinny body to the elements. Bran wondered how he could stand the cold. But Talus was strange. After two years Bran should have been used to his behaviour, but he wasn't.

Mindful of his footing, Bran peered over the cliff edge. Below them the sea breathed, not stormy like the one in his dream, just restless under the stars. Even at this distance its presence made him uneasy. Once he'd loved the ocean. Not any more.

Bran took a deep, cold breath. Gradually his heart slowed. But the screaming grew louder.

A little way offshore lay a small island, a random collision of cliff and turf and stunted willow, all of it smoothed white by snow. It looked like a submerged and sleeping beast.

A village crowded the island's lower slopes. It looked like many he and Talus had seen on their long journey north: solid protection in this icebound land. The houses were sunk into the landscape, so that only the low domed roofs were visible. Smoke rose from holes in the roofs. Inland, a long barrow marked the place where the tribe communed with the dead.

People were pouring out of the houses. They looked tiny, ants fleeing the nest. It was they who were screaming.

'I suppose you want to go down there,' Bran said, knowing the answer already.

'Of course! If we set off now, we will reach the causeway at low tide. Then it will be easy to cross.'

Bran rubbed his aching head. Whatever tragedy had struck these villagers, it felt remote to him. He had troubles of his own. 'Causeway?'

'Look with your eyes, Bran. See? That dark line beneath the water?'

'All I see is an island, Talus.'

'Looking is more than just seeing. I suppose it is possible you might learn that one day.'

Bran's fist tightened on the axe's haft. This wasn't the first time he'd felt the urge to bury it in his friend's head. Not that he would ever hurt Talus.

Except hurting Talus was exactly what he was planning to do.

How would Talus react when Bran told him what he'd decided? Bran didn't know. He just knew the time had come to say what he needed to say.

He opened his mouth, but the words refused to come out.

Talus took a step nearer the edge of the cliff. He was a head taller than Bran, and stick-thin. His eyes, bright and alert, stared down at the sea. It confounded Bran that in the middle of winter his travelling companion never wore a hat, despite having not a single hair on his head.

'That island is surrounded by more than just water, Bran,' Talus said. 'It is surrounded by fear and mistrust. Its people are alone and afraid. They need help.'

'How can you possibly know that?'

'How can you not? Think about the other tribes we have met in this northern land. Where do they live?'

Bran wasn't in the mood for Talus's games. Nor did he have the energy to argue.

'I don't know. In the glens, I suppose.'

'Exactly! In the glens. I see you are at least half-awake. The glens offer shelter from the hard weather and the hunting is good. But these people choose to live on an island. Instead of comfort, they choose isolation. Why?'

Bran regarded the snowbound landscape. High hills rose swiftly into even higher mountains. The skyline was coarse and craggy, like a row of broken teeth.

'I wouldn't call any part of this land comfortable,' he said.

'Look near the island shore. See the maze they have built there?'

All Bran could see was a pattern of shadows marking the island's terrain. If Talus said it was a maze, who was he to argue?

'And you will of course see the totems placed around the shore.' Talus pointed.

Bran saw little dots. Maybe they had faces. 'Spirits of the afterdream. Nothing unusual in that.'

'Indeed. But do you see their expressions? They are twisted and their mouths are wide open. They are screaming, Bran.'

Bran shivered, not just at the winter wind. Maybe the screams they could hear weren't coming from the villagers at all. Maybe they were coming from the totems. Not the screams of the living, but the screams of the dead.

'You can see all that from here?'

'How can you not? Come! We must hurry. It will soon be dawn. But... I do not believe you will be needing that.'

Talus placed his hand on Bran's axe and pushed it down to his side. Bran hadn't even realised he was still brandishing it. Feeling a little foolish, he hooked the weapon back on his belt while Talus went to kick snow on the fire. The flames sputtered and died, and black smoke wafted skywards. The peat that had fuelled the fire hadn't burned well, but he was already missing its warmth.

Bran took a deep breath and held it in his chest. The air was ice in his lungs. He exhaled, making a fist of white vapour that crackled into frost the instant it touched the air. The screams were still rising from the island, chopped by the wind into staccato bursts of anguish. They were nothing to do with him.

Time to speak.

'I'm not going.'

Talus was busying himself with their packs, stowing their few belongings and making ready to leave. He didn't look up.

Bran stroked the flint head of the axe with the fingers of his right hand. His left hand was curled in a useless fist in the folds of his bearskin. The cold made it ache.

'I don't mean I'm not going to the island,' he went on. 'Well, I do mean that. I'm not going there either. I mean I'm not going anywhere. North, I mean. Talus...'

Bran stopped. How could he say this without it getting all tangled up? And why wasn't Talus helping him out?

He began again.

'It's nearly the solstice. It's been two years since we set out on this journey, Talus. On this search. And we're no nearer the end. I can't do this any more. Two years is... Talus, it's long enough.'

'Long enough for what?' Talus was rummaging in his rabbitskin pouch.

'Long enough to grow very tired.'

Bran wanted to say more, but he didn't have the words. Talus was the one who was clever with words.

* * *

TWO YEARS HAD passed since the night Bran had met Talus, that night when the winter storm had whipped the sea to a frenzy. When fire had rained down from the sky and Bran's life had changed forever. The fire had burned his left hand and turned it into a useless, scarred claw, but that wasn't the worst of it. The fire had taken his beautiful Keyli away from this world and into the next. Sometimes Bran's crippled hand still ached, but the ache of Keyli's absence was one that never went away.

Bran pinched his eyes shut and wished the memory gone. Keyli's death lived in his dreams but he couldn't bear to have it in his waking mind. Talus knew what had happened—he'd been there, after all—but Bran had never told the story to another living soul. Had never even told it to himself, not really.

Maybe one day...

This was his true burden, so much heavier than the leather pack he carried on his back: the old memory of that terrible night. He'd carried the memory a long way north already—so far. With every dawn he'd seen the land around them grow colder and more bleak, settlements more sparse, prey animals harder to find.

Now the land itself was beginning to break apart. The coast had become a shattered mess of inlets and islands. Even the mountains were breaking up. Yet north they continued to trek, even as the solid ground fell away beneath them. Soon the land would be altogether gone, and only the sea would remain.

And Bran was weary—more weary than he'd ever been before.

'I DON'T THINK there's any point in going on,' Bran said. 'The journey gets harder each day. I think... the time has come to end it.'

Talus faced him, his face unreadable, saying nothing.

'We don't even know if it's possible to get where we're going,' Bran went on. 'And even if it is, what will we find there? What if the old tales are... well, just tales?'

Talus continued to say nothing.

'What if there's nothing in the north at all?'

Still no response.

Confounded by his friend's silence, Bran looked out to sea again. 'We haven't seen the northlight for six whole moons now,' he said. 'We followed it all this way but now it's abandoned us. We were wrong. *I* was wrong. If you want to go on, that's all right, but I...'

Talus drew himself up to his full height. He smoothed his hand over his bald head. He was looking past Bran, for some reason unable to meet his friend's eye.

'Are you trying to say goodbye, Bran?'

Bran pressed the heel of his good hand against his eyes. He would not cry.

'Two years,' he said, substituting anger for grief. 'I've followed you on this cursed trail for two whole years. Well, now the trail's gone cold. You go on if you want, but I'm going back. I'm going home, Talus. I can't follow you any more.'

Three long strides brought Talus close. He was

smiling. He put his bony hands on Bran's shoulders. Still he was looking not at his companion but past him.

'Bran,' he said. 'Don't you know it is I who am following you?'

Bran's tears turned slowly to crystals of ice. 'You can't even look me in the eye,' he said.

'Why would I,' said Talus, 'when I can look at that?' He turned Bran round to face the ocean. There was unexpected strength in those scrawny arms.

Bran gasped. Something was happening in the pre-dawn sky. Something glorious. Green streamers rose from the northern horizon, expanded, became vast glowing rivers of light. The light was in constant motion, like flowing liquid. Its colour shifted from green to blue to orange to red.

It came towards them.

There were moving images inside the light: a string of women dancing in line, a shoal of iridescent fish, an eye, a skein of blood, beads of silver dew or sweat, a burning horse. The pictures formed and flowed and melted away, always changing, never still. Were they spirits or dreams? It didn't matter.

The shining parade rolled ever nearer, giddy in its ever-changing round. Now it was vast, all-encompassing. It poured around the little island and exploded over the cliff, over Bran's head. It met the mountains and dwarfed them. It was unearthly and welcome and entirely wonderful.

'The northlight,' Bran murmured.

The ache had gone from his hand, and from his head. Even from his heart. He still felt exhausted, but the coldness of the air, suddenly, was exhilarating.

'It's beautiful,' he said.

'It always was,' said Talus.

The sea continued to breathe below them, in and out, caressing the shore. Above them flowed another ocean: an ocean of light. Its power rained down on Bran, filling him from his toes to the crown of his head. Suddenly anything was possible.

Talus handed Bran his pack. 'Do you still wish to say goodbye?'

Already the eerie light was fading, washed away by the dawn that had started to creep over the mountains. Such fleeting magic. Bran didn't care. He'd seen it again. The northlight had returned.

'Is it true what they say, Talus? That love survives death?'

The last traces of the northlight danced in Talus's eyes.

'On the night we first met, Bran, you did me a great service, at enormous cost to yourself. In return, I promised to show you a sight no man has seen, to tell you a story no man has heard, to set you walking on a path no man has trod. A path, perhaps, that will lead you to the peace you crave. It is a promise I intend to keep. And so I ask you again: do you still wish to say goodbye?'

The last shreds of the northlight vanished into the brightening sky. Pale pink tendrils twisted briefly, making a shape that might have been a ghostly face, a phantom hand: a woman, beckoning.

Bran hefted his pack onto his shoulder. 'I suppose I could go a little further. But, Talus, what do we do when we run out of land?'

Talus clapped him on the back.

'Why, Bran, isn't it obvious? We find ourselves a boat! Now, shall we see what all that screaming is about?'

As they followed the narrow track down the cliff towards the shore, the sky to the east turned livid red. Once, when he looked that way, Bran thought he saw a figure standing on a ridgetop, silhouetted against the dawn, watching them.

But he couldn't be sure.

CHAPTER TWO

By THE TIME they reached the shore, the rising sun had appeared through a cleft in the mountains. The sky was crimson. Restless waves stroked the coarse grey shingle of the beach. Bran stood at the water's edge, his shadow fleeing from his feet and over the choppy sea.

The tide had ebbed enough to reveal a weed-strewn path extending through the shallows all the way to the island: Talus's causeway. It was made of six-sided stones, dark like slate. Bran had never seen anything like it before.

'Did they make this?' he said, momentarily distracted from the screaming and wailing that still filled the morning air.

'No man made this,' said Talus.

'You're sure about going over there?'

'We might help. And, perhaps, they might help us.'

Talus stepped out onto the peculiar stone path. The receding tide had left it wet and glossy. He walked fast, as he always did. Following carefully over the strange and slippery stones, Bran considered his options. Seeing the northlight again had energised him. Yet his sadness remained. His heart simply wasn't in this any more.

Torn by indecision, he asked himself a simple question: what would Keyli have done?

Well, he knew the answer to that. Keyli would have investigated. In life, her curiosity had been a match even for Talus's. She would have wanted to know what was going on here.

One more day, then. He would give Talus one day on this wretched island. Then he'd make up his mind, once and for all.

Bran's moccasins skidded on a patch of seaweed. Talus caught him before he could fall. Bran nodded his thanks and they moved on.

A pair of totems awaited them on the island's snow-dusted shingle beach: disembodied faces standing each as tall as Bran. They were slick with ice. Their jaws gaped; in their necks, stone tendons bulged. They were clearly the work of a skilled craftsman. Possibly a deranged one. Talus had been right. As usual.

Bran kept his head lowered and his eyes averted as they passed between the monolithic statues. The last thing he wanted to do was offend the island's ancestor spirits. These days, Bran didn't much care for the dead.

As always, Talus walked with his head high.

The defensive maze they'd seen from the cliff took the form of a network of trenches cut into the island's peaty soil. Rough stone walls kept the soil from spilling onto the paths, although, at this time of year, the earth was frozen solid.

They marched through the snow, Talus leading the way.

'We'll get lost,' said Bran. He tried to peer over the walls of the maze, but they reached above his head. The yawning faces of the totems had unnerved him. It was one whole turn of the moon since they'd last taken shelter in such a place, and he was getting used to the solitary life.

'That is impossible,' Talus replied. 'I can already see the pattern of the maze. It is a simple one.'

'If you say so.'

Talus chose turns seemingly at random. Bran followed, knowing better than to offer suggestions. The wailing grew steadily louder. Bran grew steadily more unhappy.

The way narrowed, the turns tightened. Bran was convinced Talus was leading them down a dead end. Surely now they must turn back.

He was about to tap Talus's shoulder when, without warning, the maze spun them round and ejected them into a wide arena.

Like the trenches, the open space was sunken and lined with stone. At the far end, a low passage led—Bran guessed—into the village itself. Numerous totems were spaced evenly around the arena's circular perimeter, some twice the height of a man. At least they had their mouths closed. Overhead, the crimson sky was laced with orange.

A crowd had gathered in the arena. Most wore thick furs; a few wore simple skins, layered against the cold. Many of the men held spears with stone tips. Their cheeks were purple in the cold. All looked grim. The women knelt in a ring around a seated man; it was they who were wailing.

Nobody seemed to notice their arrival. All attention was on the man on the ground. Like Bran, he was big, red-bearded. He was also naked, his bare skin rimed with ice. Around his head was a simple circlet of woven willow twigs. He was utterly still.

Bran felt an almost overwhelming urge to run away.

'Talus!' he hissed. 'I really think we should...'

'You!' A man stepped out of the crowd. The wailing of the women stopped abruptly.

The man stood as tall as Talus, and the deer-skull strapped to his head made him taller still. Eagle feathers adorned its giant antlers. Animal teeth rattled on a leather thong around his neck. His face was caked with blue paint, striped with yellow, reducing his features to an abstract pattern. He walked with a slight limp, aided by a long staff dressed with jangling shells.

He glanced at Bran, and stared at Talus.

'I am Mishina,' he said at last. 'I am shaman. Who are you?'

Talus sank to his knees and opened his robe. Unlike Bran's simple bearskin, Talus's clothing was a random patchwork of different animal hides: rabbit, seal, even wolf. Some weren't familiar to Bran at all.

Exposed to the cold air, Talus's bare chest began to resemble a plucked fowl, but he held firm without shivering.

'We come without weapons,' he said, 'in only our skins.'

Bran—who liked magic-men about as much as he liked totems—just glared.

'Without weapons?' said Mishina. 'Your friend carries an axe.'

'To make a fire, a man must cut wood,' Talus replied. 'We ask only to share words with you, and perhaps a little food.' He stood, wrapping his robe around his thin body again. 'And to offer what help we can. You have troubles.'

'Stay where you are,' the shaman said. He tossed his head. The antlers turned the gesture into a challenge. 'Say nothing. Do nothing.'

Talus dipped his head. 'As you wish.'

Meanwhile, several young men had pushed their way into the circle of women and were trying to lift the seated man. But he was heavy, and their fingers slipped on his icy skin. Bran wondered why the man wasn't able to stand himself. What kind of fool chose to sit unclothed in the snow in weather like this?

One particularly brawny character managed to wedge his hands under the man's thighs. He gave a grunt and lifted. At the same time, someone on the other side pushed, and the brawny man lost his grip. The seated man—who'd rocked momentarily onto one haunch—fell back to earth, hitting the ground with unexpected solidity. At last Bran realised what it was they'd stumbled upon, and scolded himself for not having seen the obvious at once.

The man in the snow was dead.

MORE MEN CROWDED round the corpse, practically fighting each other in their efforts to raise it up. The women started wailing again. The scene descended into absurdity. At last the shaman called a halt. He spoke quietly to one of the observers—a stocky man with thick sandy hair—who ran into the village. Moments later, the man returned dragging a litter woven from branches.

The women shuffled aside, still on their knees. They'd fallen quiet again, though several were now tearing their hair. With some effort, the men managed to slide the frozen corpse onto the litter. Its flesh was as unyielding as stone. When the body was finally in place, Mishina thumped his staff on the icy ground.

'Hashath has left this living land,' he cried. 'Our warrior-king hunts now with his fathers in the afterdream.'

The sandy-haired man clamped his arms across his chest. His face worked with emotion.

'I have run with the spirits,' the shaman went on. 'The spirits say that Hashath was tired of this world. They say that he knew his time had come, that he shed his clothes and walked into the night. That he gave his body to the ice. The spirits tell us now to honour the will of Hashath, and set the next warrior-king on his path.'

The men were nodding, and grunting agreement. The women began a slow, soft chanting. The men bent to the litter.

Talus coughed and stepped forward. Bran tried to grab him, but his crippled fingers slipped through his friend's robe.

'Whatever you're going to do, Talus,' he hissed, 'don't do it.'

'Forgive me for saying so,' said Talus to the shaman, 'but I think your spirits may be wrong.'

Mishina whirled round, his grip tightening on his staff. The bones around his neck rattled. The thick paint on his face made his expression impossible to read, but Bran guessed that Talus had made the shaman angry.

He sympathised. Talus did that to people a lot.

Five enormous strides carried Talus into the middle of the throng. The women shuffled aside to give him room; even some of the men fell back. Bran had seen this before: Talus looked frail, but there was something in his manner that could part crowds quicker than a charging boar. Bran's trepidation dissolved into a kind of fascinated pride.

The shaman was unimpressed by Talus's boldness. 'Back!' He raised his staff.

'Before you strike me,' said Talus, lifting his hands in placation, 'let me share my thoughts with you. They concern your king. You would do well to hear them.'

'You are a gull-of-the-storm in the guise of a man!' Cracked paint showered from Mishina's cheeks. He swung his staff—the tip of which was studded with flint shards—straight at Talus's head.

The sandy-haired man grabbed the staff just before it made contact. Thick muscles bunched in his forearm. Mishina grunted. Talus didn't move a muscle.

'Let the stranger speak,' said the man. 'If it concerns my father's death, I would know his wisdom. If not, then you may kill him.'

Talus beamed. 'Thank you. I will be brief. Mishina believes your king welcomed his own death – perhaps even brought it upon himself. I never knew your king in the living flesh, so I cannot know if he was a man to do such a thing. But I can look with my eyes. As an animal leaves its spoor on the ground, so a man leaves his marks everywhere he goes. Are there marks here that nobody has yet seen? I believe there may be.'

Here was another sight Bran had seen too many times to count: the faces of strangers growing slack and confused before one of Talus's bewildering speeches. He rubbed his beard to hide his smile.

'See these tracks!' said Talus. His sudden shout made several of the onlookers jump. He bounded around the corpse on its litter, pointing at scuffs and scrapes in the snow. Wherever he strode, the crowd opened to let him through. 'In your rush to see your dead king, many of you have trodden the snow.' He stopped, triumphant. 'But look: these two furrows lead exactly to where the body was resting.'

Talus crouched beside a pair of parallel grooves running back towards the village entrance. They were shallow and almost invisible amid the many footprints. Bran hadn't spotted them—nor, he suspected, had any of the islanders—but, now that Talus had pointed them out, they were impossible to miss.

'A heavy object was dragged here. Someone tried to cover the tracks it left. They failed. This tells me they were in a hurry.'

'You say "object,"' said the sandy-haired man. 'You mean my father?'

Talus stood. 'What is your name?'

The man squared his shoulders. 'I am Tharn. I am the eldest son of Hashath and warrior-king now to be. I would know what you have to say!'

'Well, Tharn, king-to-be, I believe your father was

24

either dead or asleep before he reached his final resting place. He did not walk here. He was dragged.'

'Asleep?'

'The kind of sleep from which you do not wake.'

'If someone found him dead, they would not have dragged him here,' said Tharn. 'They would have raised an alarm.'

'Mmm.' Talus bent to the corpse. Mishina hissed and raised his staff again, but Tharn waved him back.

Talus ran his bony fingers over the dead king's right shoulder. He explored the back of the neck, the broad chest. He stood, circled the body, stroked his own chin. He touched the king's right elbow, then the left.

Throughout this, Bran watched Tharn's brow descend further and further down over his eyes. At last it was too much.

'You insult my father!' Tharn shouted, seizing Talus.

In the same moment, Talus grabbed the wrist of the frozen king and yanked the dead man's left arm all the way up until it was pointing at the blood-red sky. There was a hideous cracking sound, and ice shards sprayed the crowd. Several of the women screamed. There was a collective bellow from the men. Tharn drew back his bunched fist.

'There!' Talus seemed oblivious to the uproar he'd caused. 'Please, Tharn, would you hold your father's arm for a moment?'

Bran was convinced the young man would punch Talus. Instead—looking dumbfounded—Tharn did as he was told.

Talus knelt and pointed to the hollow under the dead

king Hashath's arm. The skin there was pale and hard, bristling with frozen hairs.

There was also a small red hole.

'See?' said Talus. 'The blood froze quickly, so the wound was hidden beneath the king's upper arm. Here, this slight swelling in the muscle of his chest, this was how I knew to look. The wound is small, but deep. The edges of the wound are clean. The weapon was almost certainly carved from bone.'

Tharn placed his dead father's hand into Mishina's grasp. It was a strangely tender gesture. A lump rose in Bran's throat.

Gently, Tharn knelt beside Talus. He touched the tip of his finger to the wound under his dead father's arm. When he withdrew it, it came away clean. Just as Talus had said, the blood had frozen solid.

'What has happened?' said Tharn. His voice was gruff, unsteady.

Talus placed his hand on the young man's shoulder.

'I am sorry, Tharn,' he said. 'Your father was murdered.'

CHAPTER THREE

AT THARN'S COMMAND, a small group of men carried the litter away. Talus had thought Tharn would accompany his father's body; instead, after a brief consultation with Mishina, he came over to where Talus and Bran were standing. Five other men followed him.

'You will come with me,' said the dead king's son.

Tharn's companions closed around Talus and Bran. Talus read their faces, one after the next. All looked to be in a state of shock, from the lanky one who had trouble keeping his limbs folded, to the stout one who'd been first to try and lift the king. The third man repeatedly tossed his mane of unkempt hair; angry lines were etched into his cheeks. The youngest of the five was a beardless lad, striking for the darting, dazzling green of his eyes, and the hugeness of their pupils. Close beside him stood a dour, thick-set youth whose face was painted entirely black.

Despite their differences, all the men looked a little like each other, and a little like Tharn. Talus had no doubt the six of them were brothers.

Tharn led the group out of the arena and into the village. His brothers drove Talus and Bran, as horned aurochs might herd their calves to protect them from wolves. Mishina brought up the rear.

The route took them along narrow winding passages roofed with willow and turf. The village was another maze, this one fully enclosed. Piercing the passage walls were the entrances to the island's half-buried houses. Most of the doorways were blocked by heavy stone slabs; in a few, the slabs had been pushed aside to reveal firelit interiors.

Faces peered out to watch as they passed. Many were painted with coloured mud—yellow, brown, grey—and their expressions were hard to read. On the rest there was fear, shock, suspicion. Grief.

The procession stopped outside a house much bigger than its neighbours. The men passed one at a time inside. Overhead, the sky was red, the northlight long gone.

TALUS KNEW BRAN would be worried by the disappearance of the northlight. That was understandable. Bran believed the northlight was a river of spirits whose source lay at the outermost edge of the living world. Talus was prepared to accept that as a possibility.

He also knew it might just be colourful weather.

Most people thought weather was down to the spirits, too. Talus didn't agree. It wasn't that he didn't accept the possibility of the spirit world. It was just that, on this particular subject, he was uncertain.

Talus hated uncertainty.

For Bran, the northlight was bound up with his grief for Keyli. Over the course of the journey, Talus had watch that grief deepen. Bran's urge to reach the source of the northlight—where he hoped he might make contact with his dead wife for one final time—had grown with it. Bran was like a ripening fruit, so swollen now with emotion that one day soon he would surely burst.

So why Bran's sudden desire to turn back? It was a puzzle.

Talus relished puzzles.

Something hard jabbed into the small of Talus's back: Mishina's staff. Talus put questions about Bran to the back of his mind and stepped inside.

THE KING'S HOUSE was impressive, although Talus had seen much grander structures elsewhere. The low doorway led into a single circular room, big enough to hold twenty people. In the middle of the floor, a fire blazed on a stone hearth. Around the walls, alcoves held beds with straw mattresses and deerskin covers. Broad stone shelves reared opposite the doorway; on them were displayed skulls and shells and all manner of bone tools and knives. If the status of a man could be gauged by his possessions, the king had commanded great regard.

The roof was a wonder. Arcs of whalebone rose from the low stone walls to meet at a central point. Willow rafters spanned the gaps between the bones, and the whole structure was covered with thatched seaweed. Off-centre was a small smoke-hole. Even so, the air in the room was sooty and hot.

Talus wondered why—when the architecture was so clever—the ventilation was so poor. Then he spied a broken piece of driftwood dangling near the smoke-hole. Once, a screen must have hung there, cunningly shaped to guide the smoke out of the house. The breakage wasn't unusual, but it was odd that, in the house of the king, it had gone unrepaired.

The six brothers seated themselves, leaving Talus and Bran isolated near the doorway. Mishina stood behind them, tall and aloof, blocking the exit.

In one of the alcoves, a woman loitered, her face lost in shadow.

'Say nothing,' Talus said to Bran. Addressing the others, he said, 'We thank you for admitting us into your circle.'

Tharn waved his hand dismissively. He was seated alone on a stone chair beside the rack of shelves: the king's throne. His brothers sat cross-legged on the floor around the central fire.

'Sit,' said Tharn. His face betrayed no emotion.

Talus and Bran joined the men at the fire. The murky air was stifling, but the heat was welcome after endless days on the tundra.

The woman slipped out of the alcove, and Bran gasped. Talus saw why: the woman had red hair and pale skin, just like Keyli.

Talus considered advising Bran this was not his wife. But Bran's muscles, which had tightened upon sight of the woman, had already relaxed. Bran might be hot-headed, but he wasn't stupid.

The red-haired woman carried shallow clay dishes filled with liquid. She handed them round, then slipped away, passing Mishina and vanishing into the morning light. Bran's eyes remained fixed on the doorway for some breaths after she'd gone. Relishing the look of her, perhaps, but also gauging the distance to their only escape route.

Talus hoped his companion didn't do anything foolish.

He took a sip from his dish: it was a shellfish stew, salty and flavoured heavily with herbs. Bran took up his own dish and drained it in one gulp. Talus heard the growling as the hot food entered the big man's belly. He put his own stew down unfinished. Even without looking, he knew his friend was eyeing it with hunger.

'My father is dead,' said Tharn. His voice was quiet, but it filled the room. 'Someone has killed him. Someone has killed the king.'

Silence fell in the dead king's house. Every face was grim. And no wonder: these were his sons. But there was more to it than that. Even Talus had been shocked by the slaying. To kill a man was wrong. To kill a king was... unthinkable.

A king was spirit-chosen, more than a man. To kill a king was to do than merely snuff out a man's life: it was to invite the wrath of every ancestor who'd ever lived. When the murderer's turn finally came to pass into the afterdream, he would be hounded and tortured by his enraged ancestors for all eternity. What man would consign himself to such an unspeakable torment?

'If I may speak...' Talus began.

'You will be silent,' snapped Mishina from the doorway. 'You are alive only by the word of Tharn the king-to-be.'

'Then I will address myself to Tharn.'

31

Tharn silenced them both with a brisk chop of his hand. 'Stranger, you will not speak unless I say.'

Talus nodded. Bran fidgeted. He was right to be uneasy: they were lucky to have made it this far alive.

'Two strangers come to Creyak,' said Tharn, 'and my father dies. It worries me that these two things happen on the same night. It is a...' Tharn frowned.

'A coincidence?' said Talus.

'It makes me suspicious. Here in Creyak we enjoy a peaceful life, but we are not without our enemies. What I do not yet know is this: are *you* my enemy?' He glared first at Talus, then at Bran. 'And *you*?'

'You don't want to call me an enemy,' said Bran.

'Easy, my friend,' Talus murmured. The tension had returned to Bran's body. Talus hoped his temper wasn't returning with it.

'I will hear your names,' said Tharn. He held Bran's gaze. 'Then I will hear your tale. Though I doubt such vagabonds have any skill in the art of telling.'

'My name is Bran. And I'm no vagabond.'

Bran snapped out the words. Tharn continued to glare at him. Talus waited for the explosion, but it didn't come.

'Go on,' said Tharn.

'We're travellers, if you must know. We've been walking for a very long time. We want to... we are walking towards... look, it's better if I let my companion tell you. He's... better with words.'

All attention turned to Talus. Bran let out a long, slow breath. Talus nodded, acknowledging the big man's self-control.

Tharn seized a long bone knife from the shelf beside him and twirled it in his fingers. 'Then tell,' he said. 'But be quick. My father is dead and my mood is dark.'

'As my friend has said, we are travellers,' Talus said. 'We are in search of a great prize. We travel in peace and make company where we find it. We are not the cause of your troubles.'

'Prize?' said Tharn. 'What prize?'

'We seek the place where the northlight touches the world.'

Tharn snorted. 'The northlight? What madness is this? As for making company, what trade do you have for the food and shelter you no doubt take from those you visit? You are old and unmuscled, and your friend is a cripple.'

As soon as the word left Tharn's lips, Talus knew they were in trouble. He tried to hold Bran down, but there was no stopping him. Bran's face, always ruddy, turned purple. He leaped to his feet, drew his flint axe and slashed it through the air. Its blade caught the edge of the flames licking out from the hearth, stirring them to a frenzy.

'I am no cripple!' he bellowed, and pointed his axe straight at Tharn.

Before Bran could make another move, the brother with the wild hair surged forward and threw an arm round his neck. With his free hand he grabbed the haft of Bran's axe. Unbalanced, the two men lurched backwards; if Bran's weight had been on his other foot, they'd have both tumbled straight into the fire.

Locked together, Bran and his assailant spun towards

33

the far wall. Talus began to rise, only to be pulled back down by the long-limbed man beside him. The lad with the green eyes was standing too, but a curt gesture from Tharn made him thump back down to the floor, resigned simply to watching like the others.

The two combatants continued to grapple. It was a strange contest. Limbs were flexed, grunts were expelled, but no actual blows were traded. They circled the room like dancers, locked together. Despite Bran's apparent advantage of weight, they seemed perfectly matched in strength.

'Pull him down, Fethan!' called the youngster. If he couldn't join in, at least he could shout his support.

'Arak!' warned Tharn.

The lad hugged his knees. His eyes were wide with excitement.

Stumbling sideways, Bran and Fethan came close to a stone slab lying askew on the floor. The slab was clearly designed to cover the square pit beneath it, but it had been left askew and the pit was partially uncovered. Talus had already guessed what was stored down there.

Bran tried to trip Fethan, but the Creyak man resisted. Distracted, he lost his grip on Bran's axe. Bran seized the advantage, pulling briefly back from his opponent and raising his weapon ready to strike.

But, in retreating, Bran planted his foot on the stone slab. It tipped, throwing him backwards. His left leg plunged into the pit, raising a huge splash of water. He scrabbled, desperate to free himself, but he was stuck half in and half out of the pit, his axe trapped beneath his body.

The youngster could no longer contain himself. He jumped up and waved his arms. 'Kill him, Fethan! Kill the killer!'

Fethan dropped to his knees and yanked at something dangling round his neck on a leather thong: a bonespike. The little weapon flashed in the firelight as Fethan thrust it hard against Bran's throat. Bran froze. A tiny bead of blood gathered at the tip of the bonespike.

Silence descended on the room.

CHAPTER FOUR

DESPITE HIS DESPERATE position, Bran was coiled and ready to turn on his attacker. If he tried it, he would certainly die. The tiny movements in his throat increased the pressure of the smooth, ivory spike on his neck, and the red bead there gradually swelled. With detached curiosity, Talus wondered how long it would be before Bran's blood started to gush.

Talus looked at Tharn. The son of the dead king was staring right back at him.

Talus rose to his feet. He stretched out his hands, palms down.

'I ask you to forgive my friend,' he said. 'He acts before he thinks.'

'He is a senseless idiot who deserves to die.'

'Perhaps. But he also happens to be a fisherman of great skill and experience. This might interest you: I see you keep limpets for bait.'

The sudden change of subject confused Tharn, just as Talus had hoped it would. The other men around the fire glanced at each other uncertainly. Fethan glowered.

By way of explanation, Talus indicated the water-filled pit into which Bran had plunged. Jostling against Bran's submerged leg were hundreds of shellfish.

'Bran is very good with boats. He knows both pole-fishing and the spear. He has also learned the way of nets, is that not right, Bran?'

Bran nodded as best he could without impaling himself on the bonespike.

'What are... *nets*?' said Tharn.

Talus smiled. 'Perhaps we have something to trade after all. Bran, and... Fethan, I believe that is your name? Please, stop fighting and join us again. Drink more of this delicious broth.'

Slowly, Bran lifted his right hand, his good hand, the hand in which he'd held his axe. Then he raised his left, the one forever curled into a useless fist. Talus recognised the effort of will it took his companion to offer surrender, and respected him for it.

But Fethan was having none of it. Raising his shoulders, he increased the pressure of the bonespike on Bran's throat. His mouth was contorted into a ferocious grin. He looked deranged.

'Fethan,' said Tharn. 'Let him go.'

For a long moment, Fethan did nothing. Then, with a sudden flourish, he hung the bonespike back round his neck and rejoined his companions by the fire.

A low sigh passed round the circle, and the tension drained out of the room. The lad with the restless green eyes nudged his black-faced neighbour, whispered something in his ear. The other boy didn't respond. If anything, he looked half asleep.

Bran clambered out of the pit. The furs on his left leg were sodden.

'I'm sorry,' he said, addressing Tharn.

Without speaking, Tharn pointed to the gap in the circle where Bran had been sitting. Bran took his place there and stared at the flames in the hearth. He looked defeated.

Shells rattled as Mishina left his post at the door. He limped up to Talus and jabbed him with the end of his staff.

'When I first saw your shambling friend—this fishing man who calls himself Bran—I thought him a bear,' the shaman said. 'His behaviour in the house of the king shows that is exactly what he is: a red-haired, angry bear. Be glad of the mercy of the king-to-be, for that is the only reason he is still alive.'

'We are grateful,' Talus agreed.

'And you? You are no fishing man. What is your name, and what do you bring to Creyak? Apart from trouble, that is.'

'I bring you no trouble. Nor does my friend, who is not a bear but just an ordinary man. As am I.'

'Then what do you offer? Speak well: you are speaking for your life.'

Talus considered his options and decided the moment had come to introduce himself properly. In a single, fluid movement, he stood and opened his arms. He made his voice very loud.

'I bring you tales! I bring you stories from now and to be and ago. Where there are hearts to beat, I bring the adventure to make them race. Where there are ears to hear, I bring the music of song. My tales may be long or short, but they will never be tall. I bring laughter and sorrow, wonder and despair, tragedy and triumph. I am the word-that-wanders, the riddle-that-rhymes.' He executed a deep bow. 'I am Talus, the bard.'

Tharn drew back his arm and hurled the knife he'd been twirling. It landed in a far corner with an echoing clatter.

'*Bards and fishermen!*' he roared. 'The king of Creyak is dead! Show me you did not kill him, or I will kill you myself!'

Talus bowed again. 'I will show you what you ask for. But first, may I ask a question?'

Tharn was shaking from head to toe. His hands compressed into fists, relaxed, compressed again.

'My question is this,' said Talus before Tharn could protest. 'Tharn, you have already had your father's body taken to the burial cairn. Do you intend to begin the funeral rites today?'

'Of course!' said Tharn. 'My father is dead. His journey to the afterdream starts at once.'

'Mmm.' Talus stepped out of the circle. He started pacing up and down the room. 'It is just that, before the king's journey begins, I believe there is a story here that should be heard. Unfortunately that story is in knots. Before it can be told, it must be untied.'

'My father's story is over.'

'But that of his murderer is not.'

'It will be. When you are dead.'

'And if Bran and I are not the ones who killed the king?'

'Then it will remain a mystery.'

'Does that not bother you?'

'No. It is not my concern. Whoever killed the king will receive his punishment when his own life ends and he enters the afterdream himself, as every man must when he closes the last of his eyes and steps through the smallest door. There he will face a punishment I cannot comprehend. My concern now is to send my father to the afterdream, and to become king in his place.'

In roaming around the room, Talus had contrived to end up near the furthest alcove from the throne. He stopped there and picked up the knife Tharn had thrown. Holding it by the blade, he advanced towards the dead king's son.

'I disagree with you,' Talus said. In the circle, the stoutest of the brothers gasped. Talus handed over the knife and resumed his pacing. 'There is a tale to be told here, one that only the king can tell.'

'A dead man has no voice,' said Tharn.

'Your father will speak, but not in words.' Talus beamed. 'Come with me now.'

'Come? Where?'

'To the cairn.'

'For what purpose?'

'To examine the body of the king. The dead do speak, you see, and your father is no exception. Are you not curious to hear what he has to say?'

THIS WAS THE moment. Tharn would either swallow Talus's bait or swim away from his line. Or kill him on the spot. Talus wondered if the king's eldest son knew that he was being charmed. That, in a way, bards were fishermen too.

Everything depended on how curious he was.

Every moment of every day, Talus's thoughts buzzed with questions. He knew it was an unusual trait; most people he'd met moved through their lives like leaves on a breeze, content to let the wind blow them wherever it chose. Content not to ask why.

Not Talus.

Sometimes, the only way to release the pressure in his head was to share his thoughts with those around him. In his rare moments of whimsy, he imagined his curiosity like a swarm of bees, spilling from his mouth to carry his endless questions out into the world.

It was only natural, then, that he should have become a bard. Stories were all about curiosity, after all. Being a bard allowed Talus first to snare people, then to take them down mysterious paths to unknown destinations. Whenever a new tale spun itself out of his mouth— seemingly with a life of its own—Talus felt a wonder unmatched by anything else.

Being a bard also gave him freedom to travel. Most settlements welcomed a wandering teller of tales. People liked to hear news of other lands, and they liked the comfort of a familiar story told well—or the excitement of a new one told to thrill. In his time, Talus's feet had taken him far across the world. This wasn't the only journey he'd made in his life.

If Talus's thoughts were bees, Tharn looked well and truly stung. The watching men exchanged their thoughts in hushed voices, but Talus paid them little heed. His attention was on the king-to-be.

'You have earned yourself the right to live a little longer,' Tharn said at last. 'We will go to the cairn. We will see if this... this *bard* is as clever as he thinks.'

Talus allowed himself to relax.

There was a flurry of activity as the brothers rose from the fire, reformed their cordon around Talus and Bran and steered them out of the house. Bran plodded with his shoulders slumped and his head down. Talus walked with him, tolerating the jabs and nudges delivered by the shaman whenever their pace slowed.

'It does not surprise me that you walk slowly, bard,' said Mishina, poking Talus with his staff. 'You are walking towards your death.'

'I do not fear death,' said Talus. 'And I am used to walking.'

'Enjoy it while you can. Your journey will be a short one.'

'No. I have a long way yet to travel.'

The shaman continued to taunt him, but Talus ignored him. His thoughts were flying again, this time travelling into the past, to a very different place...

IN A SOUTHERN land where a vast desert met a great river, Talus had once met a tribe of people—the biggest tribe he'd ever encountered. The desert people had planted crops in vast irrigated fields and raised extraordinary stone structures towards the sky. It was like nothing Talus had seen anywhere else in the world. Its beauty had seduced him.

The desert realm was ruled by a warrior queen called

Tia. When Talus was first brought before her as an interloper, he thought she would kill him. Instead, she listened to what he had to say. She enjoyed hearing Talus's tales of other lands, and allowed him to stay. Over time, they became friends.

Talus was especially interested in the desert people's attitude to the afterlife. They'd developed the art of preserving bodies after death: they drained blood, removed organs, wrapped skin and interred corpses in dry desert tombs, all to maintain the body's integrity when it finally entered the next world.

So much effort, so much belief. Yet still they had no answer to the one question that had confounded Talus for most of his life.

Is the afterlife real?

His curiosity on this subject fascinated Tia. Her attention flattered him. She admitted to finding him strange (most people Talus had met seemed to share that opinion) but she never judged him. Instead, she responded to his inquiries with questions of her own.

Talus loved questions.

'If there is no afterlife,' Tia said once, 'where do people go when they die?'

'Perhaps nowhere,' Talus replied. 'When a tree falls, it simply lies there, slowly rotting into the ground until it is gone. Perhaps it is the same for us.'

'There are those who would say that, just like people, trees have spirits. If that is so, then where do the tree-spirits go?'

'Perhaps they rot too.'

'So all men who claim they can speak with the spirits

of the dead are lying? All the priests of my temple, all the shamans of all the many lands you claim to have seen, they are all frauds?'

'No. I think priests and shamans believe in what they do—believe very strongly, in fact. But everything they do can be explained in other ways. Before a shaman can run with the spirits he must first beat drums, or descend into holes in the ground and breathe the smoke of the fire he has set there, or he eats a certain kind of toadstool... all these rituals can bend the shaman's mind and make him see things that are not there.'

'But what if they *are* there?'

'I am not saying they are not.'

'Then what are you saying?'

'*That I have never seen them.*'

Their discussions went on day after day. The hot sun baked their backs. In Tia's company, Talus discovered a fellowship he'd never known could exist, and a kind of peace. Tia didn't agree with everything he said, but she understood why he was saying it.

But then war had come crashing down on Tia's realm, and everything had changed. Tia had changed, shedding the woman to become once more the warrior queen. She told Talus to leave, but he stayed, promising to advise her as the war developed. But she was strong in battle and needed no advice.

Towards the end, they found themselves together at the very top of the biggest of the desert tombs. The tomb's stepped sides sloped away towards the sand far below. The noise of battle surrounded them.

'I heard a story once,' Tia said hurriedly, 'from another

travelling man, not unlike you. He spoke of a place far in the north, where the world is all made of ice. There, it is said that a river of light comes down from the sky to meet the frozen sea. The light is made of spirits. In the place where it touches down, all the worlds meet. This world, the next. Perhaps many others. He said he was going there, to see what he could see.'

'What was his name?' said Talus.

'It does not matter. Men like him use names and cast them aside. I often wonder if he will ever find what he is looking for.'

It was only later that Talus understood she was saying goodbye.

Shortly afterwards, Tia's enemies stormed the tomb, led by their king and his warrior-priest. Tia's soldiers were no match for them. Rather than watch her people die, she led them into exile.

Talus went too, and for a while he thought he would stay with his desert queen. But Tia had planted a thought in him.

What if there really was such a thing as the northlight? What if there really was a place where it came down from the clouds to touch the living world? Wouldn't that be a place where a curious man might learn once and for all if the spirit world was real?

He tried to talk more to Tia about it, but she'd lost interest in his questions. All she cared about now was reclaiming her lost kingdom. Her patience gone, she told Talus to choose: it was either her, or the long journey north.

Talus chose north.

CHAPTER FIVE

THARN LED THE way to the burial cairn, which lay at the northern extremity of the village. Here, the maze of passages converged on a single, winding way. This path, though still sunk into the ground, had no roof. The red light had faded from the sky, leaving it bright and laced with the fish-scale clouds that told Talus a storm was coming.

Bran—who'd started out sullen—now looked nervous. His hands were trembling; his face was a mask. Talus knew exactly what was making his companion uncomfortable.

They were approaching the land of the dead.

The path widened. Ahead rose a dome skinned with turf: a hill made by men. The island's burial cairn. It resembled many cairns Talus had seen before, but was remarkably symmetrical. Whoever had built it had known his craft.

Tharn brought the procession to a halt. The cairn entrance gaped, a bleak, black square standing no higher than Talus's shoulder. It looked grim and foreboding.

The shaking in Bran's hands had descended to his legs. Talus gripped his companion's arm.

'There is no need to be afraid.'

'Tell it to my knees.'

Tharn called forward his brother with the lanky arms and legs. With his long limbs unfolded, the man was astonishingly tall. A whispered conversation ensued.

Talus studied the cairn's mouth. The king lay inside, awaiting his final passage to the afterdream. This place—like all such places—was a threshold, packed with potential. What answers must it hold, to what countless questions?

'Come,' said Tharn. 'Let us enter.'

Talus leaned close to Bran. 'It is an interesting family, do you not think?'

Bran's expression remained glum. 'You mean you've only just realised they're brothers? Talus—you're usually much quicker than that.'

One by one they entered the cairn. Talus ducked quickly under the stone lintel, but Bran pulled up short. Fethan jabbed him with the blunt end of a flint axe similar to Bran's own. Talus was about to intervene when the tall brother slipped between the two men.

'Be easy, Fethan.'

'Out of my way, Cabarrath.'

Cabarrath placed his hand on Fethan's heaving shoulder. 'Let us not take more death over the border.'

'This one's trouble.' Fethan's eyes—as dark as his tangled hair—flicked restlessly from side to side. 'Let me have my fun.'

'No, brother.' Cabarrath was older than Fethan, Talus had decided—almost certainly the next oldest after Tharn.

Cabarrath turned his touch into a brother's embrace, tightening his arm around Fethan's neck and squeezing amiably. With his free hand, he rapped his younger brother on the top of his head. After this little ritual, he let go and gave Fethan a gentle shove into the cairn. Suddenly grinning, Fethan ducked past Talus and plunged into the darkness.

'Forgive my brother,' Cabarrath said to Bran. He extended his hand. 'After you.'

One after the other they crossed the invisible threshold into the land of the dead.

IT TOOK TALUS'S eyes a while to adjust to the darkness, but gradually he began to make out shapes. He was standing at the end of a long underground chamber— almost a tunnel. Stone pillars rose at regular intervals, dividing the interior into stalls. Each must contain the bones of many dead. Talus breathed in and tasted the herbs that hung here to sweeten the air. Beneath their aroma lurked the stench of decay.

The tunnel grew narrower as it progressed, and the ceiling lower, making the cairn seem much longer than it really was. At the far end stood a stone door so small even a child would have struggled to use it. Not that any living person would have dreamed of trying to pass through that door: it was the final barrier between this world and the next.

'I've got to get out of here,' muttered Bran.

'There is nothing to fear,' said Talus. 'We have not left the world. This is not the afterdream.'

'I haven't been near one of these places since Keyli died.'

'It is just a place.'

'That's just it. It isn't.'

The king's body lay in an empty stall halfway along the cairn's interior. Tharn and his brothers crowded rounded it, their shoulders hunched to stop their heads banging on the low ceiling.

The corpse lay on its back with its legs still frozen as though sitting—a pathetically comic posture. It was not quite cold enough in here to freeze water. As the body thawed and the stiffness of death departed, its limbs would relax. By then, the smell in the cairn would be rich indeed.

'I am Tharn,' said the king's eldest son. His words resounded. Echoes bounced back, rich and hollow, as if many people were speaking at once. Talus listened to the harmonies, intrigued. 'I come with my brothers: Cabarrath, Gantor, Fethan, Sigathon, Arak. We come to honour our king and father, who has left us to join his wife, our mother, in the afterdream. This is Hashath of Creyak, who is dead.'

He took a step back. With a brisk wave, he beckoned Talus forward.

Talus stroked his bald head with one bony hand. He'd come here with no real idea of what he would do. But that was his way; if you wanted to measure the currents of a river, what better strategy than to plunge headfirst into its waters?

He turned to Fethan, raised his hand and snapped his fingers. Fethan's eyes darted naturally to the sound. With his other hand, Talus snatched up the bonespike Fethan was wearing on a thong around his neck—the same weapon with which Fethan had threatened Bran in the king's house.

'Hey!' said Fethan as the thong's knot parted. His fingers became claws and he lunged for Talus. Cabarrath seized his younger brother round the middle, pinning his arms to his waist. Fethan thrashed, but Cabarrath was strong. His height was against him, though; he kept cracking his head on the low ceiling, and cursing.

'Enough!' said Tharn. 'Fethan, be still! Bard, whatever it is you intend to do, be quick about it. I have no patience for this. The afterdream is not a place to linger when the solstice is near.'

Fethan grew sulky and his limbs stopped working. Cabarrath's face carried the ghost of a smile, but there was no humour behind it.

For the second time that morning, Talus bent to the corpse of the frozen king of Creyak. What would he do? Still he had no idea.

He ran his fingers over Hashath's skin. The flesh was hard like stone, and very cold. He explored the king's shoulder, then the frozen hands. He examined the tips of the king's fingers. Something was stuck under the nails. Interesting.

He let his touch linger there.

Finally, he raised Hashath's left arm to expose again the single tiny wound that—if his theory was correct— had killed the king. Moving the arm was difficult, but Talus was strong.

Talus tilted his head. Bran sometimes told him he looked like a bird. He wondered if it was true.

Then he took Fethan's bonespike and plunged it straight into the bloody hole in the king's side.

With a roar, Tharn made a grab for Talus. But Bran

was in the way. The fisherman set his feet and held back the king-to-be, letting his shoulders accept the blows. Talus was glad his companion was built like a bear.

Mishina stepped forward. For a moment, Talus thought the shaman would pull him away from the frozen king. Instead, Mishina began to chant and bang his staff on the floor of the cairn. The combined sounds—the deep repetitive thudding of the staff, the thin rattle of the shells that hung from it, the guttural hum of Mishina's voice—echoed and re-echoed inside the enclosed space. Soon a pattern of sound had built up that turned Talus's insides to water.

Fascinating. But Talus had other things to attend to.

Using his forefinger, he pushed the bonespike deeper into the wound. It sank a long way into Hashath's stiff flesh. So did Talus's finger: all the way up to the second knuckle. Talus supposed the onlookers would consider it gruesome.

Tharn was bellowing like an ox, but Bran wasn't moving.

And Talus had already learned what he needed to know.

With a hideous sucking sound, he withdrew his finger. Then he used the leather thong to draw out the buried bonespike. Once this was done, he offered the bonespike to Fethan. Cabarrath relaxed his grip enough for his brother to snatch it back.

'Why do you do this?' said Tharn. His chest was heaving. His breath steamed in a cloud that wafted over Bran's head and towards Talus's face.

Talus turned to Mishina. 'Forgive me,' he said, 'but that noise makes it very difficult to concentrate.'

The shaman stopped in mid-chant. His painted face contracted into a cataclysmic frown. Talus wondered what he looked like without the thick daubs of mud.

To Talus's surprise, Mishina laughed.

'You are clever,' he said. 'A very clever man.'

'No,' said Talus. 'Merely observant.'

'I do not understand,' said Tharn.

'Then let him explain,' said Bran. Protecting Talus appeared to have robbed him of his fear.

'It is clear,' Talus said, 'that young Fethan here has a temper.'

'You dare...!' said Fethan.

'It's nothing we don't already know,' said Cabarrath.

'A man with both a temper *and* a bonespike might be the killer we are looking for,' Talus elaborated.

'You believe Fethan killed the king?' said Tharn. 'It cannot be true.'

'The truth is what we are here to find. That is why I did what I did.'

'Explain yourself,' said Mishina.

'Gladly. The shape of a wound carries the shape of the weapon that made it. Any hunter knows this. That is why I brought Fethan's bonespike to the wound that killed the king—to see if the shapes match. They do not. The king's wound is much deeper than Fethan's bonespike is long. This means the murder weapon—which is certainly a bonespike or something similar—was much longer than the one Fethan carries round his neck.'

Silence fell as the six brothers digested this. At last, one of them spoke: Arak, the pale youth with the green eyes. The runt of the litter.

'Seems to me this wandering bard's just telling us what the women of Creyak have known for years,' he said. His voice was high but strong.

'What is that?' said Tharn.

Arak grinned. 'That what Fethan really needs is a bigger weapon.'

Laughter exploded round the group. Tharn did his best to keep his face straight, but in the end even he couldn't suppress a smile. Mishina was smiling too. He nodded at Talus, just once. A salute or a warning? Even Talus couldn't tell.

The uproar continued until Tharn waved his hands.

'This is not the place for laughter,' he said. 'Your ways are strange, Talus-of-the-tale. Is your curiosity satisfied?'

'On this particular subject, yes.'

'Well,' Tharn went on, 'mine is not. It is still strange to me that you chose to come among us on such an ill-omened day. You show me that Fethan did not kill my father, but you might still be the killer yourself. You will stay, therefore. My brother Gantor will prepare a house for you and your companion. You will not leave until I am satisfied of your good will. None of these things I have said are requests.'

Bran turned on him, his good hand straying to the haft of his axe.

'We accept your hospitality,' said Talus quickly. 'And we understand your suspicion. You have my word that we will not leave this island until the mystery is solved.'

'If you try to leave,' said Tharn, 'I will stop you.'

*   *   *

AS THEY LEFT the cairn, Talus knew he should feel satisfied. Seeking the truth was like telling a story: each small step took the seeker—or the teller—one stage nearer the conclusion. Eliminating Fethan was just such a step.

Satisfying Tharn of their innocence was another.

Yet... bonespikes were common things. And what killer would carry his guilt in plain view on a thong around his neck? For all his cleverness, Talus knew Fethan might still be guilty. Instead of triumph, then, he felt frustration. There was more to learn here in the cairn, he was sure of it.

On his way to the exit, Talus feigned breathlessness. His mime was unconvincing, and earned him a dig in the ribs from the shaman, but it gained him just enough time for a final look around the interior. He lingered as long as he dared and finally, as his keen eyes scanned for the second time the corridor with the little stone door at the end, he spotted something. It was a tiny thing; not surprising he'd missed it until now.

Added to what Talus had discovered under the dead king's fingernails, it might mean their trip here had been worthwhile after all.

His patience gone, Mishina shoved Talus outside. The bard sprawled on the icy ground, cursing; not because he'd fallen, but because he'd left it too late to act on his discoveries.

Bran helped him to his feet.

'I'm glad I don't have to go back in there again,' he said.

Talus brushed flakes of snow from his robe. 'It is interesting that you say that,' he replied.

CHAPTER SIX

GANTOR WAS A great boulder of a man. He wore a long cloak of grey caribou hide, shaped and leather-stitched to fit his robust body. White stoat pelts ran around the collar and down the sleeves. It was a fine garment. Footwear in Creyak ran to simple fur-lined moccasins similar to Bran's own; for some inexplicable reason, Gantor went barefoot.

The shoeless guide guided Bran and Talus back through the labyrinthine trenches. As he had in the island's defensive maze, Bran soon lost all sense of direction. Not that he was really paying attention. He was still recovering from being inside the cairn.

Actually, the experience hadn't been as bad as he'd anticipated. The cairn in his home village of Arvon had been a poor, dead place, just a cold hole carved out of the earth. But the Creyak cairn was different. Rich, and somehow alive.

Not that Bran had any intention of setting foot in it again. Nor of staying on Creyak for a single breath longer than he had to. He'd made up his mind. As soon as an opportunity presented itself, he was leaving.

* * *

GANTOR LED THEM to a narrow dead end. Directly in front of them was one of Creyak's ubiquitous door-stones. Beside it was a gap in the trench wall, looking out on a wide, shallow pit piled high with rough stones and lengths of whalebone. Thick ropes were wrapped around the stones, preventing the piles from collapsing.

Gantor was so broad he practically filled the passage behind them, cutting off any possibility of escape. Bran briefly considered taking the blunt end of his axe to the back of Gantor's head; with the big man insensible, he and Talus could make a run for it. But Talus showed no sign of wanting to run anywhere.

Besides, Gantor's head—not to mention the rest of him—looked extremely hard.

Gantor set his shoulder to the door-stone and heaved. It moved smoothly on a track of polished granite to reveal an interior like the king's house, only on a much smaller scale. It was clearly unoccupied: there were no beds in the alcoves and the stone shelves standing opposite the door were bare. The hearth was empty.

'I build houses,' said Gantor. 'This one is new. You will stay here now. At sunset I will take you to eat with the people.'

He adjusted his cloak and straightened the stoat-fur pouch at his waist. He frowned and rummaged inside, but came out empty-handed.

'Lost something?' said Bran.

Gantor turned his back and folded his arms. Bran loitered, trying to devise a way of carrying on the conversation. Perhaps if they could gain his trust...

Talus seized Bran's arm and dragged him through the open doorway.

'The first thing we must do,' said the bard, 'is get a fire going.'

'What you mean,' Bran replied, 'is you want *me* to get a fire going.'

But Talus, like Gantor, had already lost interest. And the thought of a fire was attractive: the act of building one was almost as warming as sitting in front of its flames. The sooner he started, the sooner he'd shake off the cold.

And keeping busy might stop him thinking about death.

After a brief search, Bran found a stack of peat bricks and a bundle of dry willow bark in a pit in the floor, similar to the shellfish pond in the king's house. He hefted three of the bricks over to the hearth and propped them one against the other, leaving an open space beneath. Into this space he placed a handful of bark strips. Finally, he reached into the small pouch he carried under his bearskin, but not before throwing an uneasy glance back at the door.

Gantor's body blocked most of the fragmented light filtering down through the passageway's woven roof. The big man stood motionless, showing no interest in anything they might be getting up to.

From his pouch, Bran extracted a blunt block of grey flint and a shiny nodule of a heavy substance Talus called *pyr*. Kneeling, Bran held the chunk of pyr as close to the bark as he could and struck it with the flint. There was a faint *chink*. A spark leaped from the pyr to the bark, which started to smoulder. Bran puffed air gently over the bark. After a few breaths, a tongue of orange flame sprang into life. Soon all the bark was alight; shortly after that the peat bricks began to smoke, filling the house with swampy fumes that wound their way slowly towards the hole in the roof. There the whalebone rafters came together in an artful spiral that drew the smoke effortlessly into the sky.

Gantor's head swivelled on his squat neck. He cast his baleful gaze over the flames, then turned away without comment.

Bran stowed both flint and pyr back in his pouch. He'd journeyed far enough with Talus to know that every tribe had its own unique relationship with fire. Some conjured it with tools like the ones he carried. Others used bows to spin pointed sticks in wooden bowls. Some appointed guardians whose sole task it was to prevent the tribe's precious heartfire from ever dying out, so that every new fire they made was seeded from the flames of the one, true original.

Until he'd met Talus, Bran had been of the bow-and-stick persuasion. He'd once asked Talus where he'd learned to use the pyr, but the bard had refused to tell.

'Far from here, a long time ago,' was all Talus had said. This was his usual answer to such questions.

They sat in silence, warming themselves before the flames. A gust of wind blew across the smoke hole, sucking away the fumes. Bran breathed deep, enjoying the clean, warm air. The fire warmed his heart too, reassuring him the world around him was vital and real.

It also reminded him just how tired he was. Well, it had hardly been the most restful of nights.

✳   ✳   ✳

THE WIND ROSE and the whalebone rafters began to
creak. The creaking was joined by the dull spattering
sound of fresh snow falling on the roof. Before long, the
gusts had all joined into one and Bran and Talus found
themselves sitting underneath a winter storm.

'I'm not happy about being a prisoner here,' said
Bran, stifling a yawn. Outside, Gantor had raised his
fur hood against the wind stealing through the passage
roof. He looked like a stone blocking a mountain pass.
'We could get away, you know, if we really wanted to.'

'Tharn's caution is natural.' Talus was rubbing his
hands before the flames. 'But he and the others will
come to trust us soon.'

'How do you know?'

Talus delved into one of the many pouches he carried.
He took out his hand and opened it to reveal a scattering
of tiny red flakes, almost dust, dark against the bard's
pale skin.

'Is it blood?' said Bran.

'That is one wrong guess against you. Instead of
guessing, Bran, try to look.'

'I'm too cold for your games. Just tell me.'

'Cold is no excuse for lazy thinking. Look, but with
more than just your eyes.'

Bran shuffled round the hearth until he was sitting
right next to Talus. The storm battered against the roof.
He sniffed the red flakes, but all he could smell was the
peaty aroma of the fire. He licked the end of his finger,
dabbed it into the little pile and touched it to his tongue.

He'd been so convinced it was blood that what he actually tasted surprised him. 'It's just mud. Dried mud.'

'Better,' said Talus. 'Now it is your turn to ask me a question.'

Bran spat and wiped his finger clean on his bearskin. What he really wanted to do was lie down and sleep. But Talus wasn't going to let this rest.

Actually, Talus was good company when his curiosity was aroused. Bran had lost count of the number of times his friend had involved himself with the affairs of strangers like this. And the bard had a knack of finding his way to the truth.

It was the part of Talus he was going to miss the most when they went their separate ways.

'Where did it come from?'

'Excellent! I found it beneath the fingernails of the dead king. I should have seen it when I first examined his body in the arena.'

'Why didn't you?'

'It was a difficult situation.'

'You mean the great Talus actually overlooked something?'

'I knew we would learn more by visiting the cairn.'

'You're not answering my question.'

'Not all questions deserve an answer.'

'All right, never mind. What does the mud tell us?'

'Something, perhaps. The king may have struggled with his assailant before his death. Clawed at his attacker, for example. If so, it is possible that is where this mud came from. Or perhaps it simply came from the ground.'

'The shaman paints his face with mud,' said Bran. 'Talus—surely you don't think *he* did it?'

He was horrified. As king, Hashath would have been a living vessel for the spirits of all the tribe's ancestors. To strike out at such a man was to strike out at every Creyak villager who had ever lived and died, all the way back to the first dawn. Killing a king wasn't just murder; it was genocide.

No tribesman would have been more aware of this than Mishina. As shaman, he was in constant contact with the ancestors. He would know better than most the consequences of such a desperate crime.

Those consequences were simple and stark. When the king's murderer eventually faced his own death (for all men must one day pass beyond the smallest door and enter the everlasting dream) he would be immediately seized by the twice-killed ancestors and trapped in a place of torture. The ancestors would send blizzard-wolves to tear out his liver. They would send storm-eagles to rip out his eyes. They would set flood-fires to drown him with flames. His heart they would throw to the giant carrion crows who lived in the black walls of night-ice bounding the wilderness that lay beyond the afterdream's furthest borders. The murderer's soul they would keep for themselves, pinned out for all the spirits to see.

Despite such dire punishments, king-killers were not unheard of. But usually they were men who'd lost their wits, or who for some reason didn't comprehend the appalling fate that awaited them.

Mishina was not such a man. As shaman, he simply *couldn't* be.

'The pigment on the shaman's face is blue and yellow, not red,' said Talus. 'But colours can be changed. We cannot discount him yet. Nor is he the only inhabitant of Creyak to hide behind a mask of mud—did you not see the many faces watching us from the houses earlier?'

'Well, whoever this man is...'

'Or woman.'

'You think it was a woman?'

'I do not know enough to think that. But we have learned from Tharn that the king outlived his wife. Perhaps he found another woman to love. Love is like a moon, Bran, waxing with passion and waning with hate. Most murders are driven by love. I have said this to you before. Yet there are other forms of love than that between a man and a woman.'

'And you're the expert on love?'

Talus threw him an inscrutable look and blew the flakes of mud into the fire, where they flashed and vanished. 'All this talk has made me tired. I will conserve my strength now. I will be needing it tonight.'

'What for? Anyway, you never get tired.'

'Gantor said we would be eating with the rest of the villagers. It is likely to be a large gathering. Knowing I am a bard, they will want me to tell stories. This I will do, not only because it is *what* I do, but also because it will help us gain their trust.'

'Do you think so?'

'It will also help in another way.'

'And what's that?'

'It will distract them.'

'From what?'

'From you.'

'Talus, what do you...?'

'I will explain, but first I have an important question to ask you.'

If he'd been less tired himself, Bran would have let his temper loose on his infuriating friend. For some reason, his temper was nowhere to be found. 'Then ask me,' he sighed.

'Ever since the day your wife died, you have been afraid of death.'

'Well, is it any wonder when...?'

'Please, let me speak. When we entered the cairn today, you looked like a man stepping off the edge of a cliff. The task I have for you... Bran, this is not something I will tell you to do. I will merely ask it. Because I believe it will be very difficult for you.'

Bran swallowed. As always, the mention of Keyli had tightened his gut and stabbed needles down the length of his spine. Despite the fire's heat, he felt as if he'd plunged through a fishing hole into ice-cold water.

'Just tell me what it is you want me to do.'

'I want you to go back into the cairn. I want you to go to its end, all the way to the door that opens on the afterdream.'

Something had sucked all the breath out of Bran's lungs. 'What then?'

'I want you to open it.'

CHAPTER SEVEN

SHORTLY BEFORE SUNSET, Gantor stirred from his post at the door. He clapped his hands together, then beckoned Talus and Bran outside.

The passage roof was clogged with fresh snowfall. Talus could see its white blanket through the cracks in the willow rafters. They rattled in the wind, and some of the snow filtered through.

'It is time to eat,' Gantor said. Dusted with snow, he resembled one of the white northern bears Talus had heard of in legend.

Their guard marched them down a long, curving passage so low they had to bend double. Bran kept glancing around, no doubt checking for escape routes. Well, the task Talus had planned for him would give Bran the perfect opportunity to use one.

The question was, would he take it?

At the end of the low passage was a large open space: another arena. Its perimeter was sheltered by a whalebone canopy hanging with no apparent means of support.

'An interesting structure,' said Talus.

'Rawhide ties carry the weight of the bone back to heavy stones set deep in the ground,' said Gantor.

'You speak with great knowledge.'

'I built it.'

The arena was packed with people; it looked as if the entire village had turned out. Gantor's canopy protected only the arena's outer edge, so the centre lay exposed beneath what was effectively a gigantic smoke hole. With the storm gathering, Talus questioned the wisdom of holding a meeting here tonight, but beneath the hole in the roof was one of the biggest fires he'd ever seen. Flames rose from an enormous stack of driftwood, their heat repelling the worst of the weather.

Gantor led them to a spot near the fire. The heat scorched Talus's face, but he didn't care. Fire was always welcome, especially during a winter such as this. They sat on mats woven from reeds between groups of people they didn't know and who regarded them with naked fascination. Gantor sat beside Talus and said nothing.

A woman moved through the crowd carrying a large dish of hollowed bark. Smaller dishes clattered on a leather thong around her neck. As she drew nearer, Talus recognised her as the woman who'd served them broth in the king's house.

When she reached Gantor, the woman plucked three of the small dishes free and filled them with broth. As she turned to leave, she threw Talus a shy smile.

Gantor handed round the dishes. Talus sniffed his: more stew-of-the-sea. He sipped, tasting clams and herbs and something smoky.

'They're burning wood,' Bran said as he tucked into his stew. 'How can they afford to do that?' In this cold and remote land, wood was a precious commodity, more prized for building than burning.

'They do it to honour their king.' Talus continued taking sips from his bowl. Bran had already emptied his. Was his appetite never satisfied?

An exploding knot of wood sent a ribbon of sparks up into the night. The sparks mingled briefly with the swirling snowflakes before the wind whipped them away.

'Do you really think I'm going to be able to sneak away?' Bran pitched his voice low. 'What if there's a guard at the cairn?'

'There will be no guard. Everyone is here. Nor will there be any need for you to sneak: Tharn's opinion of us has already changed.'

'Oh, really? What makes you think that?'

'Did you see the face of the woman who brought the food?'

'I did. It was a pretty face.'

'Bran—you are so easily distracted.'

Another knot cracked in the fire. A man emerged from the crowd to stand before the flames: Tharn. He was dressed in a long robe of dark leather, densely patterned with orange stitches. Beside him stood Mishina, whose face was now painted an unbroken yellow. It bothered Talus that he still couldn't make out the shaman's features.

'Welcome to you, Creyak!' Tharn cried. His rumbling voice was more than a match for the wind.

The crowd murmured in response.

'Your king, Hashath, has joined the ancestors in the afterdream!'

Another murmur.

'Before I place my feet in the tracks my father made, we must say our farewells according to the ways of Creyak.' Tharn glanced at Mishina, who nodded. 'But first there is a wrong to be righted.'

Tharn made his way through the crowd. Heads turned to track his progress... all the way up to where Talus and Bran were seated. When Tharn stopped, the heads stopped too. Now the entire village was staring at them. Bran squirmed uneasily. Talus waited for Tharn to speak.

'Talus—with your strange ways, you have seeded in me an equally strange idea: that the man who killed my father may somehow be brought to... I cannot think of the word to use.'

'The word does not exist,' Talus replied. 'But the idea does. If what you wish is for this man to answer the questions his actions have raised, then yes, I wish it too.'

'To answer,' said Tharn. 'Yes, that will do. But before we can do this, I must put things right between us.'

Bran threw Talus a quizzical look.

'Here in Creyak, we do not trust strangers. Strangers who come in the midst of death are doubly dangerous. However, this afternoon I have learned something new. A woman of our village—her name is Lethriel—was out gathering herbs on the glen just before dawn. She watched you descend from the cliffs. I know you were not in Creyak last night.'

'I thought I saw someone out there!' said Bran.

'Let him finish, Bran,' said Talus. 'Tharn—what do you say this means?'

'It means you were not on this island when the king died. You did not kill him.'

The woman who'd served them was by now heading for the opposite side of the fire. As Tharn spoke she smiled their way, and Talus had no doubt this was Lethriel. The herbs in the stew were probably the very ones she'd been collecting that morning.

'I saw her,' Bran said again. 'I knew it.'

Tharn knelt. He placed his hand first on Bran's shaggy head, then on Talus's hairless one.

'Our food and fire are yours,' he said. 'You are welcome in Creyak. But we expect a reward for our hospitality.'

'Name it,' said Talus, knowing exactly what was coming.

'A story,' said Tharn. 'Tell us a tale, bard. Make it about life and death, because that is what concerns us here tonight.'

With that, he stepped away, returning to the core of his family and leaving Talus and Bran to face the crowd.

'Leave this to me,' said Talus.

'I intend to,' said Bran.

TALUS LOOKED OUT over the sea of faces. Lightning flashed above the smoke hole, reflecting off several hundred pairs of eyes: eyes that were looking only at him. Somewhere among them was the killer.

He wondered briefly which story he would tell. Would it be an old one, or a new one that came to him even as he spoke it? He wouldn't know until he opened his mouth.

'Once, a boy dreamed his father was dead'—an old story, then; that was just fine—'and the dream was so

71

real that the boy thought it was true. He became so sad that he ran away from his village. The boy ran for many days, all the way out of this world and into the next. There he found a lake. It was night and the water was black.

'Soon, a giant rose up from the water of the lake, but he was not wet. He was bigger than a thousand men, and he wore the feathers of a thousand different hawks. Many ordinary men and women gathered at the lakeside to honour him.

'The giant raised his arms and turned around many times, but he did not grow dizzy. When he stopped, his left side was facing his people. They waded into the water and swarmed over him and tore off his feathers, revealing a dreadful bloody mass of bones and meat beneath. The land turned as black as the lake water and the giant said, "This is a night of death." And, across many worlds, many thousands died.

'The boy was terrified, so he hid all through the following day until the next night. As soon as it was dark, the giant emerged from the water again. Again he turned around many times, but this time he stopped with his right side facing his people. They tore off his feathers, this time revealing a naked body shining with glossy brown skin. The moon blazed and turned the land to silver, and the giant said, "This is a night of life." And, across many worlds, many thousands were born.

'The boy ran home and found his father was not dead after all, but alive. He embraced him, but he did not tell him what he had seen. That night, when he went to sleep, he feared he would have the same bad dream.

But he did not. Nor did he ever dream of death again, throughout all his long life.'

WHEN TALUS'S WORDS had trailed away into the night, Mishina rapped his staff sharply on the ground, three times. The villagers responded by thumping the ground with their heels. Acknowledging the applause with a low bow, Talus seated himself once more at Bran's side.

'Later, when the singing has begun,' he murmured, 'pretend the food has curdled your stomach. We will say you have retired to the house. They trust us now. You will not be followed. Are you sure you are ready to do this?'

Before Bran could answer, someone landed beside them in a cloud of dust: Arak, the youngest of the king's sons. His arrival coincided with another flash of lightning, much brighter than the last. Two breaths later, thunder boomed.

Arak reached over Bran and grabbed Talus's clean hand with his grimy one.

'That was a wonderful story!' The lad's eyes were shining. His whole face glowed in the firelight. Then his expression fell. 'Is that really how death comes?'

Talus pushed Arak's hand gently away. 'It is just a story,' he said.

Arak shuffled his buttocks on the hard ground. He scratched the back of his neck. Presently, he spoke again.

'I don't know what to do.' He looked across to where his brothers were feasting. 'None of us do. Can you make it right?'

'I will do what I can,' said Talus. 'But only if the king-to-be wills it.'

'Tharn will look after us. He always does. It's the way of Creyak that he should be king now. Nothing can stop that.'

Arak continued to fidget. His eyes continued to rove. He looked lost.

'There is a reason for everything,' said Talus. 'Even death.'

'Death comes for a reason?' said Arak.

'I believe so.'

'It's hard to believe it.'

'Yes, it is.'

'Death brings more than just grief,' said Bran. 'It brings a need to know the truth. A need to close... Talus, how did you describe it to me?'

'To close the past,' said the bard.

'Closing,' murmured Arak.

'Knowing the truth closes the door that lets in the darkness,' said Talus. 'This is something time has taught me. It is why I do what I do.'

'And what's that?'

'I find truth where there appears to be none.'

'So... you will help?' said Arak. 'You will work to make this right? To make this man answer for what he has done?'

'I will work to uncover the truth. If that is what you consider to be "right," then the answer to your question is yes.'

Arak leaped to his feet, suddenly grinning. 'That's all I wanted to know!'

With that, he ran off into the throng.

'Poor boy,' said Bran. 'He's lost.'

'Death brings trials, Bran. You know that.'

Despite the blazing heat of the fire, Bran shivered. 'Yes,' he said, 'I do.'

CHAPTER EIGHT

As THE EVENING went on, fermented drinks were passed around and the proceedings grew increasingly unruly. At a wink from Talus, Bran started groaning and rubbing his belly. After Tharn's change of heart, nobody protested when he made his excuses and retired from the arena.

He went straight to the cairn.

Talus had already taken great delight in explaining to Bran about the cairn's design.

'It is cunningly built,' the bard had said. 'Its walls shape any sounds that are made inside it. Imagine! A simple footstep becomes the grunt of a sleeping giant. A single human voice swells up until it becomes the roar of an angry mob.'

Well, that explained how Mishina, simply by banging his staff on the the floor, had set up that unnerving barrage of echoes. Bran consoled himself that at least this time he'd be alone. He would move carefully, making no sound. That way, the cairn would remain silent.

He was wrong.

As SOON AS he reached the shelter of the entrance stoop, Bran heard it: an immense, liquid moaning. The sound was so deep in pitch it was scarcely sound at all. It flowed out of the cairn like thick tar. When the wind gusted, it grew immeasurably louder.

Bran quickly decided the wind was the cause of it: the air moving past the mouth of the cairn made a hooting sound, like a hunter blowing air across his cupped hands to mimic the call of an owl. It was a deduction worthy of Talus himself.

It didn't make Bran feel any less terrified.

He loitered outside the entrance. If he was going to run away, now was the time to do it. Everyone was busy at the feast; the rest of the village was deserted. Bran was confident he could find his way back through the maze. He'd even worked out that the tide would be low enough for him to cross back over the causeway.

But that would mean letting Talus down.

Did it matter, when he was planning to leave his friend anyway?

He continued to dither until eventually someone spoke in his head. It was a voice that came to him occasionally, usually in times of great trial when the weight of the world seemed to press down hard on his tired bones.

It was Keyli's voice.

'Stay, Bran,' she said. 'You can't leave him without saying goodbye.'

Bran set courage against fear and stepped inside the cairn.

Here the sound was a hundred times worse. The curved walls scooped up the drone of the wind, amplified and twisted it, gave it words where before it had none. Made it a dire song. The roar of the gale was an ocean through which swam the voices of the dead.

Bran shuddered. He shook snow from his bearskin and peered into the gloom. The light was terrible. The bright moon had guided him this far; now he was practically blind.

Slowly, shapes materialised: the regular uprights of the stone stalls; the mounds of desiccated bones; the slumped mountain that was the dead king's slowly thawing body. The tiny door Talus had sent him to open looked very far away.

Thunder boomed outside. The cairn swallowed the sound whole, compressed it, smashed it against the sides of Bran's head. He dropped to his knees, pressed his hands to his ears. The thunder became the war-cry of an army of wrathful ghosts.

'No!' Bran shouted into the darkness.

The cairn ripped his one word into a thousand pieces. He was drowning in echoes.

No—no—no!

The sound intensified. Thunder crashed again and again. The storm had eaten him. Bran pinched his eyes shut and tried to wish the noise away.

'Please stop!' he shouted.

Stop—stop—stop!

The floor shifted beneath him, trying to tip him over. The air grew thick, wrapped itself around him like a tongue and squeezed. The ceiling descended. He couldn't breathe. He could barely think.

'I can't do it!'

Do it—do it—do it!

Then Keyli said, 'You can.'

The instant he heard her voice, the cairn relaxed around him. He floated in space, in the sound. The sound gathered him up, carried him high into the storm. The wind turned him over and over, spinning him until he was dizzy and sweeping him off to another time, another place, another storm...

BRAN STANDS ON weed-slick boulders as waves hurl themselves high over his head. The furious ocean stretches before him, alive in the tempest. At his back, behind the marram dunes, squat the low huts of Arvon, his home. The huts are filled with slumbering people. They are oblivious to the drama playing out on the rocky shore and so, as far as Bran is concerned, they might as well be dead.

Behind the huts rise the white-capped grey mountains known as the Nioghe. The mountains crowd the coast as if eager to drown themselves. Like the people of Arvon, they're as still as the dead.

The sky, however, is alive. More: it's filled with fire. The stars have left their places and are shooting across the heavens. They leave thin white scratches in the night, as if big cats are trying to claw their way through from the other side of the black. It's a sight to behold.

But Bran has no time for the sky. There's a boat on the raging water. Keyli is in the boat. Her mouth is agape, but Bran can't hear what she's screaming. He has no idea why she's out there. All he knows is that earlier that evening they fell asleep in each other's arms as they always did, and that he awoke in the middle of the night to find her gone. He rose, panic in his breast, and followed her tracks to the shore.

He has no doubt that it was great Mir, guardian of the ocean, who roused him from his sleep, Mir who called him across the dunes to this place, to witness his beloved wife dying in front of him, Mir, who has watched over Bran his whole life, bringing him and his wriggling catches home safe through even the worst winter storms.

Mir, who now thinks it sport to stamp out Keyli's life right in front Bran's unbelieving eyes, with no more regard than a cruel child stamping his heel on an ant.

A fresh trail of light streaks across the night sky, wider than the rest. It's not thin and white, but yellow and jagged. The flying fire is getting closer.

As the yellow light fades, Bran finds he's no longer alone on the shore. A man is standing with him: a tall stranger dressed in motley robes. His head is bald. The stranger shouts and points.

'What?!' Bran yells.

'Rope!' says the stranger.

Bran sees it: one end of a rope thrashes in the waves; the other is tied to Keyli's boat. If he could only grab the rope, he might be able to pull her back to the shore. Pull the woman he loves to safety.

He glances behind him. There is nobody else around. The dunes are a blank and the mountains don't care.

Bran crouches, nearly loses his footing on a treacherous, weed-covered rock. The rope dances just out of reach in the foaming water. He stretches for it with both his good, strong hands. He misses.

The stranger leaps past him. He jumps into the churning waves, sinking instantly up to his shoulders. He seizes the rope and hurls it at Bran.

Bran catches the rope. It's coarse and sodden. Keyli is still screaming. The sea picks up the boat and flips it over, and Keyli flies from it into the water.

'Keyli!' Bran shouts.

Her white hands emerge from the waves and cling to the upturned boat. It's a good boat—Bran made it himself. But the storm is tearing it apart.

The stranger tries to pull himself back onto the rocks. His hands keep slipping on the weed and his bald head keeps going under. Bran grips the rope and starts to pull. The sea tries to suck the rope out of his hands, but Bran is strong, both his hands are strong, and he's pulling with all his heart, and the weight of all his life behind him, and the weight of all his life to come.

At first the boat resists. Bran howls and pulls and eventually the boat begins to come, and Keyli comes with it. Bran sees her face in agonising glimpses, now white in the water, now eclipsed by the cruel swell. He sees her hands, each slender finger making its own good grip on the sealskin hull of the boat. She's holding tight, and so is he. He's strong enough to do this, everything's going to be all right.

'Do all you can,' says the stranger. His voice is filled with water. His head sinks beneath the waves and doesn't come up.

Bran screams and pulls. If only he can be quick

enough, he can save both Keyli and the man who came to his aid. He wedges his feet into the deepest crevice he can find and *pulls*.

It's then that the stars stop flying and begin to fall...

'ENOUGH!' BRAN SHOUTED. He clamped his hands hard to his ears, took a tottering step back towards the cairn's entrance. Incredibly, the sound of the twin storms—the one outside the cairn and the one inside his head—faded completely away.

Bran stood, shaking, unbelieving, lost inside a bubble of sudden silence. What trickery was this?

Cautiously, he took a single step forwards. The thunder rumbled again; the echoes of his own shouting returned.

When he took a step back, the sounds died away to nothing.

Bran forced himself to relax. Talus had told him of such things, though he'd never actually encountered them. Builders so clever they could make chambers that turned sound into alternating stripes of fury and calm. Here was the proof of it.

Gradually Bran's heartbeat slowed. He often dreamed about Keyli's death—had dreamed about it a lot lately, in fact. Never had he relived it so intensely as he just had in the cairn. This was a place of death.

Maybe the whole island was.

He waited while the dread drained away. Slowly, his memories of that awful night—of the storm and the fire-filled sky—sank back into their hiding place. Now that he understood what made the sound act the way it did, it had no power over him. It was just noise.

He stepped forward through the alternating bands of sound and silence towards the little doorway awaiting him at the end of the cairn. As he advanced, he found himself thinking back to the story Talus had told in the arena. The tale of the feathered giant was odd—not one Bran had heard before. He couldn't decide if it was meant to be happy or sad. He supposed it was both.

He reached the end of the cairn. The ceiling was low here, forcing him to crawl.

He raised his good hand—it was trembling—to the little door. The stone was comfortably cool. This was one of the cairn's silent spots, and Bran felt curiously at peace. He bent his fingers round the edge of the stone and set his weight against it. Just as he was about to push it aside, he spotted something sticking out from beneath it.

The object was difficult to make out in the darkness. He thought it might be a bird's quill—or was he was still thinking about the feathers from Talus's story?

There was only one way to find out. Bran heaved at the little door. It slid aside with surprising ease. As it moved, he closed his eyes, not wishing to see what lay beyond.

Blind, he reached down and fumbled on the floor. At first he felt nothing but, after a moment, his fingers stumbled over the object he'd seen. It was hard and spindly. He picked it up and stuffed it into the pouch he carried at his waist. Then he slid the door shut.

Only then did he open his eyes.

He stared at the little door, glad it was sealed again. What might he have seen had he looked? Spirit eyes staring back at him, the eyes of someone dead?

Keyli's eyes?

Part of him believed there was nothing there, that the door was just a simple dam holding back the natural earth beyond.

Part of him believed he'd narrowly avoided catching a glimpse of the afterdream.

He choked back a sob. He'd already revisited the past once this night. He had no intention of doing so again. He'd come here for a single ordinary reason: to find whatever it was Talus had sent him for. Now it was done. All that remained was for him to go back the bard, hand it over and say his goodbyes.

Lightning shattered the darkness beyond the entrance to the cairn, turning the night-dark doorway briefly into a stuttering, snow-veiled square. Bran held up what he'd found. Blue flashes chased across the thing's contours, describing its shape in exquisite detail.

It was a bonespike, much longer and thicker than the one Fethan carried round his neck. Its smooth sides were blackened with a sticky substance, which Bran was certain was blood.

He was holding the murder weapon.

Bran made for the exit. On the way he brushed against the corpse of the frozen king. Fresh thunder crashed outside. He bit his lip to stifle a scream and covered the last few paces at a run.

After the strange acoustics of the cairn, the sound outside was clean and somehow wholesome. Bran raised his face and drank it in. The thunder held itself in check, exposing the roar of the ocean. The storm had whipped it to a frenzy. He wanted to be off this cursed island right now. He'd find shelter on the mainland: a cave, perhaps, or the hollow trunk of a fallen tree.

A new sound came to him, riding over the smash of wave on rock: human cries, and the sound of splintering wood.

In front of Bran was a narrow, winding path leading away from the cairn—away from the village altogether, in fact. He guessed it led to the island's western beach.

The cries came again.

Stuffing the bonespike that had killed Hashath into his pouch, Bran started running along the path.

CHAPTER NINE

THE PATH LED Bran up a steep slope through a twisting slalom of icy rocks. The wind whipped fresh snow against his face. The cold bit his ears, the tip of his nose.

Men he couldn't see shouted for help.

The slope reached its peak and started to descend, so abruptly that Bran's feet shot from under him. Just for a moment, he felt as if he was flying. Then he was down again and sliding on his backside over slick ice, finally landing on a beach of pebbles that clattered like thousands of tiny bones. The wind continued to hammer him, its monumental roar competing with the crash of the waves on the shore.

An eerie orange light burned through the swirling snow, illuminating a sweeping curve of shingle studded with craggy boulders. Looming over the beach was a tremendous weather-torn cliff. The sun had set long ago; where was the light coming from?

The shouts were much louder now. Bran picked himself up and pressed on, the wind so strong he had to lean into it to stay on his feet. The shingle sucked at him and he plodded with giant, unsteady steps, like a man wading through a swamp. At last he reached the waterline, where a slender rock pointed like a gigantic finger at the sky.

A boat wallowed in the shallows. Its hull was smooth and grey. Its prow rose high, ending in the carved likeness of a wolf's head. A hollow bowl sat between the animal's ears. Flames licked from the bowl: the source of the light.

The boat was on the brink of disaster. Huge waves hurled it against first one boulder then another. Over the sides of the hull, the faces of men now flickered into view, now vanished: the boat's crew, trying desperately to steer their vessel safely to shore. Their faces looked deformed, monstrous even, in the eerie light. Oars thrashed, but Bran could see it was hopeless. Trapped in the chasm between the rocks, the boat had fallen victim to an endless churning whirlpool.

Mir, the spirit of the sea, was angry.

Lightning connected the clouds. Bran flinched. This was too much like that other storm, that other night. Keyli's face had come and gone from view just like the faces of the boat's desperate crew, alternately exposed and concealed by the waves. Maybe he'd passed through the doorway after all, and here he was in the afterdream, where death ruled all...

'Help us!'

The voice cut through the storm: the cries of the many distilled into a single desperate plea.

Bran cupped his hands, the good and the bad, around his mouth. His beard was sodden.

'Row back!' he shouted.

The sea seized the boat and tossed it against the rocks. The hull shuddered along its entire length. Suddenly Bran understood that the boat was immense—bigger than any he'd seen. There might be as many as twenty men aboard.

He flapped his hands. 'Go back!'

He had no idea if they heard him. Then one of the oars flailing over the side of the boat started to press against the waves rather than with them. All instinct would be telling these men to beach the boat before it was wrecked; someone on board, on hearing his cry, had found the courage to do the opposite.

'Throw a rope!' Bran moved his arms, miming the act of catching and pulling. Could anyone see him?

The answer came in the form of a coiling snake-shape lashing out of the murk. It cut into the sand ten paces away from where Bran stood. At once it started slithering back towards the water's edge. Bran chased it, managed to grab it just before it vanished into the waves.

So like his dream.

The boat was retreating now, crawling back out of the whirlpool that had been holding it captive. But escape meant returning to the open sea, where the storm would sink it for certain. The rope snapped tight, threatening to drag Bran into the water. He set his weight against it, tried to wrap the rope round the finger of rock. It would make a perfect anchor, if only he could secure it. His heels scrabbled in the shingle. The rope began to slip through his good hand, burning it.

Lightning flooded the night sky, turning it entirely white.

A voice beside Bran's ear said:

'Have you noticed how low the boat sits in the water?'

It was Talus: calm, eternally bare-headed and quite unaffected by the catastrophic weather.

'Grab the rope!' Bran yelled. 'Make a fish-loop! Hurry!'

While Bran battled to stop the boat pulling him out to sea, Talus took up the loose end of the rope and circled the rock with it. For the brief moment he was hidden, Bran had the delirious sensation his friend had passed not just out of sight but out of the world altogether.

Talus reappeared from behind the rock, his teeth bared in a rictus grin. He looped the end of the rope over the place where Bran was gripping it and made a knot.

'There!' he said, dusting his hands. 'You can let go now.'

Bran did so, dropping to his knees and allowing the rope to snap tight in the air. A moment later it would have taken off his head. The rope creaked as the full weight of the stricken boat—not to mention the might of the northern ocean—tried to wrench it loose. Bran held his breath and waited.

The rope held. Bran and Talus watched together as the boat wallowed. The oarsmen laboured, forcing the boat backwards against the current while the rope held the boat like a stone in a slingshot, swinging it on a long, curving trajectory towards the only part of the beach that was clear and open.

'You have a keen eye for how shapes fit together,' said Talus. He was breathless. 'The boulder makes a... a joint, like the joint in your arm. The rope holds the boat as it turns around that joint. The oarsmen pull backwards, but the boat moves sideways.' He gestured as he spoke; Bran could sense him struggling to express the thoughts in his head.

'I just did what needed to be done,' said Bran.

Still illuminated by the fire at its prow, the boat completed its arc and slammed into the shore. The waves smacked into it, driving it home. Three men leaped out, carrying ropes, and dragged the boat further up the shingle. They tied the ropes to half-buried boulders that looked heavy enough to keep Mir himself from swimming away.

Bran watched the activity with an equal balance of exhaustion and elation. It was late, he was tired. He'd been all the way to the land of the dead and back again. No sooner had he returned than he'd found himself saving lives that would otherwise have been lost. The quick and the dead, and no border between.

He thought again of Talus's giant with the feathered coat.

'This is a night of life,' he said. For a change, the bard said nothing.

WHILE THE BOATMEN finished securing their vessel, Talus bent close to Bran.

'Did you find it?' he said.

Bran took out the bonespike from the cairn. 'Here. What you wanted.'

Talus whisked the bonespike out of sight. Bran didn't see where it went; the bard's hands were fast, and there was no telling how many pouches and pockets he was hiding under those motley robes. He was glad to be rid of it.

'Now!' Talus exclaimed. 'Let us greet these visitors!'

Talus set off towards the beached boat. Bran lumbered after him, petulant Talus hadn't congratulated him on finding the murder weapon, cross with himself for needing the bard's approval.

More men were spilling out of the boat and onto the shingle. At the same time, the people of Creyak were making their way down the path from the village. Bran wasn't surprised to see they were led by Tharn.

Last to disembark from the boat was an old man. His hair and beard were united in a single cloud of white fuzz, inside which his face glowed a shade of red so vivid it could be only partly attributed to the firelight. Like the faces of his companions, there was something wrong with it.

The old man landed well, feet planted wide, and strode up the shingle with his long arms outstretched. As he approached, Bran saw that what he'd thought a deformity was in fact a network of raised scars criss-crossing the old man's weathered face, darkened with indelible dye. They swarmed over his cheekbones, crowded the line of his jaw. Each of the men from the boat bore similar marks, though coloured differently, and arrayed in wildly varying patterns.

When the old man reached Talus, he embraced him.

'You are both brave men!' he cried. He crushed Bran with an equally boisterous hug. Bran was only slightly vexed that the old man had chosen to thank Talus first.

By now Tharn had joined them.

'Farrum,' he said. He started to drop to one knee, then seemed to think better of it. Stiffening his back, he stood tall and proud, defying the gale that was throwing snow and spindrift into his face. 'I welcome you to Creyak.'

The tone of his voice suggested the newcomer—Farrum—was about as welcome as a wolf in a child's crib.

Farrum hitched his thumbs into the narrow belt of grey leather cinched around his waist. Whale-teeth hung jostling from the belt. The wind turned his hair and beard into a dancing white froth. Sea water dripped from his scarred face.

'I hope I'm always welcome here, boy.' Farrum grinned, revealing crooked teeth that looked too big for his mouth. 'These two men of your father's served me well tonight.'

'They are not my father's men.' Tharn's voice hitched and he looked away.

'We are wanderers,' said Talus. 'Creyak is our refuge against the storm. My friend heard your shouts. We helped as we could.'

Farrum clapped Talus on the shoulder. 'You did well!' The wind slapped snow into his mouth. He spat it out. 'Now, where is the king? I would eat and drink and take company with my old friend Hashath!'

His ice-blue eyes were bright as they scanned the crowd. The whale-teeth rattled on his belt.

'You arrive at a time of sorrow, men of Sleeth,' Mishina said, materialising out of the snow. 'Ill-omened events have befallen our people.'

'Stop babbling and tell me what's wrong.' Farrum's face had turned redder than ever, and his smile had vanished. The snow hissed in the sputtering fire overlooking them all.

'My father is dead,' said Tharn.

Farrum's mouth compressed to a thin line. He grunted once, then again. He appraised the scarred faces of his men, who stood in a line nearby, swaying in the storm, then looked back at Tharn.

'Do you speak the truth? How did he die? Perhaps he fell in the hunt? Or did he drown in the ocean? Or did he die laughing, plunged deep in the loins of a woman?'

'None of these things,' Tharn replied.

'Hashath was murdered,' said Talus.

Farrum's expression turned to one of puzzlement. Nobody spoke.

'Someone killed him last night,' Bran elaborated through chattering teeth. There were tensions here he couldn't fathom, and he was keen to break through them. Keen as well to get under cover. The storm was getting worse and the chill was seeping into his bones.

Farrum lowered his chin to his breast, held it there a moment, then raised it again. He was as tall as Tharn, but leaner. His great age seemed to hang around him.

'I knew that Mir had sent me here for a purpose,' he said. 'I will share in your grief, and do all I can to celebrate the passing of my great friend and ally.'

'My father was not your friend,' said Tharn, and Bran understood at least a little of what was going on.

Farrum held the young man's gaze with his old eyes. 'What will you do, then? Will you send me on my way? My boat will go no further tonight, but I have legs to walk, and so do my men.'

'You are a king, as was my father,' said Tharn. 'It would be an insult to turn you away.'

Farrum said nothing. The wind had carried their words out among the people who were watching: the crowd of villagers from Creyak; four of Tharn's five brothers; the eleven men who'd come on the boat with Farrum, all of whom carried long knives at their belts.

There was more than just tension here. Bran suddenly understood that he and Talus were standing in the middle of a potential battlefield.

'The words I greeted you with remain true,' said Tharn. 'I bid you welcome. You are tired, and so are your men. Having heard our news, you are now sad, as are we. Tonight you will take shelter in Creyak. Tomorrow we will hear why you have come.'

The broken grin flashed back onto Farrum's face, and he closed his ancient hands over Tharn's.

'Well said, young man! Now, for Mir's sake, let's get ourselves out of this cursed storm!'

Even as Farrum beckoned his men forward, a young boy burst through the throng of villagers. He wore a massive wrap of grey fur that made him look like an animated dust-ball.

'Tharn!' he was shouting. 'Tharn! Come quick! He's crushed!'

Tharn did what he'd almost done upon first seeing Farrum: he dropped to one knee.

'What are you saying, boy?'

'He's crushed!'

'Who? Who is crushed?'

'Your brother, Gantor! You've got to come! He's bleeding! I think he's dying!'

With Tharn at their head, the villagers hurried back towards Creyak. Forgetting his exhaustion, Bran followed.

'Tonight has seen not one interesting development,' said Talus, jogging at his shoulder, 'but two. It is lucky we are here.'

Here they were indeed, and Bran had missed the perfect opportunity to depart the island unnoticed. To his surprise, he found it didn't matter. A king had been killed and now someone else was hurt—badly, by the sound of it. And what of these newcomers, these men of Sleeth?

There was a lot more going on in Creyak than they'd first realised. How could he leave without knowing what was behind it?

CHAPTER TEN

THE BOY LED them straight to the house Bran and Talus had been given to shelter in. Bran felt his stomach clench. What had happened here while they'd been absent?

But it wasn't the house that interested the boy: it was the rock-filled pit beside it—which Bran now realised was nothing more than an excavation, made in preparation for another of Gantor's house-building projects. Amid the strew of rubble and shattered whalebone, three giant stones had fallen in a heap together. The ropes that had held them back lay tangled on top.

Beneath the stones was Gantor.

The big man lay on his back, staring straight up. The pit was only partially roofed, but the snow had by now stopped falling and the same wind that had ushered in the storm clouds was now driving them away. One by one, the stars were coming out.

Gantor's chest was barely moving. A laboured, sawing sound came from his throat. With all that weight on top of him, it was a wonder he could breathe at all. Blood had run from his mouth and ears and pooled under his head. Red bubbles popped at his lips and nostrils.

Tharn scrambled down into the pit, closely followed

by his brothers. The two youngsters—Arak and Sigathon—let out identical cries of anguish. They each took one of Gantor's arms and tried to drag their brother clear, but it was no use. Tharn snapped out a command and the two youths stopped pulling. Beyond the fallen whalebones, Fethan prowled, his face dark with unreadable emotion.

Bran started forward, eager to help, but Talus held him back.

'We will wait,' said the bard.

Bran was astonished. 'What? But you're always first to get involved when people are hurt...'

Talus looked affronted. 'Are you suggesting I enjoy seeing scenes such as this?'

'...although you're even more interested when people are dead.'

'Death is interesting. Now be quiet. And be patient.'

Talus folded his arms across his narrow chest and pursed his lips. His cloak flapped in fluid silence, reminding Bran of an owl in flight.

Down in the pit, Tharn had set his shoulder to the stones. He braced himself and heaved. The stones didn't so much as move. Meanwhile, Cabarrath had knelt down and was whispering to his stricken brother. Bran was actually glad that he hadn't gone charging in: this was a private moment, and he was sorry the brothers were having to play out their grief in front of a watching crowd.

Someone muscled past Bran, knocking him into Talus's arms. It was the old man Farrum, barging into the pit. Three of his boatmen followed him. Without ceremony, they joined Tharn and pressed their collective weight against the fallen stones. Nearby, Mishina was chanting under his breath.

'They will kill him,' Talus observed.

'He's dead anyway,' said Bran.

'It seems that death is a constant visitor here.'

'Here and everywhere.'

With a dull grinding sound, the men finally succeeded in rocking the stones aside. At last Gantor lay revealed.

The big man's chest was caved in; his legs were crushed to pulp. As the stones lurched to their new resting places, a spasm ran through the wreck of his body. Blood gushed from a dozen places. A thin wheeze came from his mouth. Bran guessed he was trying to scream, but his flattened lungs would not obey him.

'Be still, Gantor,' said Cabarrath. He slipped his arm under his brother's head. Blood soaked into Cabarrath's furs, turning them dark. He didn't seem to notice.

Gantor's wheezing became a drawn-out croak. It sounded as if it was coming from very far away.

'You...' he whispered. In the silence after the storm, Bran heard it clearly, and guessed everyone listening heard it too. 'You...'

Then his body relaxed for the last time.

Cabarrath's shoulders started to heave. At the same time he drew back, glancing anxiously around. There was no knowing what Gantor had been trying to say— nor even if he'd known it was Cabarrath he was saying it to. But his last words had sounded like an accusation all the same.

Arak let out a sob and rushed into the embrace of

the glowering Fethan, leaving Sigathon to stare at his brother's body with blank eyes. Tharn looked on, his face like stone, shivering with the cold, or with anger, or with both.

Farrum waved his boatmen away and placed his hand on Tharn's shoulder. Tharn tolerated the contact. Mishina continued to chant. The sky continued to clear.

Cabarrath retreated to the far side of the pit, where the shadows were thick. Sobs wracked his body. Nobody went near him.

Talus's eyes were scanning the fallen stones, the weeping men, the scattered whalebones. Bran knew he was memorising everything he saw, marking it for future review.

'We should leave them to it,' Bran said. 'It's late. We should rest.'

'Not the best place to lay down our heads.' Talus nodded towards the house that was their temporary accommodation, and which overlooked the pit. He was right. There would be no peace here tonight.

'Well,' said Bran, gazing at the house, 'I suppose we could always...' But he had no ideas left.

When he looked round, the bard had gone.

HE FOUND TALUS at the end of the passage.

'Talus, why do you always...?' Bran broke off when he saw his friend was talking to the red-haired woman who had served them their food. Who had lifted suspicion for the king's death from their shoulders.

'Please,' said Lethriel. Her eyes were wide like a

rabbit's and bright with tears. 'I was just saying to your friend... I must talk to you. That's why I waved to you through the crowd.'

'I didn't see you wave.'

'There are many things you do not see, Bran,' said Talus. He turned back to Lethriel. 'You are talking to us now. What do you wish to say?'

'I mean alone. I don't know if I should... there are things I must tell, but I don't know who to tell them to. I don't know who to trust.'

'You can trust us,' said Bran.

She measured him with a stern look. When he'd first seen Lethriel in the king's house, Bran had thought she looked like Keyli. Only now did he realise just how much.

'Can I?' Lethriel said.

'Can you what?' Bran was finding it unaccountably hard to breathe.

'You have already decided the answer to that question,' said Talus. 'Otherwise you would not have been so eager to attract my attention. We are wasting time. Where can we go that is private?'

'I... I have a house. I live there alone. I suppose we could go there, but I'm afraid people will...'

'...talk? That is likely, and I see you do not want that. Where, then?'

Lethriel thought for a moment. 'There is a place.'

She took them through dark corridors to the eastern outskirts of the village, on the opposite side of the island from the beach where Farrum's boat had grounded. The houses here were smaller and cruder than those built by Gantor. Many were in ruins.

Soon the abandoned buildings were indistinguishable from the rocky terrain surrounding them. The path narrowed to a rough trail. A steep scramble took them up over crags and bluffs.

'Where are we going?' said Bran. But Lethriel didn't reply.

Eventually the ground levelled out. They'd reached the top of the cliffs. To the east, the mainland was clearly visible across a narrow strait, a slab of black against the starry sky. To the west, there was only the open ocean. Rising from the snow-covered ground was a great circle of massive timber posts. The circle was big enough to contain the entire population of the village. But it was overgrown with ragged sedge and stunted gorse, and Bran guessed it was many years since it had been used.

Each of the encircling posts stood twice as high as a man. Once they must have stood tall and straight, but countless years had turned them into tortured relics of their former selves. Some coiled like snakes; others bent like old men sore in the bone; many were pierced with holes through which the wind whistled, making the whole clifftop sing with a low, eerie moan.

Bran ran his fingers over the nearest post. It looked like a woman writhing in pain. The wood was embossed with intricate carvings: spirals and hatched lines and indented dots. In some places, the patterns were etched deep; in others, the weather had worn them almost to nothing.

'What is this place?' he said.

'We call it the henge. The ancestors made it when the world was younger. There's a stone in the middle—do you see it?'

'It's hard to miss it.' The stone was almost as big as the boat that had brought Farrum and his men to the island.

'They used to kill people here. They would put them on the stone and slit their throats. The blood would run out and they would drink it. In the time of *ago*, this was what the spirits wanted.'

'But they don't want it any more?' Bran tried to quell his anxiety. He and Talus had once had a narrow escape from a settlement where ritual sacrifice was still practised.

'So we believe. Nobody comes here any more. People fear it is haunted by the spirits of those who died on the stone.'

Listening to the wind sighing through the sculpted pillars, Bran could believe it. 'And this is the best place you could think of to meet?'

'The henge is my place now. The air here is just right.'

'Just right for what?'

STANDING BETWEEN TWO of the pillars—and set partially into the ground—was a small wooden shack. Bran hesitated in the doorway: this was like the cairn all over again.

'Here,' Lethriel called from the darkness inside. 'There are seats.'

Bran took a deep breath and descended rotting wooden steps into a cave-like interior. It was dry and surprisingly warm.

'This way.'

Bran walked towards the sound of her voice, waving his hands in front of him. Something coarse stroked his cheek and he bit his lip to suppress a cry. Then a bony hand took his and pulled him down onto a hard surface.

'Sit down before you bump into something,' said Talus.

Gradually, Bran's eyes adjusted to the gloom. They were sitting in a square pit roofed with gnarled wooden beams. Hanging from the beams were countless bunches of herbs and winter grass, like a summer meadow turned upside-down. It was one of the bunches that had brushed his face.

'I bring my herbs here to dry,' Lethriel explained. 'The old people built it to face the rising sun. It's warm, isn't it?'

Bran looked round uneasily. Warm or not, if people said it was haunted, it probably was.

'Gantor made it safe for me,' Lethriel said. She pointed out supporting columns that clearly weren't part of the original structure. 'It was his gift to me after Caltie died.'

'Caltie?'

Lethriel looked down. 'My man.'

'Did you know Gantor well?' said Talus.

'Yes.'

'Then what happened tonight must have upset you,' Talus said.

'A man has died!'

'Yes. And it has upset *you*.'

Lethriel picked at the edge of her fur wrap. 'It's a long story.'

'Stories are my business. Will you tell yours?'

'I suppose I will. It's why I brought you here, after all. But first I want to ask you something.'

'Ask, then. If it is a question I can answer, I will do so.'

'Are you a good man?'

There was no echo in the little shack; Lethriel's voice just soaked away into the old wooden walls like water into sand.

'I do not know what you mean by "good man."'

A breeze wafted down from the entrance, cool and dry. It seemed to spin in the enclosed space, circling each of them in turn, before fleeing again into the night. Outside, the moaning of the wind grew briefly louder. Bran shivered.

Had Gantor's death been some kind of sacrifice? The thought came to him with sudden, dreadful clarity. Had Gantor known who'd killed his father, and had the killer silenced him before he could speak?

Was Gantor's abandoned spirit even now haunting this ancient wooden henge?

The breeze rustled a string of herbs hanging directly above Bran's head. He bit his lip to stifle a scream.

'I just want to be sure I can trust you,' Lethriel was saying to Talus.

'Nothing I can say will convince you of that,' the bard replied. 'But I will tell you this: I am a man who has come. I am a man who is here. I bring nothing but myself and will take away nothing but myself when I leave. But I will do my very best to leave something behind.'

'You speak strangely,' said Lethriel. 'What will you leave behind?'

'The truth. Will you tell us your story now?'

'Is that what you think this is? A story?'

'Stories are all that we have, Lethriel. They are all that we are.'

CHAPTER ELEVEN

THE MOON ROSE, throwing its rays deep into the little shack. Her face glowing silver in its light, Lethriel began.

'Do you remember I mentioned my man, Caltie? He and Gantor were blood-brothers. They did everything together. I think Gantor was closer to Caltie than he was to any of his real brothers. They looked so alike. In the last world they must have been twins. They loved each other. They loved me too, both of them.'

'But you loved only Caltie?' said Bran. He could already see where this was going.

'Caltie was my man. Gantor was not.'

'How did Gantor feel about that?'

'If you'd known Gantor, you'd know what a ridiculous question that is.' The arch of her pale eyebrows hit Bran harder than a slap to his cheek.

'How did Caltie die?' said Talus.

Lethriel hitched in a long, shuddering breath. 'It was an accident. A common, careless thing. Caltie was a great climber. He loved it up here. I suppose that's one reason I still like to come here so much. He knew a hundred different ways up and down the cliffs. He knew them better than anyone. But it was the cliffs that killed him in the end.

'It happened when he was collecting eggs. He used to climb down to the gull nests on the west cliff. Each season he'd make it harder and harder for himself, seeking out more and more difficult routes. He always liked to push himself to do better. One day he pushed too hard.'

'He fell?'

Lethriel nodded. 'I was down on the beach. I saw it all. I never usually liked to watch him: it scared me to see him take such risks. But this day... I don't know, something made me go there.' She swallowed hard. 'It just happened. I took in one breath and he was safe, climbing up to the clifftop with a pouch full of eggs. I took another breath and the rock under his feet crumbled away—the cliffs are dangerous, they always have been. He fell—just fell from the cliff onto the rocks and the sea dragged him to the bottom. He died quickly.' She paused. 'So did I.'

'I'm sorry,' said Bran. She was so like Keyli it hurt his heart to look at her: the fiery colour of her hair, the line of freckles across her nose. Her presence confused him, filled him with passions he'd thought long-forgotten.

'I was sorry too. I still am. But time passed and other men wanted to take their turn with me. One other in particular.'

'Who?' said Talus. 'If not Gantor?'

Her eyes dropped. She hesitated. 'Fethan.'

'The king's son?' said Bran.

Up came her eyes again. 'The king had many sons, Gantor among them. But Gantor is a better man than Fethan will ever be. *Was* a better man. They all are.

Fethan is the worst of them.' Her voice had become a snarl.

'We thought at first that it might be Fethan who killed the king,' said Bran. 'Is that why you wanted to talk to us? Do you think that too?'

Lethriel shook her head. 'Not Fethan.'

'Tell us what you think,' said Talus.

She hugged herself. Bran glanced at Talus, but the bard's attention was fixed on Lethriel. 'I've been worried for Gantor for a long time. He is—was—not popular. Not with his brothers, at least. They all think themselves big men, dashing and heroic, hunters and runners, you know. But Gantor was different. He was a thinker, a planner, a man who liked silence and the company of his own heart.'

'May I ask a question?' said Talus. 'How many of the houses in Creyak are Gantor's handiwork?'

'What's that got to do with anything?' said Bran.

Lethriel shrugged. 'Not the oldest, of course. Some are nearly as old as this henge. People have lived on Creyak since before the hard snows. The old people used to hunt the mammut, or so it's said. There's a sea cave on Creyak where the paintings move with a life all their own. You can get to it from the beach.'

Bran knew of the mammut: the giant tusked beasts that once walked the world but were now gone from it. He'd once seen a mammut skull, but paintings that moved by themselves? Surely Lethriel was making that part up.

'In his life, I suppose Gantor made twenty houses,' Lethriel went on. 'He was very skilled. As you saw, most of the old dwellings here stand empty. Folk would rather live in one of Gantor's houses than out here in the eastern reaches. Gantor knew how to make a home.'

'If his son was so talented,' said Talus, 'why did Hashath choose to live in a house built by someone else?'

'How do you know Gantor didn't build the king's house?' said Bran. All the houses looked the same to him.

Lethriel was smiling, just a little. 'Yes, bard. How can you know such a thing?'

Talus laced his fingers. 'We have been given a house built by Gantor. The bones in its roof have been twisted into a spiral. The spiral shape both pleases the eye and takes out the smoke. Many of the other Creyak houses I have been able to look into are the same. The king's house is not. In fact, the smoke does not move well in the king's house at all. Did you not notice that, Bran?'

'It was stuffy,' Bran agreed.

'The problem could be easily fixed: a wooden screen once hung around the smoke hole. A skilled builder like Gantor could have repaired it in a breath or two, I have no doubt. For some reason he chose not to. Or perhaps the king never asked him.'

'You see much,' said Lethriel.

'I see that Gantor was a lonely man. I see that you and Caltie were his only friends. Gantor was a stranger to his brothers, to his father, to all of Creyak.'

'You speak as if you knew him,' said Lethriel.

'I observed him briefly.'

'For Talus, it amounts to the same thing,' said Bran.

'His father hated him,' said Lethriel. 'When Gantor

offered to build the king a new house, Hashath laughed in his face. Gantor's brothers laughed too. They thought him... they called Gantor an oaf with fancy ways. Only Cabarrath came close to showing him kindness.'

'You said that Gantor loved you.'

'In his way, yes.'

'But not as deeply as he loved Caltie?' Talus let his words float on the still, dry air. 'Is that why his father despised him? Because he was the kind of man whose heart turns not to women but to other men?'

Lethriel didn't answer. Bran wondered how he could have been so stupid: when Lethriel had said Gantor loved Caltie, she'd been speaking the absolute truth.

'Let us turn our attention to the night the king died,' said Talus. 'What do you believe happened?'

Lethriel took a deep, shuddering breath. 'I know they argued, Gantor and his father. That was nothing unusual. They argued all the time.'

'What was the argument about that night?'

'I don't know. Gantor came to me afterwards. He told me he was never going to speak to his father again. He was crying. But he didn't tell me what they'd said to each other.'

Bran tried to imagine tears on the face of that solid slab of a man who spent his days hewing stone and bending whalebone. It was difficult.

'When he came to me, Gantor was... he was carrying a bonespike. One of the long ones he used to scribe the stones. He kept spinning it in his hands. I told him to go home and sleep. I told him everything would look brighter in the morning.' She looked first to Talus, then to Bran. The moonlight turned the tears on her cheeks to stars. 'But I don't think it did.'

Talus slipped his hand inside his cloak. He brought out the bonespike Bran had retrieved from the cairn. The bonespike that had been used to murder the king. Bran was relieved to see Talus had cleaned the blood from it.

As soon as she saw it, Lethriel let out a cry. 'Where did you find that?'

'That is not important,' said Talus. He held it out. 'A bonespike is a common enough thing. Do you know this one? I believe you do.'

Lethriel took the bonespike. She traced a trembling finger all the way from the weapon's blunt end to its lethal tip. She turned it in the silver light.

'Here,' she said. She pointed to an engraved mark. Bran peered at it; it looked a little like a bird in flight. 'It's a gull. One of the black ones that haunts the cliffs. It was Caltie's mark. He used to scribe this shape on the rock face whenever he raided a nest. Sometimes he would open his arms and pretend he was about to jump off. He used to boast he could fly. It scared me.'

'So the bonespike belonged to Caltie,' said Talus.

'Yes. After Caltie died, I gave it to Gantor. As a memory. He thanked me. It became... very precious to him.'

'What happened last night?' Talus's voice was barely audible. Outside the shack, the wind moaned.

'I don't know for certain. But after Gantor left me, I think he went back to his father's house. I think he used the bonespike to kill the king, then dragged his body out into the maze so it would freeze in the snow, and nobody would know who had done this dreadful thing.' Lethriel hitched in a breath, wiped her eyes. 'Gantor was a good man. He came to the feast to honour his father—the man he'd killed—but he couldn't bear it and left early. He must have roamed through Creyak in torture, unable to live with the thought of what he'd done. So he went to the place he knew best and brought those stones crashing down on himself.'

The tears had dried on her cheeks. Despite the softness of the moonlight her skin looked raw, as if the wind had burned it. Her shoulders were square and somehow proud.

'He punished himself for what he had done,' said Talus.

Lethriel showed no sign of having heard him. 'Gantor knew exactly what would be waiting for him in the afterdream,' she said. 'The ancestors, baying for him like wolves. He couldn't bear the thought of living his life in anticipation of that hell, and decided to go to it with open arms. Gantor was always the bravest of them. He had to be.'

'Brave indeed,' said Talus. He lifted the bonespike from Lethriel's limp hand and stowed it away. 'Bran— have I not said to you before that most murders are committed through passion? We should not be surprised if the killer proves to be the king's own son.'

Bran felt deflated. After all the drama he'd witnessed here, the truth seemed desperately ordinary.

'What will I do?' said Lethriel. 'Now they're both gone, what will I do?'

Talus jumped to his feet. His bald head brushed against the hanging herbs and grasses, setting them swinging to and fro. At the same time, the breeze strengthened, making his motley robes flutter around him. Its moaning transformed into a high-pitched whistle.

'You will help us, Lethriel! Tonight you have shown that you are clever. And, like Gantor, you are brave. Bran and I will need your help if we are to track down the real killer!'

Bran and Lethriel gaped at him.

'Talus, what are you talking about?' said Bran. 'She just told us...'

'Lethriel has told us what she *believes*. Not what she *knows*. The two are not the same.'

'So you don't believe me,' said Lethriel, 'when I say the king was killed by his son?'

'On the contrary,' said Talus. 'I believe that is exactly what has happened. However, I do not believe poor Gantor is the son in question.'

'Then which one of them is?' said Bran.

Talus reached up and plucked a clump of dried grass from the ceiling. He waved it in front of Bran's face.

'The answer lies exactly where such answers always lie,' he said. 'Beneath our noses.'

CHAPTER TWELVE

TALUS DARTED FROM one side of the shack to the other, yanking down bundles of herbs from the ceiling and tossing them on the floor. He was only vaguely aware of the bemused looks on the faces of his companions. The buzzing of his thoughts had elevated to a kind of screech. He knew from experience that the only way to dampen the sound was to work.

Soon he'd covered the dirt floor with herbs. He hopped among them, kicking here, scuffing there, making patterns from the debris. Every so often he stopped to survey his work. Was it good enough? He supposed it would have to do.

Clapping his hands, he ran outside into the moonlight.

'Talus?' Bran's voice floated out of the shack. 'Where are you going?'

Talus didn't reply. Speaking would only divert him from his task. He picked his way across the frozen grass, scooping up as many stones and pebbles as he could find. When his hands were full, he dashed back inside and dropped his collection in a pile just inside the doorway.

'Do we have to guess what you're up to?' said Bran.

'All will become clear,' Talus replied.

He picked a stone from the pile and placed it beside the nearest bundle of herbs. He took more stones and positioned them at different locations on the floor, some singly, some in groups. Where necessary, he made adjustments to the arrangement of the herb bundles. When he was done, he stood back with his hands on his hips, assessing his work.

Lethriel had been watching all this with her mouth agape. Bran was shaking his head. Talus supposed his performance must strike them as odd.

'Now,' he said, 'we can make a start.'

'Talus,' said Bran, 'what you've made is a mess.'

'Be quiet, Bran. Look at the...'

'At the mess?'

Talus waved his hands, exasperated. Why did he always have to explain?

'Wait,' said Lethriel. She rose to her feet and slowly circled the pattern Talus had made on the floor. 'It's not a mess.'

'At last!' said Talus. 'Somebody who knows how to look.'

'Looks like a mess to me,' said Bran.

'No,' said Lethriel. 'It's a picture. This'—she pointed to a bundle of purple heather—'this is the king's house. And here is where Tharn and Cabarrath live.' She looked at Talus. 'I'm right, aren't I? This is a picture, isn't it? A picture of Creyak?'

Talus smiled. He couldn't help himself. 'Each herb bundle is a house. The spaces between them are passages. Yes, this is Creyak, laid out for us to study.'

'What are the stones for?' said Bran.

'I know,' said Lethriel. She picked up one of the stones—a coarse chunk of shale—and turned it in her fingers. 'This is Gantor.' Before replacing the stone, she kissed it.

'You are correct,' said Talus. The first time he'd encountered Lethriel, he'd seen intelligence in her eyes. It was pleasing to see it at work.

'Here is the house of the king.' Lethriel pointed to some bound strips of willow bark. Three stones lay beside the bundle: smooth grey pebbles from the beach, one large, two small. 'The big pebble is Hashath. The smaller pebbles are the youngest brothers: Sigathon and Arak.'

Warming to his task, Talus traced his finger through the gaps he'd left between the herbs. He reached a bunch of lavender and two lumps of green jade.

'Tharn and Cabarrath, the elder sons. They share the home of the huntsmen. They live at the entrance to the maze, strong men guarding the settlement's most vulnerable spot.'

He was no longer looking at herbs and stones, but at walls and faces. The map wasn't just a picture; it was real.

'*Here* stands Fethan's house. He is the only man in a home occupied by artisan women. Gantor lived *here*, remote from the rest, close to the burial cairn.'

'All very clever,' said Bran. 'But how is playing with stones going to help us?'

'Playing with stones turned out to be very important to Gantor,' said Talus.

'You think he was murdered too,' said Lethriel slowly. 'Gantor, I mean. Do you think it was the same person?

Do you think whoever who killed the king tipped those stones down over poor Gantor too?'

'I thought you said Gantor killed himself,' said Bran. Lethriel flinched.

'That is not what I believe,' said Talus.

Bran sighed. 'Talus, we've only been here a day and we've spent most of that time under guard. How do you suddenly know exactly where everyone in Creyak lives?'

Delighted by Bran's question, Talus laced his fingers and stretched them until his knuckles cracked.

'As you must have noticed, Bran, most of the people in Creyak leave their doorways open. On our various trips around the village, therefore, I have been able to look inside most of the houses. Shall I tell you what I have seen?'

'Will it make a difference if I say no?'

'In the house that stands beside the maze, a cloak was clearly visible lying on the nearest bed. I later saw Tharn wearing that same cloak. The house is therefore his. Above the next bed, the low roof was badly dented, so Tharn clearly shares his home with an unusually tall man: almost certainly his brother, Cabarrath.'

'He's right,' said Lethriel. 'In Creyak, older brothers live together until both have married.'

'The custom is common. It was therefore likely that the youngest brothers, Sigathon and Arak, lived with their father. This was proved when I saw mock-weapons—driftwood axes and so on—stored beside two of the beds in the king's house: the same weapons the two youths wore at tonight's feast.'

'Again, he's right.' Lethriel couldn't have looked more excited. Bran, on the other hand, just looked bored.

'Which brings us to Gantor. Lethriel has already told us he lived alone. That puts him in this isolated house near the cairn. As for Fethan: he clearly enjoys female company.'

'I did notice how all the women at the feast kept smiling at him,' said Bran.

'Not all of them,' said Lethriel with a scowl.

'This house'—Talus pointed to a bundle of dried samphire and its accompanying stone—'contains five beds for women and only one for a man. The man who lives there has long black hair; I saw strands of it spread over not just one bed but all of them.'

'Have you finished?' said Bran.

'You asked me to explain.'

'All right, Talus, you've proved you're just as clever as you always were. But this still doesn't tell us anything useful.'

'I disagree,' said Talus. 'It proves that Gantor did not kill the king.'

Tears welled in Lethriel's eyes. 'What? How?'

Talus stepped into the middle of his map. He felt like a giant stepping onto the world. The patterns he'd made on the floor were vivid, and told him much. Why couldn't they *see*?

'As heirs to the king, Tharn and Cabarrath could have lived in any house they chose. They chose this one, which lies to the left of the maze. Inside the house, they chose beds in positions that favour the left hand. Their cloaks and possessions lie at their left side.'

'So they're left-handed?' said Bran. 'That's unusual, I suppose.'

'Sigathon and Arak carry their mock-weapons at the left side. Fethan, when he threatened you with his bonespike, Bran, held his weapon in his left hand. Tell me, Lethriel, did Hashath favour his left hand too?'

She nodded. 'He did.'

'The king and his sons: a strange family, whose hands work in strange ways.'

Bran's good right hand stole across to cover his useless left. Talus knew that he too had been left-handed once.

'I still don't understand,' said Bran.

'All the sons are left-handed except Gantor.' He stepped, light-footed, across the map. 'Do you see how he built his house on this side of the cairn and not the other? And did you not notice which hand he used to take his bowl of broth from Lethriel at the feast?'

'It must have slipped my attention.'

'Why does that not surprise me?'

'Why does it matter?'

'Stand up,' said Talus. He stepped out of the miniature Creyak he'd made. Bran heaved himself to his feet. 'Pretend you hold a bonespike in your right hand and stab me under the left arm.'

'But why...?'

'Do as I say.'

Bran bunched his fist and lunged towards him. Talus blocked him easily with his upraised hand. Bran tried several times more, but each time the bard fended him off.

'Enough,' said Talus. Bran backed away. 'You are stronger than me, Bran, and heavier. Yet I held you off. For Hashath the warrior-king, fending off such an attack would have been even easier.'

'It would be different if his attacker came from behind.' Now they were talking about fighting, Bran's interest was aroused.

'At last you are thinking for yourself! Very well, then, come behind me!'

Again they played out the little scene. Lethriel watched, her mouth a thin, tight line. Again they parted.

'You landed five blows out of six,' said Talus.

'Proving?' said Bran, panting a little.

'You landed them on my right side. The wound that killed the king was on his left,' said Talus. 'This play-fight—and the shape of the king's wound—tell me that the king's attacker was left-handed. Gantor was innocent.'

'All right,' said Bran. 'I believe you. But Gantor could still have killed himself.'

Talus closed his eyes. He recalled the image of the pit he'd fixed in his mind: Gantor lying crushed; the angle of the big man's body; the resting places of the gigantic stones; the way the heaviest one had first landed, then rocked back under its own weight.

In seeing how the stones must have fallen, he saw too what must have driven them to fall.

He opened his eyes again.

'Gantor had his back to the boulders as they fell. The position of his legs tells me he tried to run. It was not Gantor who brought down the stones.'

'An accident, then?'

'Did you not see the ends of the ropes? They were cut

clean. And the largest of the stones could not possibly have fallen unless it was pushed from behind. No, I am certain Gantor was murdered.'

Bran gave a vast yawn. 'Talus, I'm tired. I'm sure Lethriel is, too...'

'I can speak for myself! Who killed them, Talus? Gantor and the king. Do you think it was the same person?'

'It is likely. Just as it is likely the murderer placed this behind the door to the afterdream.' Talus brought out the bonespike again. 'Are the people of Creyak allowed to enter the cairn at all times?'

'No,' said Lethriel slowly. 'On ritual days, the villagers may enter for the ceremony. Otherwise only the king and his heirs are allowed inside.'

'Nobody else? Not even the shaman?'

'Well, obviously him.'

Lethriel looked agitated. Talus decided not to pursue it—for now.

'Very well,' he said. 'Let us talk about the shaman for a moment. Where does Mishina live?'

'Don't you know? I thought you knew everything.'

'If I passed the shaman's house, its door was closed to me.'

Lethriel stabbed a finger towards an empty space in the exact centre of Talus's map. 'There. And there's a reason you won't have seen into his house. But this... this has nothing to do with the killings. Please, can't you put that bonespike away?'

'If you had to choose a herb to mark the house of the shaman, which would it be?'

Talus spun the bonespike in his fingers, enduring her glare. Finally she stomped over to where Bran was sitting. Her agitation was fascinating.

'Out of my way,' she said.

Bran stood. She shoved aside the stone he'd been sitting on, revealing a deep hollow. She rummaged in it for a moment before holding up a tiny, wizened object.

'What is it?' said Bran. 'Does the shaman like dried fruit?'

'Hardly,' said Lethriel. 'It's a kind of fungus, very rare. I gather them along with my herbs, but it's better if people don't know where I keep them.'

She threw the hideous thing down in the middle of the map. Her distress was obvious.

'Greycap,' said Talus. It was just what he'd been expecting. He wondered if Bran knew of the mushroom's special properties—and why, therefore, Lethriel kept it hidden. 'Thank you, Lethriel. You have answered my question and explained a great deal.'

'Have you finished your games?' said Lethriel. 'Are you going to take my question seriously now?'

'I take all questions seriously.'

'Who killed them?'

Her voice cracked with a sound like splintering wood. Her eyes were filled with anguish. No wonder: she'd just lost a man she held dear. Talus felt pity for her. But it was a distant emotion, overshadowed by his own overwhelming curiosity. What was she holding back?

'Ah, we come back to the question!' Talus rubbed his hands. 'Sad to say, I do not know—yet. But we have this!'

Again he brandished the bonespike. Again Lethriel flinched.

'Whoever hid this in the cairn either killed the king or knew the killer. So our eyes turn back to the king's sons. Unless... Lethriel, are you sure you told me the truth about the cairn?'

'I don't know what you mean.'

'Are there any others, apart from the king's sons, who are allowed inside? Any women, for example?'

'Why would I know such a thing?'

'You know it. That is all that concerns me.'

Lethriel's eyes flared with defiance. 'Say what you mean to say!'

'Very well. As the keeper of herbs, are you, Lethriel, able to come and go as you please, in and out of the cairn, so as to keep the dead smelling sweet?'

'You know I am!'

'And as a server of food to the king, do you also come and go in his house, whenever you choose?'

'Yes!'

'Catch!'

Talus tossed the bonespike to her. She raised her hand instinctively to catch it.

Her left hand.

CHAPTER THIRTEEN

LETHRIEL STARED AT her fingers as if they'd betrayed her. She opened her hand and let the bonespike fall to the floor.

'Talus, surely you don't think...' said Bran. Talus raised a finger to silence him. A blush was rising up Lethriel's face.

'If either of you think it,' she said, 'you can leave this place right now.' Her hands and voice trembled as she spoke.

Talus rubbed the top of his head. 'It does not matter what I *believe*,' he said. 'All that matters is what I *know*.'

Lethriel's cheeks shone scarlet. 'You are a strange man.'

'Yes.'

'But clever.'

'Yes.'

'Then tell me, clever man, what is it you *really* want from me?'

'You claim you are innocent of murder, Lethriel. I want you to prove it.'

'If you think I killed the king, you're no smarter than a starfish.' Lethriel's body shook as she spoke.

'Why do you say that?' said Talus.

'Do I look strong enough to drag a man the size of Hashath through the snow?'

'Perhaps you were not alone.'

'I didn't do it.'

'So you say.'

Lethriel stamped her foot. 'You really *are* stupid!'

'Is that what you *believe*? Or is it what you *know*?'

Talus's face was calm. Bran wasn't surprised at Lethriel's reaction. Sometimes, when he was arguing with the bard, Bran felt like the ocean beating itself to a froth against a particularly smug rock.

'Does it give you pleasure to do this to people, Talus?' he said.

'I do not know what you mean,' the bard replied. 'She claims she wants to help. That is what I am helping her to do.'

'You're not helping her. You're driving her. You might as well take a stick and...'

'You're talking about me as if I'm not here!' said Lethriel.

'Then speak for yourself!' said Talus, matching Lethriel's suddenly sharp tone.

'What I *know* is this: at the moment the king was killed, the two of you were plodding down the south cliff making ready to cross the causeway and stir up trouble. I know this because I was on the south cliff too, gathering the herbs you've so gleefully scattered across my floor. I saw you. Earlier this evening you accepted my word on this.'

'You spoke the truth,' Talus agreed. 'For that we are grateful.'

'Then believe what I have to say now.' She took a deep, snuffling breath. Little by little, the hectic colour was fading from her face. 'Like you, I heard the screams of my people across the water. As I said, I was high on the moorside path, looking down. At the same time, I saw you both, like insects, stepping out across the causeway. The sun was low, barely risen. It looked as if you were walking on water.'

'Go on,' said Talus.

'I gathered my bundles and ran. I knew something was wrong. By the time I reached Creyak, Hashath had already been carried to the tomb. I was too late to do anything. Too late to help. So, you see, it doesn't matter that I use my left hand or my right. I wasn't there. I couldn't have been, not if I saw you as I say I did. I couldn't have killed the king.'

'I know,' said Talus.

'What?'

'Just as you saw us on the cliff, so I saw you on the moor. When I saw you again later, first in the king's house and then at the feast, I recognised you.'

'Recognised me? But you can't have seen my face. I was so far away.'

'Your hair gives you away. And your height. And the way you walk. Faces are just the surface of people.'

'You... so why did you make me go through all this?'

'It is not your innocence that interests me, Lethriel. It is your ability to prove it.'

The blush gathered anew round Lethriel's bare neck. Bran hated Talus for teasing her. But he was relieved to know she wasn't a killer.

'You were testing me.' To Bran's amazement, Lethriel laughed. 'You cruel, clever man—you were *testing* me!'

Talus clapped his hands. 'So. Now it is time for us *really* to get to work!'

He crouched over his map and started sketching lines in the dirt floor. Lethriel watched him for a while with wide, appraising eyes. Finally she joined him. The moon rose out of sight and the chamber grew dark again. The moan of the wind drifted in and out, sounding more than ever like the voices of the dead.

As the night rolled on, Talus tossed out one theory after the next, describing any number of possible ways in which the king might have been killed. Bran added his own thoughts when they occurred to him, but mostly he left Talus to it. The bard's mind was like a running horse: get too close and you risked a kick to the head. Lethriel, however, seemed to be keeping up.

He found himself watching Lethriel. So like Keyli, yet unlike her too. Bran had never met a woman more gentle than the wife he'd lost; Keyli had been the calm to his storm. Lethriel had a temper to rival the fiercest warrior. To rival Bran's own, actually. Was it her grief, he wondered, making her like this, or her nature?

He imagined lying with her. What would it be like? There had been nobody since Keyli's death. In the dark of the night, Lethriel would look just like the woman he'd lost. He imagined caressing her, saying nothing to her for fear of calling her the wrong name. Did she bring her temper to her bed? The thought excited him.

Bran suddenly realised Talus was speaking to him. 'What was that?'

'If you were not listening,' said Talus, 'then clearly you have nothing of value to add to the discussion.'

'I was thinking.'

'About what?'

'Nothing important.'

'I thought not. However, I will ask you again: have you noticed anything unusual about the behaviour of any of the king's sons?'

'You mean apart from Fethan trying to kill me?'

'I am aware of what Fethan did. Is there anything else?'

Bran thought hard. 'Cabarrath looked nervous when Gantor spoke to him, just before he died. More than nervous; he looked guilty.'

Talus nodded. 'Gantor said, "You." Do you know why?' he said to Lethriel. She shook her head. 'Is there anything else, Bran?'

'I don't know. The youngster—Arak—is twitchy. And the other one... Sigathon, is it? The one who paints his face black. He hasn't said a single word since we arrived here.'

'Sigathon is a quiet one,' said Lethriel. 'Talus, are you certain it was one of the king's sons that killed Hashath? There's a whole village of people here. It could have been anyone.'

'No,' said Talus. 'It could not. Bran will tell you why.'

Bran sat up straight. It was typical of Talus to put him on the spot—punishment for his daydreaming, he supposed. Sometimes the bard made him feel like a child in need of correction.

'Well...' he said slowly, trying to gather his thoughts. It was hard, when his mind kept filling up with images of Lethriel unwrapped from her furs. 'I suppose it's like you said before: most killings are done with passion. The killer is usually family, or a close friend... or a lover.'

Talus raised his eyebrows. 'Did Hashath have a lover?'

Lethriel shook her head. 'After his wife died, the king was alone.'

'Very well. What Bran says is true. We must also remember that this is no ordinary murder. This is the murder of a *king*. In order to do the deed, the killer must have found a way to put aside all fear of his eventual punishment in the spirit world. Either that, or he was mad.'

'There are no madmen on Creyak,' said Lethriel firmly. 'Hashath drove out anyone who was not... to his liking.'

'Really?' Talus stared at her. 'That is interesting. We will talk more of it later.'

'There's another possibility,' said Bran.

'Yes?'

'The killer doesn't believe the spirits can hurt him. Maybe he doesn't believe they exist at all.'

Both Talus and Lethriel looked at him in surprise.

'That is quite a thing to say,' said Talus slowly. 'Have you ever met anyone who thinks that way, Bran?'

'No, but...'

'Then it is settled.' Talus was suddenly all briskness and efficiency. Bran wondered why he was so keen to change the subject. 'While nothing is certain, it remains likely our killer is one of the king's sons. Nothing, however, is certain.'

'You mean none of this has been any use?' said Bran, indicating the sprawl of stones and herbs.

'It is just a picture,' said Talus. 'When you look into a picture, patterns are revealed. Ideas come to life. Just as when you look into a fire; have you not noticed this?'

Bran shrugged. Lethriel mimicked his gesture; he caught her eye and they both smiled.

Talus started breaking up his map. Lethriel helped him hook the various bundles back in place on the ceiling. Bran carried the stones outside and scattered them on the ground.

Fog had obscured the mainland. It seemed to glow with a light of its own. Somewhere, unseen, the sun had risen, heralding a new day. The wooden pillars of the henge were twisted phantoms looming from swirling cloud. A gust of wind touched Bran's face and he flinched.

A figure stepped out from behind one of the pillars: Mishina. His face, striped yellow and white, seemed to float in the fog.

Bran pressed his hand to his chest. For a moment he'd thought his heart had stopped.

'The bard is summoned,' said Mishina.

Something about Mishina's presence here unsettled Bran. The thought of meeting ghosts had been bad. Meeting the shaman was somehow worse.

Bran had never met a shaman he liked. He understood the value of these spirit-walkers, the way they mediated between a settlement's people and their ancestors. But Bran was—or had been—a fisherman. If he'd had a connection to the spirit world it had always been through the sea, through Mir himself. Every day he'd ridden the waves, in direct and intimate contact with everything he believed, everything he trusted, everything he dreamed.

Bran had never just fished with his hands. He'd always fished with his heart.

Those days were long gone.

'Who exactly is doing the summoning?' he said. 'And how did you know we were here?'

'The spirits know everything.' Cool eyes blinked from behind Mishina's painted mask. 'The bard is summoned by the king-to-be.'

'We will come,' said Talus, stepping up out of the shack. He straightened his robe and bowed his head. A few breaths later, Lethriel joined him.

'The king-to-be requires the company of the bard alone,' said Mishina.

'As I said, we will come. All three of us.'

Mishina's gaze slid first over Lethriel, then Bran. Bran's good fist clenched at his side. Sometimes he was glad he had only one working hand. It meant he could get into only half as much trouble.

'Have you got a problem with that?' Bran said.

Yellow eyelids descended, flickered, lifted. The paint cracked around Mishina's lips as the shaman smiled.

'You entertain me,' he said. He dipped his head in mimicry of Talus's bow. 'You will all come.'

With the coming of the fog, the breeze had dropped to nothing. As they left the henge, a cry followed them through the still, damp air. It might have been a gull on the wing, or a seal moving through the surf, or some final breath of wind through one of the ancient sculpted columns.

Or it might have been the voice of the lonely dead.

ChAPTER FOURTEEN

MISHINA LED THEM back through Creyak's eastern
quarter to the house of the king. Talus walked at his
side, though as far as Bran could tell the two men
exchanged not a single word. There was an awkward
moment when the passage narrowed, forcing them to
walk in single file. Bran and Lethriel each stopped to let
the other through.

'After you,' they both said at the same time.

They looked at each other and laughed. Bran's laugh
turned into a yawn. So did Lethriel's, and then they
were laughing again.

'I was tired before the night began,' said Bran. 'My
head will be in a fog today.'

'We will all be in a fog,' said Lethriel. 'See?'

She fluttered her hands through the thin grey mist
drifting through the passage.

'It's come off the sea. You can taste it.'

'You know the ocean?'

'I'm a fisherman. Or was. Now I...' Bran halted. What
exactly *was* he these days? 'Now I travel.'

'Where are you travelling to?'

'The north.'

'Why?'

Which brought him all the way back round to Keyli again. 'Perhaps I'll tell you another time. I'm sorry about your friend. About Gantor.'

'Thank you. Death surrounds us.'

She started to squeeze through the narrow part of the passage, but Bran pulled her back.

'Wait,' he said.

'What is it?'

'When you said that Fethan was interested in you, but that you weren't interested in him, I just wondered if... after Caltie, has there been...?'

'Anyone else?' Her smile was broad now. Bran didn't know if it was her expression or the way the light caught it, but suddenly she didn't look like Keyli any more. He found that a relief. 'Why do you ask me that question, fisherman?'

'I... I know how it feels to lose someone you love.'

'I know.'

'You... how do you...?'

'I can see it in your eyes. What was her name?'

'Keyli.'

'Was she beautiful?'

'Yes. Yes, she was.'

'How did she die?'

The directness of Lethriel's questions unnerved Bran. This wasn't how he'd imagined the conversation going. 'It's not something I like to talk about.'

'Maybe you should. But if I've offended you, I'm sorry.' She touched the side of his cheek: a brief, surprising contact. 'Now, what was it you wanted to ask me?'

'Nothing. It's...'

'Yes?'

'It's good to see you looking happier.'

'It's your friend—he makes me smile. He's strange and exasperating, but there's something about him that makes you believe that... that everything's going to be all right? Do you know what I mean?'

Bran nodded. 'I do.'

'Sometimes love comes again. We have to believe that, people like you and me, don't you think?'

Bran didn't dare answer. Incredibly, a new possibility had presented itself to him: abandoning the quest didn't necessarily have to mean going home.

WHEN THEY ARRIVED at the king's house, they heard raised voices coming from within. Inside, they found Tharn and Farrum standing on opposite sides of the hearth in which the remains of a fire guttered and spat. The two men looked like bulls ready to clash horns. They seemed oblivious to their visitors.

'You've been king for just one day and already you've lost control of your people,' Farrum was saying. As he spoke, the scars on his old, lined face moved with a life of their own.

'The people of Creyak are my business, not yours,' said Tharn, fighting to remain calm. 'Nor am I yet their king.'

'No,' said Farrum. His wiry body twitched beneath a cloak still damp and caked with salt from his ocean voyage. 'There is only one king in this house, boy.'

'You have your own people, your own isle. You have no power here.'

'Power lies where it chooses.'

'Tell me why you have come. Or leave now.'

Mishina knocked his staff on the floor. It was no more than a tap, but it turned the heads of the arguing men. Farrum's face flashed with momentary annoyance before cracking into a broad smile.

'You didn't tell me you had other guests, young Tharn,' he boomed.

'I invited them,' said Tharn. Bran thought he looked relieved. 'I did not invite you.'

'Oh, you fret too much, Tharn. Take your father and me—there was always fire between us. Most days we could never agree on anything at all!'

'I know.'

Mishina tapped his staff again, harder this time. The shells hanging from it jangled. Farrum scratched his hands through his massive white beard.

'I suppose we can continue this argument later.'

'Is that the only reason you came to Creyak?' said Tharn. 'To argue?'

'No indeed, boy. I had hoped to speak with your father about certain matters suitable only for the ears of a king.'

With deceptive speed, Farrum darted round the fire. Before Tharn could react, the old man had grabbed both his ears.

'But, as you said yourself, you're only the king-to-be. Once these precious little flowers have grown into the ears of a true warrior, then perhaps I'll say what I've really come to say.'

Tharn shook himself free, pushed Farrum away. Bran was impressed by his ability to stay calm.

'Get out, Farrum. You have been given a house. Use it. Soon my father's spirit will pass through the final door to the afterdream. Then I will be king, and these ears that cause you such amusement will be ready to hear your words. Until then, you have nothing to say to me.'

'You've got your father's spirit, Tharn. There's hope for you yet.' Farrum strode across the room, stopping in the doorway. 'By the way, if you really do want me to go, you'll have to send someone out to fix my boat. There's a gash the length of its hull, and here I am with no artisans on my crew.'

Robe flapping, he stepped out into the misty dawn.

'That man!' said Tharn. 'He can turn me to anger quicker than anyone I know. No artisans indeed! He will use that excuse to remain in Creyak as long as he desires.'

Mishina advanced. 'I have brought the bard as you asked.'

Tharn eyed Lethriel. 'And what is she doing here?'

'I'm here with Talus,' she replied. 'I want to help.'

Something passed between the two of them. Bran couldn't tell what it was. Residual anger perhaps; both were recovering from losing their tempers.

Then he noticed Tharn's cheeks were puffed and red. The man had been crying. Well, no wonder. In a space of less than two days he'd lost both a father and a brother.

Lost them. Or killed them himself. Was it possible that here before them was the killer they were looking for?

139

'Stay then, Lethriel,' said Tharn, his voice softer. 'You are always welcome here.'

'May I ask why you summoned me?' said Talus. He looked like he already knew the answer.

'You have shown yourself to be both clever and curious, Talus. Ever since I learned of my father's death, I find myself full of questions.'

'And grief, I suppose,' said Bran. He studied Tharn's expression closely.

'I loved the king! Do you not think I would feel grief?'

Bran bowed his head. 'Any son would mourn his father's death.'

'Indeed. But the questions remain. Who killed him, and why?'

'When we first arrived on Creyak,' said Talus, 'you showed little interest in such things. You wished only to send your father on his final journey. What has changed you, Tharn?'

'You, bard. You have changed me. The questions came first from you, but I find myself unable to sleep for thinking about them. If I do not find the answers'— Tharn struck the heels of his hands against his temples— 'I will go mad!'

'Be calm, Tharn,' murmured Lethriel.

The king-to-be lowered his hands. 'Will you help me, Talus? *Can* you help?'

'Do you wish me to?'

'With all my beating heart.'

'Then it pleases me to offer you my services. Come: we have much to discuss.'

Talus seated himself before the dying fire and extended

his hand, inviting Tharn to join him. Bran suppressed a smile. Already the bard was acting as if the place belonged to him.

'Lethriel,' said Talus, 'you will sit on my other side. And Mishina—you will do well just here. Your voice is a powerful one, and must be heard.'

Mishina propped his staff against the wall and seated himself in the very spot Bran had been planning to occupy: beside Lethriel. Now she was squeezed between shaman and bard.

'I'll just sit here then,' Bran said, kicking a flat spot on the floor beside Mishina.

'On the contrary,' said Talus. 'You, Bran, will not be sitting at all.'

'I won't?'

'No. You will return to the beach.'

'What? Why?'

'You are good with boats. If anyone is able to help Farrum out of his difficulties, you are.'

'You want me to fix the boat?'

'I doubt there is anybody here who can do it.'

'Why would you say such a thing?' said Tharn.

'I say only what I see. In Creyak, I have seen many paths climbing up to the cliffs, but only one leading down to the shore. I have seen a beach that is wild and untended. I have seen no boats.'

'We have boats.' Tharn sounded defensive.

'Dugouts?'

'Of course.'

'How many?'

Tharn squirmed. 'Not many.'

'Farrum's craft is not a dugout. It is made from a wooden frame covered in sealskin. It is big: thirty paces long, by my estimate. To repair it, an expert boat-builder is needed. That is why Bran must go.'

It had been quite the night for tempers; Bran could feel his beginning to build yet again. Controlling himself, he said, 'I could take a look. But do I have to do it right now?'

'The sooner the boat is mended, the sooner Farrum will be able to leave.'

'So you too think Farrum should go?' said Tharn. He seemed eager for Talus's approval. Perhaps the bard reminded him of something he'd lost in his father.

'I did not say that. But it is clear Farrum is making excuses for not leaving. If we take those excuses away, we may learn what he is doing here in the first place.'

'You say he is lying?'

'I say we do not yet know the truth.'

'I suppose it wouldn't do any harm,' said Bran. He was talking to Lethriel, he realised. 'If there's nobody else here capable of mending it, I mean. It is sort of my speciality.'

If Lethriel was impressed, she didn't show it.

'So I'll be going,' he added.

'Take care on the path,' said Talus. 'It will still be icy.'

Talus turned his back on Bran and began to tell Tharn about the model of Creyak they'd made, and of the various theories they'd discussed concerning the murders. Soon Lethriel was joining in, then the shaman and finally Tharn himself.

Feeling thoroughly rejected, Bran set off for the beach.

CHAPTER FIFTEEN

BRAN HAD ONCE considered himself a child of the sea. He'd been born and grown up in Arvon, living safe between the water and the high Nioghe mountains. His father had been a fisherman, and his fathers before him, all the way back to the dreaming shadows of older, colder times. Those fathers, like Bran, had dedicated their lives to Mir, who had blessed them in turn with his bounty; in feeding them, Mir had proved himself a bringer of life.

But Mir was also a destroyer.

On the night Keyli had died, Bran had turned his back on the sea that had claimed her life. Had turned his back on Mir. He and Talus had walked inland until the walking had become a habit, the habit a friendship. Their journey north from Arvon had taken them through fair land and foul, but never once back to the sea.

Until now. Now they were finally approaching the place where the land stopped and the great northern ocean began. If they wanted to continue their travels, they would have to give themselves over to the sea. Over to Mir.

And that was the problem. Even the promise of the northlight—Bran's dream of reaching its source and holding Keyli in his arms again—even that wasn't enough to overcome his fear that the instant he ventured out on the water Mir would take him too.

This was the real reason Bran wanted to abandon the quest.

He was afraid.

Rounding the final corner of the path to the beach, Bran stepped from ice onto coarse shingle. All was grey in the morning fog. Low cloud hugged the clifftop. The waves were heavy, growling things.

Well, he didn't have to go near them.

Farrum's boat lay half on its side, just above the waterline. It looked as Bran imagined a stranded whale would look—though he'd never seen such a thing— and it was the main reason Bran hadn't put up much protest when Talus had sent him out here. He might have rejected the sea, but that didn't stop him loving boats. And this one was a real beauty.

He approached with caution, keeping as quiet as he could on the shingle. Farrum was certain to have left someone on guard, and Bran didn't want to be heard. Sure enough, there at the prow was the bulky shape of a seated man, bundled in furs. Snores rose with the steam of his breath.

Bran stood for a moment, staring at the boat and forgetting to breathe. Apart from that wolf's head, it was very like the fishing boat he'd used in Arvon. Something about it made him want to cry.

The cold bit into him, prompting him to move. He circled behind the sleeping guard and walked the length of the boat. Its construction was familiar to him, but its tremendous size made it truly a wonder. As Talus had observed, its hull was seal-pelt stretched taut over a sturdy wooden frame. A complex internal structure was visible through the pair of gashes halfway down its length: curved timbers, notched and lashed.

The wolf's-head burner at the prow was an unusual feature. Bran hadn't seen anything like it before. It gave the boat a cunning, animal quality. Boats were bound close to the spirit world, everyone knew that; but this was different. The wolf's carved snarl disturbed Bran, and thrilled him too.

The tears in the boat's hull were long, spanning four or five pelts. No doubt they looked bad to the untrained eye, but Bran saw immediately how they could be repaired. Given the right materials, he could do it himself, nor would it take him long. Farrum's claim that he was stuck here was at best an exaggeration, at worst an outright lie.

The boat was lying against a large rock, which Bran used as a stepping stone to help him climb aboard. Sea spray misted his face. Silently he dropped down into the hull.

Inside, woven slats overlapped to make a flat deck raised up from the curve of the hull. The design was new to Bran. The deck was crammed with clutter: poorly-shipped oars; sodden furs and food pouches; sharp chert tools. Bran waded through the mess, the raised deck giving slightly under his feet. If this had been his boat, he would have kept it a lot tidier.

At the stern was a lop-sided structure made of willow panels. Somewhere to shelter in a storm. Another new concept. Bran was simultaneously impressed and contemptuous: such a wonderful idea, so crudely executed.

He lifted the flap of sealskin that served as a door and peered inside. It was too dark to see anything.

A hand shot out of the gloom and slapped his face.

Bran grabbed the flailing wrist and twisted it. A pained yelp emerged from the darkness. He yanked, dragging the hand's owner into the light. In doing so, he nearly lost his balance. He took two awkward steps around a sloshing waterskin, narrowly missed breaking his ankle on a badly-placed oar. But he held on.

His captive was a tall woman wrapped in thick, ivory fur. Her face was angular and seemed very dark under the pale hood. She might have been beautiful if not for the scars crowding her cheeks. She stood erect, shoulders back, a proud posture revealing the long lines of her neck. Hanging from a thong necklace was a fine wooden amulet in the shape of a howling wolf.

Bran released his grip on her wrist. 'I won't hurt you,' he said. He glanced behind him, half-expecting the guard to come vaulting over the boat's weather-edge to the woman's defence. 'Just please don't scream.'

'Why would I scream?'

The question took him by surprise. 'Because I grabbed you.'

'You won't do it again.' Her voice was certain, imperious. A force in its own right.

'Is that some kind of threat? Or are you just waiting for your friend to come and knock me out?'

'Who, Lath?' said the woman with undisguised

contempt. 'Don't expect him to come running. He drank more last night than most men drink in a year.'

'If you shout loud enough, I daresay he'll hear,' said Bran. His good hand was ready to clamp her mouth if she tried.

She bared her teeth.

'I won't hurt you,' Bran repeated. His eyes strayed to the fur she wore. 'Is that ice-bear?'

'Yes.' She looked defiant.

'Where did you get it?'

'It's a long story.'

'I'm sure it is. Now, you're really not going to scream, are you?'

She stared a moment longer. Then her shoulders relaxed, and she seemed to shrink. 'No. I... I hope you won't either.'

'Why would *I* scream?'

She shrugged. 'To warn someone I'm here. I'm not, you see. Not supposed to be. Here, I mean.' Her eyes flicked first to one side, then to the other.

'You've been hiding on the boat?' Bran looked doubtfully into the willow shanty. 'You sailed all the way from this other island—Sleeth, is it called?—and you're asking me to believe nobody noticed you were in there?'

'There's a secret space.' She ducked back inside and peeled back a long strip of sealskin to reveal a compartment between the back of the shanty and the ribs of the boat's stern. 'And they're men. Men don't see much. You won't tell anyone, will you?'

Bran felt his heart soften, so pained was her expression.

'Why do it in the first place? Why take the risk? Surely if Farrum found you...'

'He'd have hauled me out and handed me round his crew. They'd have used me up, all of them, and hurled me over the side of the boat and into the jaws of Mir. He's cruel, you know.'

'It's a big risk you've taken.'

'It was worth it. There's somebody I had to see. Somebody in Creyak. A... a man. He... I...'

Bran raised his good hand. 'All right, I understand. Was it worth risking your life to see him?'

Without hesitation, she nodded. In the shanty's gloom, her ice-bear fur seemed to shine with a light of its own. 'This *is* my life. This voyage, here and now. I've left everything I've ever known to be with him.' Back went her shoulders again. 'I love him. Without him, I am dead. If you've ever known such love, you'll know why I'm here, and why I did it!'

'I know of love.' Bran sat down heavily, tired all over again. 'So what are you still doing in the boat? I'd have thought this would be the perfect time to make your escape, what with Farrum and his men all sleeping after the feast.'

'I would have done, if Farrum hadn't left Lath watching over the boat.'

'I thought you said Lath was drunk.'

'He is. But that doesn't stop me being cautious. All it would take is one slip. He mustn't tell Farrum I'm here.' Her eyes widened. 'You could help me! Would you? Will you?'

Bran tried to imagine the crossing from Sleeth. How

many days had it taken? It must have been dreadful cooped up in the hull like that, especially during the storm. While the boat was throwing itself against the rocks, it would have been nothing short of terrifying.

'What's your name?'

'Alayin.'

'I'm Bran. You're safe now, Alayin.'

'Only if I can get out of here without Lath seeing me.'

Bran frowned. 'Things are not well here. The king is dead.'

'I know. I overheard what was said when we landed. It is very sad.'

'What I mean is... this isn't a good time to be stirring things up.'

'I don't want to stir anything. I just want to be with the man I love.'

THEY TALKED A little longer, but Bran's mind was already made up. Alayin knew it too: he'd already seen the hope spring into her eyes. Now it was there, he couldn't bear to see it depart.

'Stay here,' he said. 'You'll know when to make your move.'

He dropped lightly back onto the beach and circled back round the boat. He saw no other damage than those two long gashes. It was testament to the quality of Sleeth craftsmanship that the hull wasn't in worse shape.

Reaching the prow, Bran stood over Lath's slumbering form. He planted his feet wide in the shingle and coughed. When Lath didn't move, he kicked him.

Grumbles and curses rose up from the tightly-wrapped furs. Slowly, the big man unfolded himself. He stood, tottering, and glared at Bran with red-rimmed eyes.

'Who're you?'

'I'm the one who saved your boat from being smashed to pieces on the rocks last night. Remember?'

A frown descended over Lath's wide, flat face. He too bore the familiar Sleeth pattern of scars. On Alayin's face they'd carried a certain elegance; on his they resembled a landslide.

'Remember?' Lath repeated.

'The rope. We anchored you on the rock. Me and my friend.'

An enormous grin broke Lath's face wide open. He burped out meaty fumes and slapped Bran on the back.

'You're a mighty, mighty man!' The second slap nearly knocked Bran over.

'Thank you. Now, how would you like to be mighty too?'

Expressions came and went on Lath's craggy face, settling finally into puzzlement. 'Mighty? Me?'

'How happy do you think Farrum's going to be if we mend his boat?'

'Mend it?'

'You and me together. What do you say?'

After more uncertainty, the grin returned. 'I say you're a mighty man.'

'All right. I'm not going to disagree. It's not a difficult job, but we're going to need some tools and some materials. I'm going back into Creyak now to see what I can find. Will you come with me?'

The frown descended again. 'I'm on duty.'

'Of course you are. But this is a duty too, isn't it? And, like I said, just imagine how pleased Farrum's going to be. What would you rather see: a happy Farrum, or an angry Farrum?'

Another monumental belch. Some consideration. 'Happy Farrum.'

'Exactly. So, are you coming?'

'Coming, aye.'

Bran helped Lath stagger up the beach. When they reached the path, he glanced back towards the boat, hoping to spot Alayin slinking over the side and losing herself in the fog. He saw nothing. That was all right: it would be safer for her to wait until they were out of sight.

They hadn't even reached the first of the Creyak houses when Lath tripped and fell. He landed hard, cracking his head on a stone. He groaned and vomited last night's liquor onto the icy ground, then staggered to his feet, a red blotch shining on his forehead. He stood swaying, his rolling eyes occasionally making contact with Bran's.

'Why don't you have a rest?' said Bran.

'Good idea,' said Lath. He sat heavily. Within five breaths he was snoring again.

Bran wrapped Lath's furs around his body and secured his hood over his head; the last thing they needed was another frozen corpse on their hands.

The fog had penetrated deep into the settlement, and Bran stood briefly still, unnerved by the trails of vapour curling through the stone-lined corridors. The sound of the sea had been replaced by a low moaning. At first he thought it was wind. Then, unaccountably, wolves. Eventually he recognised it as human sobbing. It came from the houses, all of them, the collective private grief of the people of Creyak.

ChAPTER SIXTEEN

THE FEELINGS THARN and Lethriel shared for one another showed in countless tiny ways: each holding the other's gaze just a little longer than necessary; each letting the other speak just a little more than they might; the way their postures matched. Talus wondered if Bran had noticed, and resolved to ask his companion when the opportunity next arose.

Talus was as curious about love as he was about all other human affairs. It fascinated him in a way no other subject could... perhaps because he understood it so poorly. Why did love lead so often to anger, to betrayal and yes, even to death? Talus didn't know. Only by studying it could he ever hope to learn.

Once, he'd undertaken the study in earnest, although he feared that, before the end, he'd allowed his emotions to interfere with his objectivity. Memories stirred of strange passions and hot stone and hard desert light. Memories, perhaps, of love.

Had Tia loved him back? He had no idea. In any case, it had been long ago.

As for Tharn and Lethriel, it interested him that they felt the need to keep their affair secret. Why would the king's heir—a man of considerable status—choose to hide his passions? To what acts might those suppressed passions lead him, if he was driven beyond his ability to restrain them?

And what about Lethriel? She wanted desperately to learn the truth about Gantor's murder, for the sake of both him and Caltie, the man she'd loved. But what about this new man she loved now? If it turned out that Tharn had been involved with the king's murder, how would she deal with it?

Many questions, to which Talus had no answers. So he did what he did best: he talked.

Throughout the discussion, he tried hard to gauge Tharn's reactions to his ideas. But the king-to-be was hard to read, responding for the most part with grunts and shrugs. For a man who'd said he wanted to find the killer, he showed little interest in what Talus had to say.

'What do you make of Gantor's last words?' Talus said. 'Do you believe Cabarrath could be the killer?'

'Cabarrath was closer to Gantor than the rest of us.' Tharn glanced at Lethriel as if for approval. She responded with an almost imperceptible nod. 'They had their differences, but...' Again he shrugged, and that was the end of that.

At last, Talus could take no more of it. Forcing himself to smile, he stood and spread his hands. 'This has been most useful,' he said. He turned to the shaman. 'I am especially interested in what you have had to say, Mishina.'

Mishina gazed up at him. The heat of the fire had dried his painted mask so that the slightest movement caused it to flake away. Much more of that and Talus would be able to see what the shaman really looked like.

'I have been of little use,' said Mishina.

'I disagree,' said Talus. 'In fact, I would very much like to speak with you further, away from here.'

The corner of the shaman's mouth twitched. 'That would be... entertaining. If the king-to-be agrees, of course.'

'I am sure he will,' said Talus before Tharn could object. 'Perhaps Lethriel will remain to keep him company. She proved helpful to me earlier when I was shaping my thoughts. I will be interested to learn what truths they may uncover between them.'

Tharn nodded.

'When you are finished,' Talus concluded, 'will you send your brothers to me? I would like to speak with each of them in turn, alone.'

'Will that help?' said Tharn.

'It might.'

As he helped Mishina out into the fog (the shaman's limp seemed quite bad this morning), Talus wondered if Lethriel had understood the message he'd been trying to send her. If she really wanted to help with the investigation, he'd just presented her with the perfect opportunity. Tharn might say things to her that he didn't want to say in front of a stranger—nor even his own medicine man.

And if Tharn let slip something that connected him to the murders? What would she do then? Would Lethriel protect the man she loved today, or seek justice for those she'd loved before?

Which was stronger: the love of *now*, or the love of *ago*?

UNLIKE THE OTHER dwellings Talus had seen, Mishina's house had no door-stone. Instead, the entrance was concealed by an extra length of corridor that doubled back on itself, splitting twice into short dead-ends. This tiny maze was far too small to get lost in, but it was a reminder that visiting the shaman was a ritual in itself. It also explained why Talus hadn't identified it on his travels around Creyak so far.

The interior delivered quite a surprise. Talus had expected it to be sombre and austere; instead it was a riot of colour. The walls and ceiling were painted with intricate swirls and patterns. Carved wooden animals— also brightly painted—swung on cords from the rafters. There were hanging chains of beads, and hollow gourds that gave out low chimes as they jostled against each other. Decorated masks and bone-white skulls stared from the corners.

There was light here too, and lots of it, both orange from the fire blazing in the hearth and white from cunning vents in the roof, which somehow captured the foggy daylight from outside and channelled it in narrow beams into the building's interior.

Mishina removed the antlers from his head and busied himself in a corner while Talus warmed himself by the fire. There was something scratched into the dirt floor by the hearth; he crouched to study it. It was an angular figure made up of one straight line and two jagged ones. Beside it were dozens of tiny marks that might have been people. If they were, the angular shape represented something truly enormous.

Talus recognised it at once.

'I was remembering something I saw once, in a far-off land,' said Mishina.

Talus looked up to see the shaman standing over him. He held a bowl that Talus assumed must contain food; when Mishina sat down, he saw it was full of a thick black liquid.

'If this is meant to be a building,' said Talus, pointing to the shape, 'then I have seen such things too. They build structures like this in the deserts of the southern continent. Tombs for the dead. The sides of the structure slope and the stone is cut with deep steps so that a man may climb to the top.'

He couldn't take his eyes off the image of the desert tomb. How strange that Mishina should have drawn it when, not long before, Talus had been thinking about his own travels in that distant land. And the woman he'd met there.

'They are cairns,' said Mishina, 'just like the cairn of Creyak and all the settlements of this land. Only, in the desert, the cairns are much bigger. The people of the desert believe their king is also the spirit of the sun. And so they build their cairns...'

'...to reach for the sun. I know of this belief.'

'So you too have crossed the world, Talus. Have you also seen the cairns of the jungle realms that lie far to the west, over the sea? They are very like those of the desert.'

Jungles over the sea? This was news to Talus.

'It is a dangerous land,' Mishina went on. 'Once, I was attacked by a big cat with fur as black as midnight.' He pulled up his robe to expose a leg ruined by scars. 'That is why I limp.'

'I have never heard of such a place.'

'Well, at least you have seen the desert. Perhaps we have more in common than we imagined.'

'Perhaps.'

Mishina dipped the first two fingers of each hand into his bowl. When he brought them out, they were black. He started smearing the paint methodically across his forehead.

'So tell me, bard. What is it that you wish to discuss?'

Talus regarded the little drawing scratched into the floor. 'Spirits and kings. I am interested to know, Mishina, what you think of such things.'

'In the desert, men believe in the sun,' said Mishina, daubing the black paint over the blue that was already there. 'In other places, beliefs are different. If you have travelled, you will know this. In the high mountain lands of...'

'I am not interested in mountains. I would rather hear about Creyak.'

'Very well. In Creyak, men believe their king is like the trunk of a tree. His living subjects are the branches, and his ancestral spirits are the roots. When a king dies, another must take his place, or else all communication must end between those who live in the air and those who are dead in the ground.'

'Is it what *all* the people here believe?'

Now the entire top half of Mishina's face was black. His old eyes stared deep into the fire.

'I do not understand what you mean.'

'To kill a king, a man must first rid himself of fear. Fear of the ancestors. Fear of the spirit world and all the power it holds over him. This is a very difficult thing to do.'

'Difficult indeed.'

'But not if that man does not believe in the spirit world to begin with.'

Mishina looked up from the flames and into Talus's eyes. His half-painted face made him look like two men. The illusion made Talus feel momentarily dizzy.

Then Mishina's mouth split wide open and he let out a great guffaw of laughter. 'A man who does not believe in the spirits? Who has ever heard of such a thing? You joke with me... ah, but I should expect nothing less from a wandering bard! Tell me, what other tales of fancy do you carry in your motley travelling robes?'

Talus traced the sloping sides of the desert-cairn Mishina had drawn. 'I carry many tales. But I had rather hoped to hear one of yours.'

Mishina wiped his hands clean on a scrap of paint-clotted rabbit-skin. Then he dipped one fingertip back in the paint and began to dab black spots onto the blue paint covering the bottom half of his face. 'What would you have me tell you?'

'Tell me about Farrum. There is a feud going on here, I think. That interests me.'

Mishina nodded. 'A feud, yes, you are right. It began many years ago, when Hashath and Farrum were children together in Creyak. Farrum was the son of a warrior—this was a time when the people of Creyak fought often against their neighbours, you understand. They were violent years.'

'Creyak seems peaceful enough now,' said Talus.

'When he became king, Hashath brought calm and order. He made truces with his neighbours. He turned Creyak in on itself, and made it a haven for all those who lived there.'

'What about Farrum?'

'Farrum became frustrated. His father died in a fierce fight with a rival king and he swore to avenge him. But Hashath forbade it. So Farrum did the only thing he could think of. He challenged Hashath himself.'

'He fought the king?' In Talus's experience such challenges were rare, though not unheard of.

'The fight was brief. Hashath was a powerful man and his strength and skill made Farrum look a fool. Farrum fled in shame, taking his supporters with him. Most were his dead father's friends and their women.'

'That was when Farrum made his home instead on the island of Sleeth?'

Mishina closed his eyes. The black paint around them was already dry. 'Yes. In those days, Sleeth was all but deserted. Farrum made it his own and has lived there ever since. Others have joined him over the years— outcasts from many of the settlements along this part of the coast. Now Sleeth thrives.'

'Outcasts,' said Talus. 'Tell me—do these outcasts include other people from Creyak? People Hashath did not... approve of?'

Mishina shrugged. 'Hashath was strict. If there were people in Creyak he did not care for, he did not encourage them to stay.'

Talus's thoughts were buzzing again. He pressed his hand against the top of his head to stop them spilling out. 'If Farrum had beaten Hashath in that fight, he would have become king of Creyak and the history of this place would have been very different.'

Mishina opened his eyes again. 'For many years now, the people of Creyak have feared attack from the sea by Farrum. He is brutal and ambitious, and his people are clever boatmen. But the attack has never come.'

The shaman reached behind him and brought out another bowl. This one was filled with fresh blue pigment. He picked up a little of the colour on a clean fingertip and pressed blue dots into the new black. Soon his new face was completed; the design reminded Talus of the scarred faces of the visitors from across the sea.

'You know much about the history of this place, Mishina,' he said, 'considering you are not a native.'

'How do you know that?'

Talus pointed to the drawing. 'Like me, you are a wanderer.'

'It is my duty to seek out truth wherever it is to be found.' The shaman's eyes seemed to glow inside their rings of black paint. 'The spirits guide me in this. They take me where I need to go in order to see the things I need to see.' He rose to his feet. 'Now please, forgive me. There are rituals I must attend to.'

'May I ask one more question before I leave?'

'If you must.'

'Where do you keep your supply of greycaps?'

Mishina frowned, cracking his newly-applied mask a little. 'An odd question for a bard.'

'Indulge me.'

The shaman considered for a moment, then crossed to the far side of the room. Talus followed close behind. Mishina lifted a lid of stone to reveal a shallow pit in the floor. Mishina delved first down, then sideways. His hand came up covered in fine grey dust and holding a pale leather pouch. Mishina felt inside it. Even through the paint on his face, Talus could see his expression change to one of shock.

'Gone!' said Mishina. 'How did you know?'

'Who can say? Perhaps the spirits are guiding me too.'

chapter seventeen

As soon as he reached the king's house, Bran rolled the doorstone aside and entered. The heat of the fire struck him an almost physical blow. Someone had piled the hearth high with peat and the flames were licking halfway to the ceiling. The whole interior was thick with smoke and aglow with dancing light.

The meeting was over. Talus and Mishina were nowhere to be seen. But Tharn and Lethriel were still here. They were lying together on a bed of grey furs, their naked bodies locked together. The flickering firelight painted their movements orange. The red of Lethriel's hair was a flame all its own.

Bran couldn't move his feet. He knew it was wrong to watch, but he couldn't look away. Had he wondered what Lethriel looked like underneath her winter wraps? Well, now he knew. Countless tiny moments suddenly made sense: shared glances between her and Tharn; her speaking of love coming again. This was what she'd meant.

Lethriel's head came up. Her eyes found Bran and widened in surprise. Tharn didn't see him at all. Lethriel's hands stroked the skin of Tharn's back. Holding Bran's gaze, she shook her head. Her expression pleaded.

Bran left, rolling the doorstone back into place as quietly as he could. On his way here, he'd imagined remaining in Creyak with Lethriel after parting company with Talus. Some fantasy. He was trapped on the path after all, facing the same two choices he'd always faced: go on, or turn back.

The fog enveloped him, sucking at his thoughts. After the heat he'd felt inside the house of the king, it was very cold. He felt foolish, but he was also relieved. If his brief dream of being with Lethriel had come true, what would Keyli have thought? Would she not want him to be happy? If only he could see her one more time, he could ask her for himself.

But Keyli was dead.

BACK AT THEIR temporary home, Bran was relieved to find the hearth alive with a fire almost as vigorous as the one he'd just left. Even better, a deer haunch was roasting on a stick. Fat dripped sizzling into the flames. The smell of cooked meat was overwhelming. Bran's stomach let out a bellow and it was as much as he could do not to grab the meat right out of the hearth.

'A gift from Mishina,' said Talus. He was standing by the open doorway with his arms clasped over his chest: a meditative stance.

'Are you sure it's not poisoned?' Bran squatted by the fire. The venison was cooked to perfection. With his good hand, he tore off a hunk.

'You do not like the shaman.'

'I just don't think he likes us.' Bran sank his teeth into

the juicy meat. At that moment he didn't care if it was poisoned or not. 'Oh, this is delicious! Talus, you've got to try it.'

Like a bird taking flight, Talus unfolded himself from his position of rest and started dancing round the fire. 'And now,' he said as he pranced, 'you must tell me what you learned on the beach!'

'Slow down. Sit down. Let me fill my belly.' Bran was tired of Talus's lightning changes of mood.

'Never mind your belly, Bran. We do not have much time.'

Bran carried on eating. 'What's the rush?'

'I have asked Tharn to send his brothers here to us, each in their turn. This is our only chance to speak with them all before the final rituals begin to send Hashath to the afterdream. Once they start, days will pass before we can do any more useful work. By then, it may be too late.'

Bran looked around the empty house. 'They're not here yet.'

'Tharn will send them when he has concluded his business with Lethriel.'

'I think they might be a little while.'

Talus stopped dancing. He cocked his head on one side. 'Ah, so you know about them.'

'Now I do. I suppose you knew all along?'

'Of course! Now, tell me about the boat.'

Bran sighed. The bard was incorrigible. Well, talking about what he'd found on the beach would at least distract him from the turmoil of emotion he'd felt since seeing Tharn and Lethriel together. And he had to admit to feeling smug about having his own surprise to spring on the bard.

'The boat has a clever design,' he began. 'There's a flat deck inside. It makes it much easier to move around. Or it would have, if not for all the clutter.'

He went on to describe the vessel's internal structure in as much detail as he could remember. It felt good to talk like this; for a long time, boats had been his whole life, and he'd forgotten how much he missed being around them.

'Since when were you so interested in boats, Talus?'

'I am interested in everything. Tell me the rest.'

'There's not much more to tell.' Bran paused. 'Oh, unless you wanted to hear about the woman I found hiding in the hull.'

The bard's eyebrows rose, creasing his hairless brow. Bran suppressed a smile of satisfaction, then related his encounter with Alayin.

'A woman,' said the bard. 'Very interesting.'

'I hope she managed to get out of the boat,' said Bran. 'Lath—that's the guard—was unconscious when I left him. It was the best chance she was going to get.'

'Oh, believe me, Bran—the woman you found has not gone anywhere. She is still on the boat, precisely where you left her.'

'What?'

'Let us return to the man you found asleep: Lath.'

'Yes. He was guarding the boat.'

'Against what?'

'Well, against...' Bran could hear himself beginning to bluster. He battled on regardless. 'Theft. What if someone from Creyak wanted to steal it?'

'Steal the boat? A boat that requires at least eight men to crew it? What person, in a community that has turned its back on the sea, would want to steal such a vessel? Try again, Bran.'

'There must be valuables aboard. Farrum put Lath on guard to stop someone stealing things from inside the boat.'

'Very good. So tell me, Bran, what valuables did you find?'

'Well... none, I suppose. Just the usual clutter. Provisions, clothes, tools, that sort of thing.'

'But there *was* something, Bran, was there not? A single thing you found, surely the most valuable thing on board? The thing Lath had really been put there to guard?'

Bran shook his head. 'I don't know what you...'

Then he had it.

'Her,' he said. 'Alayin. Lath wasn't there to guard the boat at all. He was there to guard Alayin.'

'You found your way in the end!'

'Farrum didn't want anybody finding her there.'

'Yet that is exactly what you did. I think we should keep your discovery to ourselves, for now at least.'

Bran called up an image of Alayin: dark, scarred skin surrounded by white fur. 'She lied to me,' he said. 'She didn't come to Creyak to see her lover at all. So why is she here?'

'Perhaps some of her story is true,' Talus replied. 'Perhaps not. But it is an interesting development, is it not? Now, can you guess what I have been doing while you have been playing with boats?'

'You always tell me not to guess.' Bran waved the hunk of meat he was steadily working his way through. 'But if you want me to I will. Has it got something to do with the shaman?'

'I have been speaking with Mishina, yes.'

Bran put down the meat and stared out into the fog. Mention of the shaman made him feel cold again, despite the heat of the fire.

'He is unusual among shamans,' Talus went on. 'Although he serves Creyak as spirit-walker, in the past he has walked himself, far across the world. He is interested in all spirits, not just those of this land.'

'Sounds like someone else I could mention.' Bran didn't have much time for the wider world Talus often talked about. The world beneath his feet was enough for him.

'But, clever as he is, Mishina did not know his greycaps were missing.'

'Greycaps? Oh, the mushrooms. What have they got to do with...?'

Talus was up and dancing again, unable to contain himself. Bran felt himself beginning to relax. Sometimes the bard was too much like a little boy not to smile.

'There is a truth here in Creyak which nobody wishes to face, Bran, because it is too terrible to contemplate.'

'And what truth is that?'

'The fact that someone has killed a king.'

'I know. We've been over this already. I can't imagine the punishment that waits for the killer in the afterdream. Nobody in their right mind would consign themselves to it.'

Talus clapped his hands. 'Precisely, Bran! The question is therefore: how does a man remove himself from his right mind?'

Bran was pleased he was managing to keep up. 'The greycaps,' he said. 'They affect thoughts and dreams. The shaman probably uses them to enter his spirit-trance.'

'Well done, Bran. A man who eats greycaps might convince himself of anything. Might convince himself, for example, that it is perfectly safe for him to kill a king. Of course, it is only an idea.'

Talus sat on the dirt floor before the blazing hearth. Bran tore another chunk of meat from the haunch and tossed it to him. Talus caught it and started to nibble.

'How did we get mixed up in this, Talus?'

'Our path leads us where it will. You know that.'

'I suppose so. I just don't know why it had to lead us here.'

'We are where we need to be, Bran. We always are. Which reminds me of a tale I know, in which...'

'Forget the storytelling, Talus. Just tell me what you think is going on in Creyak.'

'Ah, to the point! Reliable Bran! But you forget that what we *think* is not important. All that matters is what we *know*.'

Bran finished his meat and licked the last of the juices from his good hand. 'All right. What do we know?'

'We know two men have died mysteriously.'

'And that a third man has arrived unexpectedly.'

'Farrum, yes. Good again, Bran. Farrum's arrival is certainly suspicious. And here is something else: we can guess that the king was probably killed by someone close to him. This is not something we can know, but we do know that this is how the pattern of the world is woven.'

'Now who's making guesses? I'd tuck in to this deer, Talus, while there's still some left.'

'No time, Bran!' Talus pointed outside. 'See? Our first visitor is here!'

A man emerged from the fog to fill the doorway. He was so tall he had to stoop.

'Please come in, Cabarrath,' said Talus. 'We have a little food, if you would share it with us.'

'I am not hungry,' said Cabarrath. He smiled, but it was a smile filled with sadness. Bran felt sorry for him. For them all.

CHAPTER EIGHTEEN

'THARN TELLS ME you have questions,' said Cabarrath, seating himself by the fire. He moved his long limbs with economy and grace. His face was sad and open. He did not look like a killer.

In Talus's experience that meant nothing at all.

'Yes,' said Talus. 'My questions are few, and they are simple. Are you ready to answer them?'

'I will tell you what I know. Anything to catch the demon that is loose in Creyak.'

'Demon? So do you believe the spirits are responsible for the deaths of your father and brother?'

Cabarrath shook his head. There were dark rings under his eyes. Grief could keep a man awake. So could guilt.

'All I know is that I helped carry my father's body from the snow into the cairn, and that I held my brother Gantor in my arms as he died. How these things happened, I cannot say.'

'Where were you on the night your father was murdered, Cabarrath?'

'In my own house.'

'Can you prove it?'

'I do not understand.'

'Was there anybody else there with you?'

'Tharn was there. We live in the same house.'

'I suppose that, if I asked Tharn the same question, he would say he was with you?'

'Of course.'

'Your house lies near the maze, does it not?'

'Yes.'

'And you heard nothing?'

'Not until the screaming.'

'The screaming?'

'When my father's body was found.'

'Who screamed?'

'Fethan. He told us he woke from a nightmare and went outside to clear his head. He walked out of the village towards the maze. That was when he saw it.'

'It was Fethan who found the king's body?'

'Yes.'

Tired as Cabarrath clearly was, he seemed relaxed. His answers were swift and certain. There was no guile to him, no sense that he was anything other than what Talus saw before him.

Of course, that might have been an act.

'What sort of relationship did you have with your father?'

For the first time, Cabarrath faltered.

'I was his son,' he said at last.

'Evidently. Were things well between you?'

'I don't know what you...'

'Did you fight?' said Bran.

Again Cabarrath hesitated. 'We had been through a difficult time,' he said finally. 'Do I have to say more than that?'

'I would welcome the whole truth,' said Talus.

'Very well.' Cabarrath watched the smoke from the fire spiral up through the hole in the roof. 'My father was angry with me. I had disobeyed him and he was angry. It was a serious matter. I had hoped that, in time, there would be peace again between us.' He hung his head. 'Now it is too late.'

'And for your part?' said Talus. 'Did you feel anger towards your father?'

Cabarrath stared at the bard. He was the second-eldest of the king's sons, a man in his own right. Right now he looked like a boy.

'Yes,' he said. 'It hurts me to say such a thing, but... yes.'

'What happened between you?' said Bran.

'A woman.'

'You fought over a woman?' Bran raised an eyebrow at Talus. Talus gave a tiny shrug. Such things happened sometimes between father and son.

Cabarrath shook his head. 'Not in the way you think. The woman came from Sleeth. Although my father and Farrum were always fighting, there has always been trade between our two islands. They bring fish and whalebones; the men of Sleeth are skilled on the sea. We give them carved things in return. This woman... she used to hide on the trading boats, make the voyage to Creyak without anybody knowing. She would sneak ashore and we would meet in secret. Our love was forbidden, you see.'

Talus sat forward. Was there some truth in Alayin's story after all? Was Cabarrath her secret lover? If so, did it bear on the rest of the investigation... or were they wandering down one of Creyak's many blind alleys?

'What was the woman's name?' he said.

'Alayin,' Cabarrath replied.

Both of Bran's eyebrows had risen. Ignoring him, the bard raised a finger. 'You speak of your affair with Alayin as something that happened in the past.'

'Yes. It ended last year. We realised we were spending more time arguing than... well, you know how love can end up.'

'When was the last time you saw her?' said Bran.

Cabarrath shrugged. 'Last winter, when I told her she was a spoiled brat and she told me I smelt worse than a boar's crotch. We both meant it. It was not a happy day.'

'And you have not seen her since?' said Talus.

'I hope I never do again.' Cabarrath spoke in a matter-of-fact way, without bitterness. 'Perhaps I will have a little of that meat after all.'

Cabarrath stripped a long strand of venison from the bone. His hands were both gentle and strong. Talus recalled how Cabarrath had restrained Fethan when he'd lost his temper in the cairn; clearly his younger brothers were used to him taking control. Yet, as the second-eldest, he wasn't weighed down with responsibility like Tharn. A confident man.

'Tell me about your relationship with Gantor.'

Cabarrath chewed methodically. 'We were close.'

'But Gantor was not liked by the others.'

'Who told you that?'

'It is not important. We also know that Gantor preferred the company of men to women, and that this caused trouble between him and his father.'

'Gantor was a good man. One of the best. He didn't deserve to be treated the way he was. I tried to look after him, but people were cruel to him.' A spark of ferocity had ignited in Cabarrath's eyes. So the easy-going giant had passions after all.

'When he died, he tried to say something to you.'

Cabarrath threw his unfinished meal into the fire. The meat tumbled through the flames, turning black and crisp. 'Our private words. It was what we said to each other whenever we met. It was a simple thing. It just meant we knew each other, and we understood.'

'What was it you said?' said Bran.

'"You and me,"' Cabarrath replied.

'Just that?'

'I said it was a simple thing. But that last time Gantor couldn't... he couldn't say it all.' He lowered his head. 'Now he'll never say it again.'

Talus allowed the silence to spin out. There was no doubt Cabarrath had held a grudge against his father. But what had he really felt about Gantor? He claimed they'd been close. And Lethriel had hinted the same. It was just a shame Gantor wasn't alive to confirm it.

Talus stood and clasped his hands in front of him. 'Thank you, Cabarrath, for your honesty. Your answers have been helpful.'

Cabarrath looked up, surprised. 'Is that it? Is it over?'

'If I think of any more questions I wish to ask you, I will call you back.'

'Oh. All right. And... please, I beg you, find out what happened to them. Please.'

Cabarrath's eyes filled up with tears. He stumbled to the door, his grace altogether gone.

Just as the morning fog was folding itself around Cabarrath's retreating form, Talus called, 'Actually, I have just thought of another question.'

Cabarrath turned back. 'Ask it, bard.'

'Why was your affair with Alayin forbidden?'

'Well, for a start, she came from Sleeth.'

'But there was more to it than that?'

'Oh yes. If she'd just been an ordinary Sleeth woman—a weaver, or a gatherer like Lethriel—my father might have learned to accept her. He liked to keep his back turned on the world beyond Creyak, but occasionally things slipped through. Some people.'

'So what was different about Alayin?' said Bran.

'Didn't I tell you? Alayin is Farrum's daughter.'

CHAPTER NINETEEN

WHEN FETHAN ARRIVED, five women came with him. He stopped at the threshold and whispered a few words to each of them. Only then did he enter the house, leaving the women outside with their heads bowed. All wore small hoods of white stoat fur splashed with red dye—a sign of mourning, Bran assumed. One of them was heavily pregnant.

Fethan went straight to the fire to warm his hands. His long hair was matted, his face haggard. He kept shifting his weight from one foot to the other. He didn't look at either Talus or Bran, just stared deep into the flames.

'Are you going to sit down?' said Bran.

'I will stand,' said Fethan.

'Very well,' said Talus. 'Thank you for coming.'

'Tharn gave me no choice.'

'I see you have brought friends.'

'The women will tell you what I say is true.'

'Then you have nothing to fear. Will you begin by telling us about the night the king died? I understand you found the body.'

At last Fethan looked Talus in the eye. 'Who told you that?'

'Surely everyone must know it was you who raised the alarm.'

'Look, I'm tired. I haven't slept since...'

'Then you really should sit down,' said Bran. Fethan's abrupt manner was making the hairs on his back prickle. He hadn't forgotten how this man had held a bonespike to his throat.

'I will stand,' Fethan repeated.

'Stand, then,' said Talus. 'And speak. Will you tell us what happened?'

Fethan swept his tangled hair away from his face. 'I will not tell you that I found the dead king frozen in the snow.'

'Oh? Why not?' said Bran. Fethan's petulance was beginning to annoy him. 'Are you going to tell us you were somewhere else at the time?'

'I was not somewhere else. I was right there. But I didn't find my father. I killed him!'

'What?'

'You were right to suspect me all along. It was me. I struck the deadly blow. I am the man you seek. I killed my father. I killed the king!'

Outside, three of the women turned away with audible sobs. The other two just watched, their fur-wrapped bodies like ghosts in the swirling fog.

'I knew it!' Bran jumped to his feet. 'I knew there was something wrong with you all along!'

Talus's finger went up. The tiny movement stilled Bran's anger—and made him marvel. How was the bard able to wield such power with a single gesture?

'Will each of these women confirm that what you have just told us is true?' Talus said.

'Yes,' said Fethan. There was defiance in his voice.

'Because they love you?'

'Because it's the truth.'

'Hmm.' Talus diverted his raised finger to the tip of his nose. 'Let us put aside this *truth* of yours for a moment. These women interest me. What is your relationship with them?'

Fethan's jaw hung open for a moment. 'What are you talking about? I just told you I'm the killer. What else is there to talk about?'

The bard's finger left his nose and traced a slow circle through the air. He said nothing.

'Just tell him,' said Bran.

Fethan shook his head. 'I don't understand what you mean.'

'These women are not your wives?' said Talus.

'Of course not.'

'You have never married?'

'No.'

'Nor do any of your brothers have wives?'

'That is not our way.'

Talus leaned forward. 'I suggest you sit down, Fethan,' he said sharply. 'And tell us exactly what *is* your way.'

Fethan sat with a thud. He looked around, confused, as if he couldn't work out how he'd suddenly ended up on the floor.

Bran joined him. For the first time, he felt a trace of sympathy for Fethan, despite the crime he'd just confessed to. The man looked... lost. 'It's simpler if you just tell him,' Bran said. 'He won't give up until you do.'

* * *

FOR A LONG time Fethan said nothing. The only sound was the crackle and hiss of the flames as they steadily consumed the peat in the hearth. Bran wanted to shake him, but Talus's patience scolded him to stillness.

Finally, Fethan spoke.

'The ordinary men of Creyak are allowed to take wives. The sons of the king are not. Only the eldest son, when he becomes king, may marry.'

'But you are allowed to be with women?' said Talus.

'We have to be...' Fethan frowned, searching for the word.

'Discreet?' said Talus.

'I suppose so.'

'Is that your idea of "discreet"?' said Bran, nodding towards the women outside. Fethan said nothing.

'What of babies?' Talus pointed at the pregnant woman. 'Is this one yours?'

Fethan hesitated before nodding. 'It happens. The mother and child will be taken to another village. They'll be forgotten.' He straightened his back. 'This time, the father will go too.'

'You're going to make a run for it,' said Bran. His feelings of sympathy had evaporated as quickly as they'd come. 'I suppose that's easier than paying for what you've done.'

'I don't know what you mean. My father is dead. That's the end of it, in this world at least.'

'What about your brothers? The rest of the village? If you run now, you'll leave them wondering what really happened. Don't you think they deserve to know the truth?'

Fethan's puzzled expression looked genuine. 'I've told you what happened. You in turn will tell the others. Now there's no reason for me to stay. I will leave today and live out my life. As for my punishment—I'll face that when I finally step into the afterdream.' He looked at Talus. 'You're a bard. You understand tales.'

'I am,' said Talus. 'I do.'

'Then you'll understand this: now that I've told you the truth, the tale of the dead king has come to an end.'

In the fire, a peat brick that was nearly burned through collapsed with a sigh. Bran watched sparks like fireflies rise in a cloud and out through the hole in the roof, then turned his attention back to Fethan.

There was every reason to dislike this man. His manner was surly, bordering on rude. And the bonespike incident still rankled—although, on reflection, Bran supposed he'd deserved it.

So why did Bran believe Fethan was lying?

'The customs of Creyak are strange,' Bran said. 'Talus and I have journeyed far, but I don't think we've ever come across a settlement where a king controls his sons so completely.'

Fethan shrugged. 'It was my father's way.'

'Didn't you resent him for it?'

'How can you resent a man you love?'

'You loved him so much that you killed him?' Even as he said it, Bran recalled what Talus had said about violence being driven by passion.

'I told you what I did.' Fethan stood. 'Now it is time for me to go.'

'Sit down,' said Talus. 'I am not satisfied.'

'Satisfied of what?' said Fethan.

'That what you have told us is the truth.'

Fethan barked out a short, humourless laugh. 'I will leave you to your *stories*, bard.' He ran for the door, but Bran was quicker. The fisherman clamped his left forearm around the young man's throat and snatched the axe from his own waist with his good right hand. He pressed the sharp flint blade to Fethan's neck, just as Fethan had earlier pressed the bonespike to his.

The pregnant woman darted forward, crying out. Her companions grabbed her before she could intervene.

Fethan struggled, but Bran was strong. 'Let me go or kill me,' Fethan snarled. 'I don't care which you choose.'

'Escape by any means?' said Bran. 'Is that it? Well, do you know what? I think my friend Talus is right. I don't believe you had anything to do with the king's murder.'

'Then let me go.'

'I think you should stay.'

'I know the truth, and I have told it.'

'Ah-ha!' Now Talus was on his feet. He stalked up to Fethan until the two men were practically nose to nose. 'I believe exactly half of what you just said.'

Fethan tried to wrestle his way out of Bran's grip; Bran kicked the backs of his legs, forcing him down to his knees. Now all his weight was on Fethan. He pressed harder with the axe blade, drawing blood. Fethan's struggles stopped abruptly.

'I believe you *know* the truth,' said Talus, staring

down at the subdued man. 'But what you have *said* is nothing but lies.'

'Believe what you want.'

'I will. You say you killed the king? Prove it.'

'What?'

'Tell me something only the killer could know.'

'I don't understand.'

'Tell me something about the murder—some small detail that will prove your guilt.'

'I can't think of anything.'

Talus crouched. Little popping sounds came from his knees. Again he was face to face with Fethan.

'Then I will ask a question. What was the expression on your father's face when he died?'

Bran could feel Fethan's body shaking beneath him.

'How dare you ask such a thing?'

'Tell me!' Even Bran was shocked by the sudden force in Talus's voice.

'He was surprised,' Fethan blurted. 'That was all. I came at him quickly. I saw his eyes grow wide. He had no time to speak. He just looked... surprised.'

'You saw this in his face?'

'I looked right into his eyes.'

'Very well. Bran—please describe the expression on Fethan's face.'

The question took Bran by surprise. 'Uh, I'm standing behind him, Talus. I can't see his face at all.'

Talus's voice softened. 'We know that whoever killed your father, Fethan, struck the blow from behind. That is how I know you are lying. Well done. You have just proved your innocence. Let him go, Bran.'

Bran relaxed his grip and stepped away. He remained alert, however, just in case Fethan turned on him. But the young man remained on his knees. The onlooking women whispered to each other.

'You must believe me,' Fethan said at last.

Talus laid a hand on his shoulder. 'Give me a reason to. Tell me why you chose to take the blame.'

Fethan raised his head. 'I will say no more.'

'You know who the real killer is, Fethan. Why do you want to protect him?'

'If you know, you must tell us,' said Bran.

'I will say no more.'

'Then you may go.' Talus retreated several paces, giving Fethan room to stand. 'But if you change your mind, please come to me again. My ears are always ready to hear a man's tale. Just as long as it is true.'

'Talus,' said Bran, 'you can't just...'

'Let him go,' said the bard.

'Go where?' said Fethan. 'I have no place here now.' Shoulders slumped, he stumbled towards the door.

'Tell me, Fethan,' said Talus. 'When Tharn becomes king, will the ways of Creyak change?'

'What do you mean?'

'Hashath, your father, cast a long shadow over this island when he was alive. Now that shadow is gone. Who knows, Fethan, perhaps your children may yet be able to play in the sun.'

A tremor crossed Fethan's face, and Bran thought he was going to cry. Then his back stiffened and he walked out through the door. The women gathered round him. He kissed each of them on the brow and the pregnant woman on the mouth. Arms tangled around each other, the strange group wandered away into the fog.

'Why did you let him go?' said Bran.

'He had said all he was going to say,' Talus replied. He looked strangely sad. 'His loyalty to the real killer has closed his mouth.'

'Then the killer *is* one of his brothers. It has to be.'

'Perhaps. Regardless, we have learned from Fethan everything we are going to learn.'

'Precious little, in the end.'

'On the contrary, Bran. On the contrary.'

They sat again before the fire.

'Thank you for stepping in, Bran.'

'What? Oh, that. You're welcome.'

'Even I must admit that muscles can be useful. I fear the mind is not always enough.'

'That's quite an admission from you, Talus.'

'There was a night, Bran, nearly two years ago, when it was your strength alone that saved my life. This happened at considerable cost to yourself. I have never forgotten that night, and never shall.'

'Why are you bringing this up now?'

'Because time is short. If I do not say these things now, by the time I think of them again it may be too late.'

Bran couldn't understand why his friend had turned suddenly so melancholy. 'What's wrong?'

'It is a long road to travel.'

'We've come this far. I daresay we can make it a little further.' The words caught in Bran's throat.

'I was not referring to the road we share, my friend. I

was referring to the one I walk alone. Sometimes, Bran, it feels like the longest road of all.'

CHAPTER TWENTY

TWO MORE FIGURES loomed out of the mist. They resolved themselves into the contrasting forms of the youngest brothers in the king's family: Sigathon and Arak.

Only a few breaths had passed since Fethan and his women had disappeared; the parade of suspects was so orderly that Talus wondered if Tharn was standing just out of sight, directing the whole affair. If so, that was good: Talus could hear distant drums and the beginnings of a mourning song fed by many voices as Creyak prepared to honour its dead. Soon all would be confusion, and his work would be that much more difficult to complete.

Was it even near completion? Talus couldn't tell. It was as if the fog creeping through Creyak had invaded his mind as well. He should have been concentrating on the king's sons, but suddenly all he could think about was Mishina.

Until now, Talus had never met anyone else who'd seen the great cairns of the desert. Mishina's sketch had taken his mind back to those long-gone times, the long trek across the hot white sand, the ripple of the far horizon, the way he'd teetered at the edge of death.

The way he'd found what might have been the

beginnings of answers, only to lose them before they could properly form.

Then there was the jungle realm Mishina had spoken about. Even reaching such a place was a fantasy he could scarcely imagine. What manner of boat could have carried Mishina all the way across the western ocean and back again?

Suddenly the world seemed very big, and Talus very small. So many sights to see, so many questions to answer, and only a single lifetime in which to do it all.

'Can we come in?' said Arak.

Talus forced aside thoughts of jungles and deserts and beckoned the two youngsters inside.

Although they were close in age, they were not alike. Sigathon was short and solid. This was the first time Talus had seen him without the black paint on his face. His resemblance to Gantor was striking.

Arak was the same height as Sigathon, but thin and wiry. Unlike his brother—who looked ready to fall asleep—Arak was bright-eyed and alert. He was just as much a fidget now as he had been at the feast, glancing from side to side and continually scratching the back of his neck.

'Which one of you is older?' said Bran.

Arak laughed. He had an easy grin, and an open face. Sigathon looked as if he'd never cracked a smile in his life.

'He is,' Arak said, jerking a thumb at his brother. 'By exactly twenty-one breaths. That's what our mother says, anyway.'

'So you are twins?' said Talus.

'Yes. Though we're not exactly identical, are we?'

'Likeness is not always in the skin. Do you do everything together?'

'More or less. Is it all right if you talk to us both at the same time? We've got nothing to hide.'

Just as Cabarrath and Fethan had done before them, the two young men seated themselves by the fire. Talus didn't even need to ask the first question.

'We were together all night,' said Arak. 'Sigathon and me. We sleep in our father's house. He was there too. It was just an ordinary night. Towards dawn, our father left the house. Sigathon and I had woken early and were playing a game—we scratch patterns in the ground and move coloured stones from place to place. We pretend we are the stones. The stones fight and remove each other from the pattern.'

'Is that why the king left?'

Arak squirmed. 'I suppose we were being noisy.'

'At what point did you realise something was wrong?'

'When we heard Fethan screaming.'

Arak scrubbed at his neck. Sigathon showed no more animation than one of the village totems.

'Tell me about this game,' said Talus.

'You mark out lines on the ground. Then you cross them with other lines. Each person takes a number of stones—one takes red, the other black—and you move the stones from one place to another.' Arak licked his lips, clearly excited. 'There are rules that make it difficult to move certain stones in certain directions.' He stopped, suddenly embarrassed. 'Anyway, it's a lot of fun.'

'Who told you these rules?'

Arak's embarrassment became shyness. 'Nobody. I invented them.'

'You are very clever, Arak,' said Talus. But it was Sigathon he was watching. There was a complex relationship here, one he was keen to understand. Could there be not one murderer but two? Two young men who did everything together, each perfectly placed to cover the other's tracks?

'You both still lived with your father?'

Arak looked surprised. 'Of course. We have only fifteen summers each.'

Fifteen years old. In many communities—perhaps most—they would already have had children of their own.

'Hashath liked to control his children, didn't he?' said Bran.

'It was his way,' Arak replied.

'Didn't you want a house of your own?' said Bran. Talus listened, content to let his companion take over the questioning.

'That time will come soon.'

'Not soon enough!' said Sigathon.

Bran jumped. The ferocity of the elder twin's voice startled Talus too.

'What do you mean?' said Bran.

'Be quiet,' Arak hissed at his brother.

'No!' said Sigathon. 'I've been quiet long enough!' His eyes rolled blearily, sliding over Talus before fixing on Bran. 'He said we could never leave his side. He said we were his pets, his wolf cubs. Pets? More like prisoners!' He gave a little howl, like a lost pup.

'Prisoners?' said Bran. 'What do you mean?'

Arak seized his brother's hand, but Sigathon shook him off, fighting what appeared to be exhaustion.

'Do you know when our father was happiest? When the tide was in and the causeway was covered and nobody could get to the island. In the end, he stopped talking to anyone outside Creyak. He stopped trading with them. He stopped making war. He even stopped making peace. He stopped *everything*. Winter fell on him and he just... froze.'

'He cut himself off,' Bran said slowly.

'Himself and all the rest of us,' said Sigathon. His sudden burst of energy was spent. His broad shoulders dropped and his mouth hung a little open.

Talus was beginning to understand just how much power the dead king had enjoyed here. At last the screaming totems made sense: they were perfect for scaring people away from the island. For keeping everything—and everyone—inside.

'Tell me, Arak,' he said. 'How did you feel about all this?'

'My brother is hot-tempered,' Arak said quickly. 'What he says is... well, I suppose it's true. But we don't all feel about it the way he does.'

'So you did not mind being your father's *pet*?'

'We all find ways to escape.'

'Your games?'

Arak scratched a hasty criss-cross of lines in the dirt floor. Into them he pressed dots, making a pattern. 'I suppose so,' he said at last.

'It is no wonder your hands are dirty,' said Talus, 'if

you are always scraping them on the ground.'

'They're not that bad,' said Arak, displaying grimy fingers with a lop-sided grin.

'And you,' said Talus, turning his attention to Sigathon. 'If your brother escapes into his clever thoughts, where is your haven?'

Sigathon sat, square and solid. He looked exactly like Gantor, and almost as lifeless. Slowly, he raised his left hand, extended a finger and tapped the side of his head. He lowered his hand again, tightened his lips to a thin, white line and said nothing more.

'Sigathon was with me all the time,' said Arak as the silence deepened. 'Truly he was.'

'It is a shame there was nobody else in the house,' said Talus. 'And so no way to confirm your story is true. Is there anything more you want to say?'

Arak thought for a moment, then shook his head.

'WHAT A STRANGE pair,' said Bran after Arak and Sigathon had left.

'They are damaged, I think. Both of them. Proof that the blood of family makes stains that are not always visible to the naked eye.'

The mourning song floated out of the fog, like the cry of a whale lost far out to sea. Talus imagined the entire vastness of the world hanging just out of reach.

Why was he finding it so hard to concentrate?

'It's a good job you let me ask some of the questions,' said Bran.

'Oh? Why do you say that?'

'Because it strikes me this mystery is all about real human relationships. You know, the messy kind?'

'What are you trying to say, Bran?' In the depths of the fog, shadows came and went.

'Only that human relationships aren't exactly your strong point.'

'And I suppose you are an expert?'

'I'm not saying that.'

'Then what are you saying, Bran?'

'Just that... well, I'm more experienced with that kind of thing.'

'Are you saying I have no experience of life?'

'Of course not. I'm just saying you're...'

'What?' For some unaccountable reason, Talus's eyes were stinging. 'What am I, Bran? Tell me that much! What am I?'

Under other circumstances, Bran's expression of surprise might have been amusing. Talus was more concerned with the unexpected passion their meaningless argument had kindled in his own heart.

'I'll tell you what you are,' said a woman's voice from just outside the doorway. 'You're just about the strangest man I've ever met.'

Lethriel stepped into view. Talus had had no idea she was there.

'What are you doing here?' said Bran. His words were stilted.

'I wanted to ask you not to say anything about... what you saw.'

'You mean you and Tharn together?' said Bran. 'Don't worry—Talus knows all about it too.'

'Oh.' Lethriel was blushing. Talus wondered how people could get so distressed about what was simply normal behaviour.

'But I won't tell anyone else,' said Bran hurriedly.

'Do you wish to say anything else, Lethriel?' said Talus. 'Hurry, please. The king-to-be will be arriving at any moment.'

'No, that was all.' But, instead of leaving, Lethriel loitered in the doorway.

'Really?' said Talus.

'Yes... no! I'm sorry, I was outside. I couldn't help overhearing. What Sigathon said—that little outburst of his—it reminded me of something.'

Talus felt his irritation subside. 'What did it remind you of?'

'A conversation I overheard between Sigathon and Tharn. It happened a few days ago, before Hashath was killed. I never thought to tell you about it before.'

'Then tell me now,' said Talus. 'But I beg you, be quick.'

'All right. I was delivering herbs to the king's house. Tharn and Sigathon were in there alone, talking in hushed voices. I didn't want to interrupt them, so I...'

'Listened in?' said Bran.

Lethriel's blush deepened. 'They were talking about Farrum. About Alayin, actually. Alayin is...'

'Farrum's daughter,' said Bran. 'We know.'

'Oh. Well, Sigathon said something about love being stronger than the king. It struck me as an odd thing to say. I mean, it's odd for Sigathon to say anything at all lately, but that...'

'How did Tharn reply?' said Talus.

'The sorts of things an older brother says. He told Sigathon to be sensible and do the right thing. He was placating him, I suppose. But Sigathon just kept going on and on about love being strong. As strong as a wolf, he kept saying. He talked about riding the wolf. And he talked about escape.'

'Is that all you remember?'

'Yes. I couldn't hear everything. Now I tell it back, it sounds even stranger than I thought at the time. I'm sorry, I know it's probably nothing.'

A stocky figure appeared, striding towards the house out of the fog.

'Please,' said Talus, 'will you leave now?'

Instead of obeying, Lethriel scurried over to the pit where the peat-bricks were stored and lowered herself into it.

'What are you doing?' said Talus.

'I want to hear what he's got to say.' Lethriel dragged the cover-stone halfway across the opening. 'You won't even know I'm here.'

Talus felt a flash of heat deep inside his gut. Was this what Bran felt like when he lost his temper? But... perhaps there was sense in what Lethriel was doing.

'Listen well, then,' he said. 'And afterwards, tell us if you have learned anything new about the man you love.'

Lethriel's eyes bobbed just above the level of the floor.

'I'm sorry,' she said. She wasn't talking to Talus now, but to Bran.

'What for?' he said.

Before she could respond, Tharn, the eldest son of the murdered king of Creyak, entered.

chapter twenty-one

'I HAVE LITTLE time for this,' said Tharn without preamble.

'It is necessary,' said Talus. 'You know that.'

The mourning song was louder now, an almost physical presence in the fog. There were words inside it, and a melody that seemed always to descend and never to rise: an endless low lament filled with darkness and desperation.

'The procession has begun,' said Tharn. 'Creyak is preparing to say its final goodbyes to the king. I had hoped you would be finished by now.'

'This will not take long. I simply wish to know where you were when your father died.'

'I was out walking on the cliffs near the henge. I do not sleep well. I never have. When I get restless, I go out so as not to disturb my brother.'

'Your brother, yes. Cabarrath told me something different. He said you were in the house with him all night.'

'And I tell you I was not.'

'Why do you think Cabarrath lied?'

'To protect me, I suppose.'

'Does he believe you did it?'

'Killed my father?' Tharn shuddered. It seemed a genuine reaction. 'No. Cabarrath knows I did not do it.'

'Can you say the same about him? Please, tell me only what you know to be true.'

'Cabarrath has always liked his secrets,' Tharn said at last. Tears began to roll down his cheeks. 'But he is no killer.'

'Secrets?' said Bran. 'You mean his affair with Alayin?'

'How do you know about that?'

'Go on, Bran.' Talus sat back. This was interesting.

'I think Cabarrath wasn't the only one to fall for Alayin,' said Bran. 'I think Sigathon did too. And I think he spoke to you about it. Am I right, Tharn?'

Tharn said nothing.

'Did it even stop there?' Bran spoke loud, almost as if he wanted to make sure Lethriel heard every word. 'Did she work her way through all of you, one by one?'

Talus was surprised. Bran had made a connection he himself had failed to make. Alayin and Sigathon? It made sense of the youngster's strange talk of love and wolves.

The bard was surprised all over again when Tharn started sobbing. His shoulders heaved; great, gasping moans tore their way up from his chest. They mingled with the whale-song drone of the mourning tune.

There was sudden movement as Lethriel burst out of her hiding place. She shoved the heavy cover-stone aside, ran to Tharn and wrapped her arms round him. She kissed his wet cheeks, his brow, his lips.

Talus observed the exchange with simple curiosity and considered the darkness of the deeds that could result from the brightest of passions. Bran just glared into the fire.

Gradually, Tharn's tears subsided. He wiped his eyes and squeezed Lethriel tight. Then he pushed her gently away.

'You don't have to do this now,' said Lethriel.

'I do,' said Tharn. 'If I am to be king, I must get used to grasping that which stings me.'

'Do you fear it?' said Talus. 'Becoming king?'

'It has always been my fate,' Tharn replied. 'But I have never been in a hurry to wear my father's crown.'

'You cannot prove where you were on the night of your father's murder,' said Talus. He kept his voice stern. Then he allowed it to soften. 'Nor do I see any clear reason why you would kill the king. Nothing I can ask you will change that. Instead I will ask you about Farrum and Alayin. What hold do they have over you and your family?'

In halting words, Tharn told the same story they'd already heard from Cabarrath. 'Farrum and my father hated each other,' he said. 'But their children... that was a different matter.'

'Alayin and Cabarrath?' said Bran, looking up from the fire. Lethriel had left Tharn's embrace, but they were still holding hands.

'They were first,' Tharn agreed. 'After their affair ended, Alayin stayed away. But she came back in the end. She is poison, that woman!'

'She went with Sigathon?' said Talus.

'Yes.'

'How long were they together?'

'Not long. It ended suddenly. Sigathon's mood has been black ever since.'

'When was this?'

'A few moons back. Who knows which of us she will pursue next?' He gave a bitter smile. 'Perhaps she will try setting her claws into me.'

'I'm sure Lethriel would have something to say about that,' said Bran.

With a start, Talus understood that Bran had feelings for Lethriel. How had he missed that? Was Bran right? Did he really understand so little about human nature? The idea disturbed him.

And, if he'd missed this much, what else had he failed to spot?

'Lethriel has never been afraid to say what she thinks,' said Tharn. 'Perhaps you have found that out for yourself.'

'It must be difficult keeping your feelings for each other secret,' said Talus.

'Yes,' said Lethriel, 'it is.'

Tharn kissed her cheek. 'Now everything will be different.' He took in a deep breath, let it out slowly. He rubbed his cheek, his palm rasping on the stubble growing there. 'Is our business finished here, bard?' he said. 'Has this been useful to you? Have you discovered the truth yet?'

All eyes turned to Talus, Bran's included. For a moment, Talus was lost for words: a new sensation, and not one he cared for.

'I have nothing more to ask you, Tharn,' he said at last. 'In answer to your questions, I believe I am close to knowing who the murderer is.'

Was that true? Talus really didn't know. He'd thought everything depended upon who had been where on the night of the king's murder, and who might have been sufficiently motivated to plunge a bonespike into his chest. But where did Gantor's death fit in? And what about Farrum?

His thoughts buzzed, moved, made patterns part-formed and tantalising. In time they would merge to become answers, truth. He was almost there, he could sense it. But he was almost out of time.

'There is one more thing I must do,' he said.

'Who?' said Bran. 'We've seen everyone now.'

'Can it wait until after the procession?' said Tharn.

'I fear not,' Talus replied. 'I must go to the beach immediately, in the hope that the woman hidden in Farrum's boat is still there. I need to see her.'

Tharn looked mystified. 'What do you mean? What woman?'

'Alayin.'

Lethriel gasped. Tharn drew back his lips to expose his teeth. 'The venomous snake! She has come to gloat because my father is dead.' His eyes grew wide. 'Or perhaps my father is dead because she is here!'

'Alayin did not kill your father,' said Talus. 'And neither did Farrum.'

'He's right,' said Bran. 'Think about it. Farrum's boat was at sea when father was killed. They can't possibly have...'

Tharn was having none of it. Shoving Bran aside, he stormed out of the house and into the fog. Lethriel followed him at a run.

'This day is full of surprises,' said Talus. 'Come, Bran, we must stop him before he does something reckless.'

They set off in pursuit. The fog enfolded them, as did the sound of the mourning song. Sudden claustrophobia gripped Talus. They were trapped here on Creyak. The island had swallowed them whole. They were doomed to circle its covered passages for eternity, seeking answers that were forever just out of reach.

THE MAIN THOROUGHFARE leading all the way from the entrance maze to the burial cairn was packed tight with people. Their faces were all painted white. They floated in the mist like spirits from the next world. It was they who were singing.

Talus spotted Tharn muscling his way through the crowd. Lethriel was right behind him, trying to hold him back; every few steps he had to shake her off. Cabarrath appeared and shouted something in Tharn's ear. Tharn yelled something back to his brother, but their words were drowned by the uproar.

The procession started to break apart. The mourning song fragmented. White faces swivelled in surprise as Tharn ploughed his way along the passage, gathering men along the way. Talus and Bran followed in Tharn's wake; giving up her efforts to stop Tharn, Lethriel fell back to join them. Bran scooped his arm around her, protecting her from the jostling bodies.

'Why didn't you tell me about Alayin?' Lethriel shouted. 'I could have stopped all this.'

'We didn't think it would cause this much trouble,' Bran yelled back.

'Be quiet and keep up,' said Talus. He had no time for

their bleating. 'I believe Tharn may be about to make a terrible mistake.'

Tharn and his supporters—Fethan had joined them now—rounded a corner and stopped short. Farrum and his boatmen were blocking the path.

'Stand aside,' said Tharn. By now the singing had completely died away. Tharn's words echoed down the passage, clear for all to hear.

'Where are you going?' said Farrum.

'This is my island. I will go where I choose. Not that it's any of your concern.'

'It concerns me when one of my men is attacked and left for dead!'

Farrum hauled a man into view. There was a purple bruise on the front of his head and a line of vomit running down his chin and into his furs.

'Nobody attacked Lath,' Bran called. 'He's drunk.'

'Drunk enough to club himself on the head, I suppose?' said Farrum.

'He fell down,' said Bran. 'Smell his breath if you don't believe me.'

Glowering, Farrum looked from Bran to Tharn and back again. He bent his head to Lath's and sniffed. With a growl, he shoved the big man aside.

'Let me pass,' said Tharn.

'Oh, I think not, boy.'

'Stand aside, Farrum. You have no right to power here.'

From behind Tharn came an answering rumble: the voice of Creyak rising behind its king-to-be.

'What would you do?' said Farrum. His white hair

and massive white beard almost seemed part of the fog. He looked very old. But the expression on his face was that of a wolf, wild and wary.

'I would go to the beach,' Tharn replied. 'There is something in your boat I wish to see.'

'My poor boy, I believe your grief for your father has blinded you to the...'

'Do not play with me, old man. You know exactly what I am talking about.'

Farrum's mouth twitched, sending tremors through the scars on his cheeks. 'And if I don't stand aside?'

'Then I will kill you.'

The crowd sighed.

'Your father abhorred violence.'

'My father is dead.'

Farrum muttered something to his men. Talus felt Bran tense beside him.

'This is not your fight, my friend,' Talus murmured.

'It could be.' Bran pulled Lethriel harder against him. She didn't resist.

But there was no fight. Farrum stepped aside, extended his arm along the passage and bowed his head.

'You're right, of course,' said the old man. 'Creyak is your domain. It is not my place to tell you what to do. I will just say this to you, Tharn: *have a care.*'

Tharn pressed forward, dragging his retinue with him. He passed Farrum without giving him a second glance. The rest of the crowd dithered uncertainly, then followed.

Without waiting for his companions, Talus hurried after them.

CHAPTER TWENTY-TWO

FOR THE THIRD time, Bran found himself on the icy path to the Creyak beach. Both times before he'd been alone; now he was surrounded by an angry mob. And Lethriel was at his side.

The fog lingered, damp and fluid in the pale afternoon light. It was like running along the bed of the sea, with all the weight of the ocean pressed down on top of him. As they hit the beach, Lethriel's hand caught Bran's own, and held it. Their feet crunched in unison on the shingle.

Briefly, the fog obscured everything. Then the prow of the Sleeth boat reared out of the blankness, looking just as it had before, except now it had not one figurehead but two: perched high on the weather-rail beside the carved wolf's head was Alayin.

Invisible in the fog, the sea hissed.

Tharn had run ahead of his brothers. On seeing Alayin, he skidded to a halt. Pebbles flew around his feet as he flailed his arms for balance.

'Alayin!' he shouted. 'What have you done?'

'I demand sanctuary!' Alayin called down. 'My father brought me here against my will. Will you protect me from him?'

Tharn's brothers caught up and formed a half-circle behind the king-to-be. Bran came to a halt a short distance away. Lethriel let go his hand, but stayed close. Talus materialised from nowhere and took up station at Bran's left side. Farrum and his men, and the white-faced villagers of Creyak, were still pouring down from the path behind them.

'I don't understand,' panted Bran. 'She's had every chance to escape.'

'She lied to you about her reasons for being here,' said Talus.

Tharn marched up to the boat, crouched and sprang. Arms extended, he grabbed the boat's weather-rail and hauled himself up. Cornered, Alayin cowered against the wolf's head.

'Cabarrath!' Tharn called. 'Fethan!'

The two brothers ran to stand beneath the prow. When they were in place, Tharn seized Alayin round the waist and hurled her off. She landed in their arms, struggled to free herself and fell awkwardly on her ankle. She cried out in pain.

'Get your hands off my daughter!'

Farrum, puffing a little from the exertion, strode up to Cabarrath and cuffed him across the cheek. He had to reach up to do it. Cabarrath staggered back—old as he was, Farrum was no weakling—and before he could retaliate, Fethan had drawn his bonespike. He crouched, ready to strike.

'Leave him!' roared Tharn. He jumped down from the boat, landing square in front of Farrum. 'Alayin, stand up.'

'I can't,' she said. 'My ankle...'

'*Stand up!*'

Bran, gripped by the scene playing itself out in the fog, became aware of Talus sidling forwards. What was the bard planning?

Tharn grabbed Alayin's arm and hauled her to her feet.

'Tell us again what you said,' he barked. 'So your father can hear.'

Alayin hesitated. 'I'm sorry, father,' she said. 'I know this isn't what you wanted. But I must tell the truth.'

'She doesn't know the meaning of the word,' muttered Lethriel.

'The truth is all that matters, girl,' said Farrum. 'Just tell it!'

'I choose to be here,' Alayin said. 'On Creyak. That is all.'

'I don't believe you,' said Tharn, shaking her. He glared at Farrum. 'Why did you come? Why did you *both* come?'

'A good question,' said Talus. He was now ten paces beyond Bran and Lethriel, and still advancing.

'Talus,' Bran hissed. The bard ignored him.

Farrum squared his shoulders and surveyed the crowd that had by now gathered around the boat. All possible escape routes were cut off. He stood with his daughter facing the sons of Hashath in an open arena walled with bodies.

'Let her go,' he said, ignoring Alayin and speaking directly to Tharn.

Farrum's men pushed their way out of the crowd.

One by one, they lined up behind their king. Even Lath was there, bruised and shamefaced.

'You are behind all this, Farrum,' said Tharn slowly. 'I do not understand how this can be, but I feel it. I *know* it. You are behind all of it.'

Farrum set his feet wide apart and planted his hands on his hips. The whalebones hanging from his belt sent deep musical notes through the mist. 'You're a fool, Tharn. Just like your father. *I wasn't even here when Hashath died.*'

'My father was many things,' said Tharn. 'But he was no fool. Tell your men to step back.'

'Why? So you and your brothers can kill me?'

'My brothers will do the same. There will just be the two of us.'

Tharn shoved Alayin towards Cabarrath, who caught her—more tenderly than Fethan might have done, Bran suspected. The two brothers marched her back to where Arak and Sigathon were waiting. Farrum's men retreated too, leaving Tharn and Farrum face to face in the swirling fog beneath the prow of the boat from Sleeth.

Bran held his breath... and let it out with a gasp as Talus strolled directly between the two adversaries.

'Excuse me,' said the bard.

Bran wondered who would pound Talus into the shingle first: Tharn or Farrum. But the they were too intent on each other even to notice him.

'Thank you,' said Talus.

He walked all the way over to where the king's other sons were standing. Cabarrath had placed Alayin into the custody of Arak. The lad's hands were bunched tight in the thick ivory furs she wore, and the wiry muscles in his arms were tense. He looked scared and uncertain, as if he'd rather be anywhere but here.

Ignoring her captors, Talus brushed back Alayin's fur hood to expose her scarred face. Her expression contorted; for a moment Bran thought she was going to spit at him, but she simply endured his scrutiny. The rest of the crowd looked on bemused.

Finally Talus nodded. Then he retraced his steps to stand beside Bran again.

'What were you thinking?' said Bran. 'They're ready to kill each other.'

'All the more reason to make haste.'

Talus looked anything but hasty, Bran thought. If anything, the bard looked utterly relaxed.

'You know, don't you?' Bran said. 'I don't know how, but you know. You know who killed the king.'

'Perhaps,' Talus replied. Bran felt Lethriel's hand clutch his arm. 'Yes, I believe I may. But this tree has many roots, and I have yet to expose them all.'

'Tell us!' said Lethriel. 'You must tell us, so that we...'

A low rumble passed through the crowd. Bran looked back at the boat. Tharn and Farrum had shed the furs restricting their upper bodies. Tharn's chest was broad and solid; Farrum's was white and thin, but corded with muscle.

Tharn hefted a stone axe with an ornate carved handle. The head was blue-grey flint. It was much more beautiful than Bran's own, workmanlike weapon. Tharn circled Farrum, his knees bent, sweat steaming from his skin despite the bitter cold of the damp winter air.

Farrum's weapon was strange. He must have been hiding it beneath his long robe. At first glance, it looked like nothing more than a sturdy branch. But, as the old man turned it in his hand, a thin black blade was revealed set deep into the wood. The blade was barely the width of a man's thumb, but it ran almost the entire length of the branch. Bran had thought Tharn's axe-head finely wrought—in its own peculiar way, this was exquisite.

'What is that?' he said to Talus.

'An obsidian swathe,' Talus replied. 'Volcanic glass. Very sharp.'

'You've seen one before?'

'Long ago, in another place. That weapon does not belong here. I would be very interested to know where Farrum got it.'

The two men continued to size each other up. Tharn tossed his axe from hand to hand, a grim smile on his face. Farrum's expression was lost in the fog and the mass of his snowy hair and beard.

The crowd watched in silence. The air tasted of anticipation.

Just when it seemed the adversaries would continue their dance forever, Tharn struck, feinting left before powering his axe to the right with furious intent. Farrum dodged easily. Bran had already seen how fast the old man could move; did Tharn really know what he was letting himself in for?

The dance resumed. Tongues of fog licked the

combatants' legs. Again Tharn attacked; again Farrum slipped aside. A silent shiver shook the crowd. Tharn wiped his brow with the back of his hand.

'Will you run from me all day, old man?' he said.

'I will do what I must,' Farrum replied.

Farrum's arm came round in a blur, swinging his curious weapon straight at Tharn's head. Tharn ducked. The glossy black cutting edge of the swathe whistled as it sliced through the air... and cut several hairs from Tharn's head. Farrum laughed.

'One blow is all it'll take, boy. I'd love to see your head roll!'

Tharn bellowed and ran at him, axe whirling. The Creyak king-to-be was quick too, despite his stocky build. Farrum parried. The two weapons clashed. Farrum's obsidian blade struck sparks from Tharn's axe-head, the impact accompanied by a high melodic ringing. Flint chips showered round the two men.

They parted. Farrum took a step back towards his boat. Tharn followed, sinking to a running crouch that took him under Farrum's swinging arm. He drove the wooden handle of his axe into Farrum's chest. The old man grunted and hammered his swathe down on Tharn's shoulder. In the crowd, someone cried out. Bran waited for Tharn's severed arm to drop to the ground.

But Farrum had struck with the blunt side of the swathe. Cursing, he spun the weapon and brought it down again. Except now Tharn was behind him, turning his momentum into a tremendous swing of his axe. Farrum leaped sideways, and the flint axe-head swished past his spine by less than the span of a hand.

Someone shouted Tharn's name. One of the boatmen responded: 'Farrum!' More cries rose until the whole crowd was roaring. Then the opponents came together again and a hush descended.

This time it was Farrum who attacked first, driving the swathe towards Tharn's face. Tharn blocked it just in time. The lethal glass blade bit deep into the axe handle and the two weapons locked together. Farrum tried to pull the swathe free, but Tharn was stronger. With a great bellow he heaved his arm back and wrested the weapon from Farrum's grip, to clatter across the shingle to land at the feet of Tharn's watching brothers. Fethan picked it up, regarding it with something approaching awe.

The villagers shouted approval. Farrum's boatmen started backing away. Hands emerged from the crowd to restrain them. Tharn stalked towards Farrum, who was retreating with his hands raised, palms out. When the old man fetched up against the hull of the boat, he let his arms fall to his sides again.

'Make it quick, boy,' he said.

Tharn raised his axe. There was a chunk missing from the handle where the swathe had eaten into it. The blade, too, was notched, but it still looked deadly sharp.

'This is a mistake,' said Talus. He took a step forward.

The bard had already interrupted Tharn once. Bran tried to imagine what the king-to-be would do if he tried it again. After seeing the way Tharn fought, he didn't have to try too hard. 'Tharn!' Bran shouted, pushing past Talus. 'Let the old man live!'

The villagers watched, incredulous, as Bran raced

across the shingle to where Tharn stood with his axe in the air and Farrum's life laid bare before him. The fog was no longer an ocean but a lake of sticky resin, holding Bran back. But Tharn held still. When Bran finally reached him, and clamped his good hand on Tharn's wrist, the king-to-be put up no resistance. Perhaps he'd wanted to be stopped.

'Do not kill this man,' Bran said.

'Who are you to tell me what to do?' Tharn's muscles bunched under Bran's fingers.

'If you won't take the words from me,' said Bran, 'take them from the bard.'

Tharn's eyes looked for—and found—Talus. The bard nodded, clasped his hands together and executed a small bow.

'You've pulled Farrum's claws,' said Bran. 'He's safe now.'

Tharn glared at Farrum. The visiting king's face was as white as his hair, the scars standing out even whiter. He looked frail.

'Not safe enough,' said Tharn. 'Old man, I will put you and your men in a place no man can escape from. You will stay there until I decide what is best.'

'Tharn,' said Bran. 'I don't think Farrum is...'

'Enough!' Tharn's face turned scarlet. 'I am the son of Hashath! My word is truth! Do you understand?'

He turned to face the crowd. He lifted his axe high above his head.

'Do you *all* understand?'

As one, the villagers dropped to their knees. So did Farrum and his boatmen. When Bran realised he was the only person left standing, he bent and paid his own respects to Creyak's king-to-be.

He looked round for Talus and Lethriel. They were some distance away, kneeling like the others. They were deep in conversation. As Bran watched, Lethriel nodded twice, then picked herself up and scurried away across the shingle. 'My word is truth,' Tharn said again. 'Get up, old man. Let's see if you are brave enough to face the spirits who have guarded this island since the time of the dreaming past. Let's see if you are brave enough to endure the gaze of the dead men of Creyak.'

He surveyed his people.

'Take them to the totem pit,' he said.

CHAPTER TWENTY-THREE

TALUS HAD SEEN totem pits before, but nothing on this scale. It was so artfully designed, he thought at first that Gantor must have made it. But it was much too old for that.

The pit was hidden behind the cairn in a natural cleft where, years before, the cliff had collapsed. Further excavation had created a deep chasm big enough to hold fifty men. It would swallow Farrum and his little entourage with ease.

The sides of the hole were shaped such that the floor of the pit was much wider than the opening at the top. Anyone who found themselves at the bottom would be surrounded by steeply overhanging walls that were impossible to climb. They would be trapped.

One by one the Sleeth men were lowered into the pit by rope. The first man down was Lath. He'd recovered from his drinking bout and the bruise on his forehead was beginning to turn yellow. When his feet reached the pit floor, he shook off the rope, turned and shrieked.

Talus peered down into the pit. Lining the steeply tilted walls were dozens of totems. The smallest of them was man-sized; most were much taller. They were carved from the solid rock of the cliff itself; it must have taken colossal effort to hew them out. Their faces were those of anguished souls and malicious spirits, an endless parade of monstrous visages fashioned to keep prisoners not merely subdued, but terrified out of their wits.

One look at the gibbering, cowering Lath told Talus how effective the totems were.

'Talus!' Bran's hand landed on his shoulder and spun him round. 'I thought I'd never catch up with you.'

'The people of Creyak have an effective prison, do you not think?' Talus replied.

'Never mind that. Where's Lethriel?'

'Lethriel?'

'You sent her somewhere. I saw you. What are you playing at?'

'I am not playing, Bran. It is better you do not know where Lethriel has gone. Just believe me when I say that, when she returns, I may have all the answers I need.'

Bran's hand twitched beside the haft of his axe. His cheeks flushed, telling Talus he'd made the right decision in keeping his companion and the woman apart.

'Tell me where she is!'

'I will not. To do what she needs to do, Lethriel must move like a mouse. You, Bran, as many people have already remarked, have more of the bear about you.'

'If you've put her in danger...'

'Bran—as long as we remain here, we are all in danger.'

One by one, the rest of the boatmen followed Lath into the pit. Last to go was Farrum himself. All the way down he glared up at Tharn, who regarded the old man's descent with furious intensity.

Once all the Sleeth men had been imprisoned, Mishina took over the proceedings. His face still bore the blue-and-black pattern of dots Talus had watched him apply in his house earlier. Had that really been only this morning? It seemed so long ago.

Having cleared a space at the edge of the pit, Mishina stood with his staff raised in both hands above his head. He began the same guttural chanting he'd used inside the cairn. Without echo, in the fog, the chanting sounded ghostly and unreal.

The gathered crowd took up the chant. Mishina began to sway. Tremors ran through his shoulders, his hips. The tremors became quakes. The shaman's head snapped back. Soon his entire body was gyrating, almost out of control. The shells on his staff rattled and sang, a strident percussion that cut through the somehow liquid sound of the chanting.

As the noise reached a climax, Mishina's body went rigid and he fell backwards. Nobody moved to catch him. He hit the rough ground and lay there, twitching, foam bubbling from his lips. The chanting stopped.

Mishina's eyes fluttered in their sockets, and the crowd looked on in adoration. Talus wished he could share their awe. As far as the people of Creyak were concerned, their shaman had left his body to fly with the spirits.

If that were true, why could Talus not sense it? He was proud of his ability to observe the world around him. Surely a man of his talents should be able to detect at least something of what a shaman like Mishina claimed he could experience?

But, although Talus looked as acutely as he knew how, the air surrounding Mishina was still. No rippling, no wraiths, no disturbance of any kind at all. If the spirits existed, they were entirely invisible. Nor did they make any sound, nor smell. When he flicked the end of his tongue through the air, he tasted only the salt from the sea.

Nothing. There was nothing.

Yet everyone believed there was. Bran believed it. Tia had believed it. Shamans the world over traded in those beliefs. But did that mean they believed it themselves?

Did Mishina?

'There's something not right about Mishina,' said Bran.

The words—not to mention the track of Bran's thoughts—startled Talus. 'Why do you say that?'

'I don't know. It's just a feeling. What do you think?'

'I think... I am coming to believe that Mishina may not be what he seems. He behaves differently from other shamans I have met. Most men like him use drugs to help them enter a trance. Mishina does not.'

'How do you know?'

'I have observed him.'

'Doesn't he use greycaps? I thought Lethriel collected them for him.'

'She does. But he encourages her to do this because that is what a shaman is expected to do. I do not believe he actually uses them.'

'What makes you say that?'

'The pit in in his house where he keeps them is thick with greycap dust. No true shaman would be so clumsy with such a precious item. I suspect that, after he has received them from Lethriel, he crushes the greycaps and gets rid of the remains. No, the greycaps are simply another part of Mishina's mask.'

'If Mishina isn't a shaman, what is he?' Bran took a step away from Talus, his eyes suddenly wide. 'You think he's the killer, don't you?'

'It is not as simple as that. Do you remember Arak's game of stones and grids?'

'Yes, but why...?'

'I believe Mishina plays games as well. Imagine: he takes a stone and he moves it into place. He moves another, and another. He stands back and considers the field of play. He watches over all that lies before him, decides upon which rules will be followed... and which will be broken.' Talus paused. 'But it was not Mishina's hand that drove the bonespike into the king's chest. Nor did he upset the boulders that killed Gantor.'

'Poor Gantor. He didn't deserve to die.'

' I fear his death may not be the last.'

Mishina was coming out of his trance. A pair of women helped him to his feet. Murmured conversation was beginning to break out among the villagers. The shaman's performance was over.

'Talus,' said Bran, 'are you going to tell me who...?'

Before he could finish the question, Tharn stormed up to them, dragging Alayin behind him. His brothers had joined Mishina at the edge of the totem pit. Fethan had hooked Farrum's black-bladed swathe onto his belt. Arak and Sigathon huddled close together, a little apart from the others. Cabarrath towered over them all with his arms folded, glowering down into the pit where Farrum and his men were trapped.

'The totem pit is strong,' said Tharn. 'But men are stronger. My brothers will guard the traitors. The rest of you will come with me to the feasting circle. That includes you, bard.'

TALUS WALKED WITH Bran in the footsteps of the king-to-be while the rest of the crowd followed. Whispered conversations came and went in the throng—mostly speculation about what Tharn was planning—but Talus ignored them. For now, all was well: the totem pit was secure and Lethriel was busy with the task he'd set for her.

As for Tharn himself, he was more concerned with not letting Alayin out of his sight. His hold on her arm was firm, and his expression was grim. She stumbled at his side, limping a little on the ankle she'd twisted when he'd thrown her from the boat, entirely submissive.

By the time they reached the arena, the fog had begun to disperse. Lacy afternoon light rippled down through the tremendous aperture in the overhanging roof.

Tharn dragged Alayin past the heap of ashes lying beneath the gigantic smoke-hole: the remains of the previous night's bonfire, still not cleared away. A large boulder stood on the far side of the circle. When they reached it, Tharn turned and thrust Alayin into Bran's arms.

'You will hold her,' he said.

'Do you trust me this much?'

'If you allow her to escape, I will kill the bard.'

Tharn seized Talus's wrist—his grip was strong—and hauled him up onto the boulder. The arena was filling up with the people who'd followed them from the totem pit, and with those who'd come out of their houses to see what was going on. Soon all Creyak was there.

Talus willed his body to relax. Despite Tharn's threat, he didn't believe he was in danger. In fact, he knew exactly what the king-to-be wanted him for.

Tharn raised his hands. Gradually the crowd fell silent.

'Death walks among us,' he said. His voice, soft and full of menace, carried all the way from one side of the arena to the other. 'I am here to send death away. I am here to tell you that the time of the old king is gone. The time of the new king has come.'

The crowd listened as Tharn spoke on. So did Talus. He used words well. In another place, another life, he might have been a bard.

By the time Tharn's speech reached its conclusion his voice was ragged, his face drawn with heavy lines. His breath made billowing clouds above his head. The crowd was hushed, clearly impressed by his oration. Here was Hashath's eldest son, next in line, claiming his rightful place at their head. This was the undeniable way of things.

Tharn ushered Talus to the front of the boulder. 'I am sorry I forced you here,' he murmured.

'You are king,' said Talus. 'It is your right.'

Again Tharn faced the crowd—his people.

'Talus will give us a tale to mark this day! Bard—

make it a tale of glory. A tale to fill up the king's day with fire.'

This was just what Talus had expected. But his mind was blank. As he looked out at the expectant faces, panic threatened to seize him. Was this the moment when the great river of stories ran dry? When he opened his mouth and no words came out?

Among the faces were those of Bran and Alayin. Both looked tired and defeated, as if they'd trekked a long way across strange lands. Well, they had. Alayin's fur hood trembled in the breeze blowing through the arena: a dark woman wearing the pale skin of an ice monster.

And the story came to Talus at last.

ChAPTER TWENTY-FOUR

'ONE DAY,' SAID Talus, 'a king stepped out onto the far northern ice in search of a monster.'

The entire crowd leaned in towards the boulder. Already Talus had them. With just a few words, the bard had gained their attention more completely than any king.

'The king took with him three loyal hunters,' Talus went on. 'Each was brave and wise, and each had sworn his life to his master.'

'I suppose you've heard this one before,' Alayin whispered to Bran.

'In two years I've never heard Talus tell the same tale twice,' Bran replied.

He wondered if Alayin would try to run. He didn't much care whether she did or not... except for what that might mean for Talus. Up to now, Tharn hadn't struck Bran as a cruel man. But he was no longer just a man. Now he was a king.

Having caught his audience's imagination, Talus went on to describe the characters of the king and his hunters. The crowd was captivated. Bran, however, was finding it hard to focus on Talus's words. This felt like one of those stories where nothing much happened for a very long time.

'Why did you lie to me?' he said.

'I said what I needed to say,' said Alayin, 'to protect myself.'

'So why are you *really* here? Did you have something to do with the murders? Don't lie to me, Alayin. I'm tired of all that. Just tell me the truth.'

'You already know what the truth is, Bran. It's right in front of you.'

'I don't know what you mean.'

'Tell me what you see.'

She stood back. Bran studied her: a tall, proud woman swaddled in ivory furs. Her back was straight; her chin jutted. She exuded such an air of control it was hard to believe she was his prisoner. He wanted to dislike her: she'd made him feel foolish. But something had risen in her that he hadn't noticed before.

'You're trapped,' he said slowly.

Her taut muscles relaxed. 'There,' she said. 'That wasn't so hard.'

'It's your father, isn't it?'

'My father. The men I fall for. Everyone.'

'What do you mean?'

'Some women... some women have a shape that fits the arms of men, a shape that fits this world...' Alayin worked her hands, trying to mould the thoughts she was struggling to express. 'That is not my shape. I want to be my own, Bran, but I am not. Do you understand? *I am not my own.*'

Bran shook his head. She puzzled him, this strange woman from an island he'd never seen. Her scars were a mask behind which her true face was sometimes hidden, sometimes revealed.

With a start, he realised he'd forgiven her lies.

He plucked a tuft of ivory fur from her hood.

'People talk of ice-bears,' he said, 'but you never meet anyone who's actually seen one. They're just monsters from stories.'

'I am proof they're not. Don't you believe the truth, Bran, even when it's before your eyes?'

'Did you tell Sigathon the truth? Or Cabarrath?'

'What?'

'I know you were with them both.'

'Oh. Well, that's all over with.'

'Are you sure?'

'Cabarrath was a good man. But Sigathon... he was a mistake. Besides, after all this, do you think I'd willingly pair myself with another of these wretched brothers?' Her voice filled with sudden venom. 'Do you think that's what I would *choose*?'

'I think Sigathon killed Hashath.' Bran immediately regretted saying it. But now the words were out, he rolled them through his mind, testing them.

'Sigathon?' said Alayin. 'That's ridiculous. The boy's an idiot, but a killer? Why would you think such a thing?'

'He acts as if he's drugged. Talus said...'

'Talus? Oh, your friend up there. Is he really a bard? He looks like a wading bird. Do you heed everything he says, Bran? Do you believe all his *stories*?'

Bran resisted the urge to shake her. No wonder she had no man if this was how she carried on.

Talus spread his arms wide, ready at last to launch himself into the main narrative of his epic tale.

'And so came the day,' he said, 'when the king and his three hunters finally set out on their great quest. On the first day, the first hunter found the tracks of a tremendous beast in the snow. Each paw was bigger than a house. Each claw was bigger than a man. The hunter followed the tracks into a blizzard, and was never seen again...'

Bran listened with only half an ear. The crowd pressed close against him. Suddenly he was the one who felt trapped. Death had come to Creyak, and it hadn't yet left. What were they doing standing around listening to Talus prattle on?

'I don't think I like this story,' said Alayin. She wriggled her body inside her furs. 'I don't want to hear it.'

'Well, we can't go anywhere. Anyway, what's wrong with the story?'

'It's as if he knows.'

'Knows what?' Alayin was trembling; Bran supposed she could use some comfort. But if he put his arm around her there was no telling how the watchful Tharn might react. 'Knows what, Alayin?'

'Knows about me.'

'How could Talus possibly...?'

'It doesn't matter. Be quiet and listen to the story.'

Now Talus was telling the crowd how the king and his two remaining hunters searched in vain for their companion. Normally Bran was happy to hear one of Talus's tales, but not this time.

'Why do I get the feeling you've got a story of your own?' he said.

'Everyone has a story. Don't you?'

'Will you tell me yours?'

She closed her eyes. 'Very well. My story is also about a journey across the ice. And a hunting party. There were four men altogether. And there was me. I was hidden in one of the sleds. I wasn't supposed to be there. Women aren't allowed to go on hunts.'

Bran opened his mouth, about to make some remark about her being a compulsive stowaway. The faraway expression on her face changed his mind.

'We travelled one whole day before making camp. That was when they found me. One of the hunters— an ugly man called Grantha—tried to rape me, but the others killed him before he could... before he could finish.'

'*Killed* him?'

Alayin shrugged. 'I am the king's daughter. If I'd been harmed, their lives would have been forfeit.'

'But Grantha didn't care about that?'

'He'd always had his eye on me. He thought he loved me. I suppose he thought I loved him back. Love drives men to violence, haven't you noticed that?'

'It's something Talus tells me constantly. Would the others have saved you if Farrum hadn't been your father?'

She gave him a withering look. 'What do you think?'

Talus had begun to lope back and forth on his rocky stage. Bran heard him say something about the second hunter finding a mound of dung left by their elusive quarry. The mound was as big as a mountain.

'After they killed Grantha,' Bran said. 'What happened next?'

'The men staked out Grantha's body on the ice for bait. They draped skins over the sleds and covered them with snow so they couldn't be seen. They sat in the hides and waited.'

'And you?'

'I sat with them. I remember thinking, "Is this all hunting is? Hiding under the snow and waiting for something to come?"'

'And did something come?'

Alayin's body jerked. Bran felt his good hand clamp down on her arm. But she wasn't running away. It was just the tremor of memory.

'Oh, it came,' she said. 'It wasn't what I'd expected, but it came.'

She stopped, and immediately her voice was replaced in Bran's ears by Talus's. The bard's words soared through the dank, grey air; the collective breath of the crowd rose and mingled with the fog. Bran could feel the two stories—Alayin's and Talus's—melting together in his head.

'Now two of the king's hunters had been lost to the blizzard,' said Talus. Bran had missed hearing how the second hunter had died. Knowing the way Talus's stories went, he'd probably been buried beneath the huge mound of dung. 'When the third hunter announced his intention to track down the beast, the king told him to stay. "I have lost enough of my hunters to this monster," the king said. "I will go myself."

'So the king walked out into the blizzard. He walked for many days. He passed the huge paw prints and the gigantic pile of dung, and at last he came to an enormous cave. The cave was so wide he could not see the sides of it. It was so high he could not see the top of it. It was so deep that it took the echoes of his footsteps three whole days to return to him.'

'Will he slay the monster, do you think?' said Alayin.

'Who?' said Bran, momentarily confused about which story he was listening to.

'The king in Talus's tale.'

'I thought you weren't interested in Talus's tale.'

She gave him a pale smile. 'I have one ear listening. So do you. Don't pretend you haven't.'

Bran chuckled, laughing more easily than he had for a long time. This brought him up short. Here he was surrounded by strangers, charged by a novice king to guard an unpredictable woman, on an island where sudden death lay round every corner. Yet, incredibly, he felt relaxed.

'I'm more interested in *your* story,' he said. 'Does the monster come in that one too?'

Alayin's smile vanished. 'Yes,' she said softly. 'It comes.'

'Tell me.'

She blinked. There were tiny beads of ice on the ends of her lashes.

'It came without warning,' she said. 'A great bear, gliding over the ice. It stood higher at the shoulder than a man is tall. Its jaws were stained with blood. Its fur was almost white but... richer, somehow. It roared.'

Her eyes had locked on something in the far distance. Bran was spellbound.

'One of the men stood up and called to the bear,

and it padded towards him. I could smell it. It stank of meat and death. The other men crept round behind it. But it heard them, or smelled them. It turned and charged. They hit it with their axes, but it bit them and struck them with its claws. It tore them apart. Soon it was standing there in a lake of steaming blood, and there was nothing left of them but bones and steaming meat.'

'What happened next?' Bran could still hear Talus, very faintly. In the bard's story, the king was battling his own monster, which was bigger than the world.

'The other hunter ran away. There was just me, alone, hiding in the sled. Me and the bear.'

'What did you do?'

'I waited. The bear licked the ice clean of blood. Then it started sniffing. It prowled around the sleds, swinging its head from side to side with its nose just above the ice. It must have caught my scent, because suddenly it stopped and stared right at the sled I was hiding in.

'There was a gap in the covers. It saw me; I know it did. So I waited. I just waited. The bear came towards me. It was old. I could see it in its eyes. It was limping. The blood of my father's men dripped from its teeth. Halfway to the sled it sank to its knees and started coughing. Blood came out of its mouth. It stood up and shuddered. It was like an earthquake. I could feel it through the ice. Then... then it fell over and died.'

This wasn't what Bran had expected. In Talus's tales, the final confrontation usually gave the audience a sense that what happened in the world had some meaning. Alayin's story was just...

'Sad and real,' he said aloud. She gave him a quizzical look. 'Your story. It's sad and real.'

If she agreed, she didn't show it. 'I took the hunters' knives and skinned the bear. It was still warm. Deep inside, it was hot, like a fire. I could still hear the life in it, slowly draining into the ice. It was a big animal, and it took a long, long time for all of it to die.'

'It was a monster,' said Bran.

'It was an animal.' She sighed. 'That's all there is really. I dragged the skin back to the sled, dragged the sled back to the boat, rowed the boat back to Sleeth. My father sent men to search for the missing hunter. They never found him. He must have frozen to death. Maybe he fell through a hole in the ice.'

Alayin's eyes returned from whatever distance it was they'd found. The tanned skin of her cheeks was flushed scarlet, the raised scars almost white against the colour, white like the ivory fur in which she was wrapped. The skin of the giant bear that was her trophy of that terrible day.

She nodded towards the boulder. 'Your friend's story is coming to an end too.'

And so it was. Having told how the valiant king had slain the monster by singing out its name and bringing the huge but fragile cave of ice crashing down on top of it, Talus brought his tale to a rousing conclusion by describing the great feast that was thrown upon the triumphant king's return.

'There are many monsters in this world,' the bard concluded. 'Set against every one is a man. Some of these men stand in the light, and we choose to call them kings. Others stand in the shadows, unseen, and they have no names, because they are not known. But they also do valiant deeds, and they also are kings.'

Talk of slain monsters and celebratory feasts had warmed the villagers through. But this odd little epilogue had them shifting uneasily. Bran smiled. It was so like Talus to add something enigmatic to the end of even the simplest story. Something to chew on.

Without warning, Alayin clutched him. Bran glanced at Tharn, to see if he'd noticed the sudden movement. But the eyes of the new king were fixed on the bard.

'What's wrong?' said Bran.

'You do believe me?' said Alayin. 'I need someone to believe me, Bran.'

He considered her earlier lies. There was no reason to trust anything she said. 'I believe you,' he said. To his surprise, he did.

Talus stepped back and Tharn stepped forward. Like the rest of the crowd, he looked uncertain about the way Talus's tale had ended. Gradually his frown deepened. The crowd began to murmur. Then Bran realised Tharn was looking past them at a commotion on the other side of the arena.

The new king jumped down from his platform. The crowd parted before him, and Tharn strode between them. Another man forced his way through the sea of bodies towards him. Bran grabbed Alayin with his good hand, in case she decided to run. But she didn't move.

It was Fethan. By the time he reached Tharn he was struggling to stay upright. Tharn grabbed his elbows, supporting him. Fethan's face was contorted with grief.

His hands and all the fur on his left side were dripping with blood. Farrum's weapon of black glass was gone from his belt.

'You must come,' Fethan said. His voice gargled. 'Farrum... the pit... Tharn, my king. I shouldn't have...'

Tharn shook him. 'Tell me what's happened!'

Fethan wrenched himself free. He started to stagger back the way he'd come. 'Come, my brother, my king,' he called. 'Come now!'

With an anguished cry, Tharn followed his brother out of the arena.

First to follow them, leaping off the boulder with his robe flapping wide, was Talus.

'Come on,' said Bran. He set off in pursuit of the bard, pulling Alayin with him. 'And don't try to run away.'

'I won't,' said Alayin. 'I have to see this through. After all, it's all my fault.'

CHAPTER TWENTY-FIVE

THEY CAUGHT UP with Talus in the meandering ravine that wound its way through the cliffs to the totem pit. Tharn and Fethan were somewhere ahead, hidden by the fog pouring over the sides of the ravine. The air was cold and thick with salt.

'Talus,' said Bran. 'Wait for us.'

'I have made a mistake,' said the bard.

'What do you mean?' said Bran. He could barely speak for the wheezing of his lungs. How did Talus manage to sound so calm?

'I believed the totem pit was secure. I was wrong.'

'But we don't know what's happened.'

'I think we do, Bran. I thought it was safe to leave the brothers guarding Farrum. I was wrong about that, too. Now there is blood on my hands.'

Bran wanted to reassure his friend, to tell him everything was going to be all right. But how could he convince the bard of something he didn't believe himself?

When they reached the totem pit, Alayin's shriek of horror was enough to confirm Bran's worst fears. As if what he saw wasn't all the proof he needed.

It was a slaughter. Two of Farrum's men lay sprawled at the pit's edge; from the contorted angle of their bodies, it was obvious their necks were broken. Beside them, moaning, lay Mishina. Further away, dim in the wind-torn fog, were two more bodies, one lying on the other.

Tharn stumbled through the chaos, his hands raised to his head.

Bran rushed first to Mishina. He might not care for the shaman, but the man's groans proved he, at least, was alive. His blue and black mask was twisted with pain. His hands clutched his ribs.

'What happened?' said Bran.

'I am not badly hurt,' Mishina growled. 'See to the others.'

Bran ran on to the two bodies heaped together. The uppermost of them was Sigathon, a bonespike protruding from his neck and his chest drenched with blood. On his face was the same dull expression Bran had observed every time he'd encountered the boy. He was quite dead.

Bran rolled Sigathon's body aside, expecting to uncover another corpse. Instead he found himself staring straight into Arak's wild green eyes. The boy's pupils were black and huge.

'They tried to kill me too!' Arak wailed. He burst into tears.

Bran checked Arak quickly for injuries. He seemed unhurt. He lifted the lad to his feet. Before Bran could say anything, Tharn was at his side.

'What happened?' The new king grabbed his youngest brother by the shoulders and gave him a vigorous shake. Arak's head snapped back and forth. Bran didn't care for the blankness in Tharn's eyes. If Sigathon truly was the king-killer Bran suspected him to be, then his crimes were paid for. There was no need for Tharn to take it out on Arak.

Fethan joined them, and Talus and Alayin. A few men from the village clumped in the mist behind them. All Bran could see of the villagers was angry faces and bunched fists. The majority of people had stayed behind in the arena. Creyak, it seemed, had had its fill of disaster.

'What happened?' Tharn repeated. His whole body was clenched, not least his fingers, which were digging deep into Arak's thin upper arms.

'Fethan and Cabarrath left us,' said Arak. He twitched in his brother's grip. This wasn't his usual fidgeting: the boy wanted to be off and running. Bran didn't blame him. 'They said they wouldn't be long.'

'Is this true?' said Tharn, turning on Fethan.

'What if it is?' said Fethan. He squared his body, defiant. For all the blood on him, he appeared to be uninjured.

'They went to gather brush for a fire,' said Arak, still squirming.

'A *fire?*' said Tharn. 'You were guarding our most dangerous enemies and you wanted to keep warm?'

'The fire was not for us,' said Fethan. 'It was for them. Cabarrath and I decided to be rid of Farrum and his men, once and for all. We left Arak and Sigathon with Mishina. We thought they were safe. We went to gather the summer brushwood from behind the cairn. We were going to throw it into the pit and set it on fire. We wanted to watch Farrum burn.'

Bran listened with mounting horror. Farrum might have

deserved punishment, but he didn't deserve to die. Were they all killers, all these brothers, all these sons of the king?

Tharn released Arak. 'You are a fool, Fethan!' He punched his brother in the middle of his chest: once, twice, three times. Fethan accepted the blows without flinching. 'How did they get out of the pit?'

'It was the fog,' Arak blurted. 'We couldn't see the other side of the pit. They must have climbed on each other's shoulders. When one got out he must have thrown down a rope so the others could come. When we saw what they were doing we tried to stop them, but they were too quick. We were too late.'

'Cabarrath and I heard the commotion,' said Fethan. 'We ran back as quickly as we could. We found... this. Farrum struck me down and took back his weapon. Then he and his men escaped into the fog. Cabarrath gave chase. I ran to bring you.'

'Which way did they go?' said Tharn.

'Towards the beach.'

Without warning, Tharn struck Fethan again, this time on the side of the head. Fethan reeled back, his eyes rolling. Tharn advanced, pounded him again, and again. The third time, Fethan went down. His head hit one of the slabs of stone lining the edge of the pit and he fell limp. Nearby, Mishina was sitting up, shaking his head, gradually coming to his senses.

Tharn beckoned over six of the watching men. To the rest, he said, 'We are at war with Sleeth. Go to your homes. Bring your weapons. Ask the spirits to put strength in your arms and in your hearts. Meet me at the beach. I am your king, and I tell you to do this.'

The men split as instructed. Tharn lowered his head, a look of deep anguish on his half-hidden face. For an instant the king was gone and there was only the man, young and desperate. Then Tharn straightened up. He looked around him.

'*Now where has Arak gone?*' he bellowed.

An arm rose from the cluster of men he'd picked out. 'There! Running!'

By the time they all looked, Arak was nothing more than a dissolving shadow.

'The boy wants revenge,' Tharn growled. 'He is brave, but he will only get himself killed.'

'Tharn,' said Talus. 'I must tell you...'

'Away with your stories, bard! Arak is the son of a king. He will do what needs to be done. Now we go to war for the death of our father, for the deaths of our brothers.'

He stormed past Talus, knocking him sideways. Bran caught the bard before he could fall.

'You do have a way with people,' he said. 'And don't tell me Tharn's making a big mistake, because you already said that.'

'Nevertheless,' said Talus, 'it is true. But who am I to judge him? I have'—a look of amazement rose on his face—'I have also made a mistake, Bran.'

'There's a first time for everything. But, Talus, Sigathon's dead. That's an end to it. Isn't it?'

'No, Bran. But the end is close. Tharn has set all his fury on Sleeth. He believes Farrum is behind this, but... he does not know everything. Tharn's anger blinds him to the whole truth.'

'If you know what that truth is, why don't you just come out with it?'

'Because when I tell Tharn what is really happening here, I fear his temper may drive him to become a killer himself. Did you not see what he did to Fethan? In Creyak, I fear truth and death go hand in hand.'

Bran watched the new king disappear with his men into the mist. 'Talus, he deserves to know. I know all about temper, but you can't hide the truth, however hard it is. You told me that.'

'Indeed I did, Bran.' Talus flashed a skeletal grin. 'Now, quickly, there is no time to lose. If I have made a mistake, I have no choice but to correct it. I must find Tharn and lay before him everything I know.'

'I don't suppose you'd care to lay it before me first?' said Bran without much hope.

'There is no time! We are coming to the place where all the paths we have followed meet. But there is one more path I must take first.'

'I'll come with you.'

'No! You must stay. Watch over the shaman. Tend to Fethan when he wakes. Let no man disturb Sigathon's body. I will return!'

So saying, he sprang away into the fog.

WHILE ALAYIN TENDED the shaman, Bran checked Fethan. The young man's breathing was shallow but steady, and his wounds were slight. Bran was confident he would come round soon.

'Mishina doesn't want my help,' said Alayin, coming

over to where he was crouched. 'I can't say I blame him. Will you stop me if I run?'

Her fur hood had fallen back, revealing short blonde hair cropped close to her scalp. Her head was all bone and scar. Her expression was ferocious, like that of an animal on the hunt.

'Where will you run to?'

'After them.' She tossed her head in the direction Talus had gone. 'Like I said, this is all my fault. It's up to me to put things right.'

'Why do you say that? What have you done?'

'I can't tell you. Will you stop me?'

'Talus told me to stay here.'

'Then stay!'

'Wait!' But she was already sprinting into the fog.

Bran considered the bodies surrounding him. The wounded would recover. As for the dead... Was there really any more he could do here?

Cursing, he set off after Alayin. Was he to spend all his time on Creyak rushing from one place to the next, always on the tail of death and never quite catching it?

It was all Bran could do to keep up with his quarry. Alayin was fast, and her ivory form slipped elusively from one patch of mist to another. The path she took was a tight descending spiral, craggy and treacherous. Bran pulled his arms close to his body to avoid flaying them on the sharp rock walls. His feet skipped and slid on the broken winter ground.

At last the rock peeled back, leaving him adrift in the fog. The sharp clatter of shingle and the muffled roar of the sea told him was back on the beach. He raised his hands, the good and the bad, and groped blindly forward.

'Alayin?' he called. 'Talus?'

Movement to his left. He veered that way. Something hulked in the fog, too vague to be properly seen. Then it melted away.

'Where are you?'

He continued to advance, treading cautiously. His mouth was filled with the damp salt taste of the fog. The shingle clawed at his feet.

A shape loomed in front of him. Was it a man? When he touched it, he found it was just a boulder. He circled it, skimming its surface with his hands. It was reassuring to have found something solid.

His fingers found a rope and traced its line around the boulder. It was the same rope he and Talus had used to help bring Farrum's boat ashore. Which meant the boat was nearby.

He followed the rope, good hand over bad. Any moment now he would see the boat. But the rope ran out, and the boat wasn't there.

Bran lifted the end of the rope and peered at it. It had been cut through. The cut was cleaner than any that could have been made with an ordinary stone knife.

Bran made his way in a fumbling half-crouch towards the sound of the waves. The rush of the sea grew louder and suddenly he was ankle-deep in water. He backtracked. How could he have missed something as big as Farrum's boat?

He looked down. He was standing in a gigantic rut in the shingle. He was in the right place, but the vessel had gone.

A slumped form lay at the far end of the rut. Bran hurried towards it, fear rising in him. Fear turned to revulsion as he saw it was a man—or most of one. The corpse's severed head lay an arm's length from its gaping neck, its blood-spattered face staring straight up into the invisible sky. One of Farrum's boatmen; even through the gore, the scars on its cheeks were clearly visible.

Bran heard the crunch of footsteps just in time to turn his head, but not to ward off the blow that came down on it. He glimpsed a tall, swaying shadow before his vision was driven away by a flash of dazzling light.

After that came blackness.

CHAPTER TWENTY-SIX

A WHITE FACE floated over Bran, in a halo of red hair. Somewhere, firelight flickered. The face drifted in and out of focus. Its mouth opened and it seemed to Bran that words came out, although he heard nothing.

'Keyli?' he said.

The blackness returned.

The face was still there when he woke a second time, but very dim. He was terrified it might be the spirit of his dead wife, yet part of him wanted it to be so. The face came close and he tried to lift himself towards it, but gentle hands pressed him back down.

'Don't try to move.'

The voice was a woman's. As if the words were magic, all Bran's senses filled up at once. He could hear the faint rush of the sea, taste the salt in the air, feel the hard resistance of rock against his back.

'Keyli?' He knew it wasn't her. Even with its covering of cracked white paint, he knew the face belonged to Lethriel. 'Where am I?'

The face retreated a little as Lethriel sat back. 'Thank the spirits,' she said. 'I thought for a moment you weren't breathing. We're in a cave, just up from the shore. I dragged you here. Don't ask me how I did it—

you're heavy. But the tide was coming in, and I was scared they'd find us. How's your head?'

Bran looked around. A few paces away, a driftwood fire burned. Glossy rock walls rose behind it. One wall bore an ancient painting of a hunting scene: men and deer and a giant tusked beast that could only be a mammut. The picture danced with a life of its own.

'How's your head?' Lethriel repeated.

Bran touched his good hand to the back of his skull, igniting a fire in his head. 'Hurts. How...?' The words eluded him. He tried again. 'Who...?'

Lethriel frowned. 'It was Cabarrath.'

'Cab... why did he...?'

'I don't know. I got there just as he hit you with the haft of his axe. He saw me and... just ran off into the fog.'

'Why didn't he...?'

'Finish the job? I don't know. Maybe he didn't mean to hit you. Maybe he thought you were someone else.'

Bran rubbed his head. The thoughts inside it settled a little. 'Fethan said that Cabarrath ran after Farrum and the others.'

'He obviously caught up with one of them. You saw the body?'

The sight of the headless corpse was something Bran wasn't going to forget in a hurry. 'Cabarrath wasn't in time to stop them moving the boat.'

'Either that or they left him behind.' Tears were threatening at the corners of Lethriel's eyes. 'Bran, you don't think he... you don't think Cabarrath is...?'

'I don't know what to think any more. Whatever Cabarrath was up to, we'll find out soon enough.'

'I suppose so.'

The firelight dimmed, sending a chill through the cave. A knot of wood cracked and the flames rose again, brighter than before. On the rock wall, the hunted animals seemed to be running.

'What about you, Lethriel? What were you up to?'

'I was trying to find Talus when I heard the commotion at the pit. I heard Tharn giving out his orders. By the time I got there, everyone had gone. I saw the bodies. I found tracks leading to the beach and followed them. If I hadn't found you when I did...'

'Wait a moment. Go back. You got to the pit after we'd all left. What exactly did you see there?'

Lethriel's throat worked as she swallowed. 'Sigathon. He was covered in blood. Dead. And Fethan lying at the edge of the pit. I don't know about him. Two of Farrum's men.'

'Is that all?'

'Isn't it enough?'

'What about Mishina?'

'The shaman wasn't there.'

Bran tried to sit up again. Pain stabbed into the back of his neck and he slumped back, groaning.

'I told you to lie still,' said Lethriel.

'Where have you been all this time? I haven't seen you since...' When had that been? Bran tried to remember.

A hint of a smile cracked the white paint at the corners of Lethriel's mouth. 'After the fight on the beach, Talus asked me to do something.'

Now Bran remembered their hushed conversation. 'Did he send you to the cairn?'

'No. To the king's house. He told me to search for something there. I waited until everyone was in the arena so I could be sure I wouldn't be disturbed. Then I started hunting—under the bed covers, in the food pits, anywhere I could think of.'

'What were you looking for? Did you find it?'

Lethriel held up her left hand, closed into a fist. She opened it to reveal what Bran thought at first was a clump of white hair. He brushed his fingers through it. It was too coarse to be human.

'Talus gave me this. He plucked it from Alayin's hood just before the fight began between Tharn and Farrum.' She raised her right hand, holding a braid of identical hair. 'I found this in Arak's bed.'

Bran's thoughts battled through the pain in his head. 'Arak wants her. Maybe he even loves her. Is that right? Is Arak the lover she came here to see?'

Lethriel shook her head. 'Perhaps in his mind. When Alayin and Cabarrath were together, all the brothers used to tease Arak. They said he was last in line, that he'd have to take his turn. I don't know if they realised how much he adored her, but I could see it. Women see these things.'

'When did Talus tell you this?'

'He didn't. I worked it out for myself. When I told Talus what I was thinking, he agreed with me.'

'Seems I'm always the last to know. But I still don't see how all this fits together.'

'Nor me. But this fur wasn't all I found. There were other things: a wooden trinket Cabarrath used to treasure, an old moccasin I know belonged to Tharn. Arak liked to collect all sorts of things.'

'Why?'

'I don't know. I don't think Talus was telling me everything.'

'He wouldn't. Come on, we've got to...' Bran tried once more to sit up, but another bolt of pain sent him crashing back to the floor. He rolled sideways and let a thin drool of vomit leave his lips.

'We'll go,' said Lethriel. 'But only when you're ready. We're safe here for now.'

'Safe from what?'

'Everything. Bran, Tharn's preparing for war.'

Bran closed his eyes, tried to force the pain away. Something touched his brow: Lethriel's hand.

'Tell me about her, Bran.'

'About who?' Bran didn't open his eyes. The darkness was soothing.

'About Keyli. About the woman you loved.'

'It's not a story to tell. I've never told it to anyone.'

'Maybe that's your problem.'

AND SO, JUST like that, Bran told Lethriel about the events of two years before, about the night and the storm. About how Keyli had taken the boat out onto the deadly sea. About the sudden arrival of Talus and how, in retrieving the rope, the bard too had fallen prey to the waves.

'I still don't know why she was out there,' he said, lost in the blackness behind his eyelids. The storm raged there just as it did in his dreams. 'I suppose I never will.'

'What happened after Talus fell in the water?' said

Lethriel. 'You said you had hold of the rope. Weren't you able to bring her in?'

'I tried. I pulled on the rope as hard as I could, hand over hand. Both my hands were good back then. I could see Keyli coming closer. Even the sea wasn't strong enough to keep her from me. But then... then the stars started raining down.'

'The *stars*?'

'They were moving. The stars were moving, shooting from one horizon to the other. Long lines of white light. I'd seen them move like that before. I'd never imagined they could come all the way down to the ground.

'They started falling far out to sea. Streaks of fire coming straight down out of the sky. Wherever they hit the water there was a great splash, and a cloud of steam. The sea *boiled*. The fire lit up the night. There was light everywhere. Thunder too, and lightning. I've never been more terrified. But it was beautiful as well, somehow.

'The stars began falling closer to the shore. Keyli was very near to me now. I could hear her calling. Her voice was nearly drowned by the storm, but I could hear her. I pulled with all my strength. Talus was still in the water, scrambling to get a foothold on the rocks, but he kept slipping on the weeds and the waves kept dragging him back down.'

Bright shapes moved in the darkness behind Bran's closed eyes. He saw it all: the tiny boat and the monstrous ocean and the blazing sky, memory and dream uniting to make the past real once more. It was like splinters in his vision, jagged and agonising.

'I kept pulling. The palms of my hands were red and raw. I couldn't feel my fingers, they were so cold. I was soaked from head to toe. I pulled until the boat was almost close enough to touch. Keyli's hand was stretching towards me. I kept hold of the rope with my right hand, reached out with my left.

'I heard a hissing, screaming sound. Keyli and I looked up into the sky together. It was as if the sun itself was falling on us. Something threw me down onto the rock, pounding me like a fist of air. It knocked Keyli backwards into the boat. Her face was lit up by the fire. Then it hit the water—the falling star. It landed a rope's length away, but pieces of it had broken off. They cut into the waves, hot and white, whistling as they came. They threw up plumes of water that rose as high as an oak tree. One of them went straight through the bottom of the boat; I think it went straight through Keyli too. The boat folded up and the waves collapsed over it and it was gone, *she* was gone, just like that. She was gone. In the same breath, another piece of the star touched my left hand, the one I'd been using to reach out for Keyli. The star only brushed it, but it was enough to burn all the skin away. I didn't even feel it, didn't realise until later how bad the injury was. All I could think of was to keep pulling on the rope. But when I finally brought it ashore there was nothing on the end of it. It was burned through.'

Bran stopped. The images behind his eyes were fading. The darkness was coming back. The pain of the memory, incredibly, was easing.

'And then?'

Bran opened his eyes. Lethriel's face was there, drenched in firelight. The drip-drip of the water in the cave echoed around her.

'I tossed the rope aside. I scanned the waves for signs of the boat, signs of Keyli, but she was gone. The stars had stopped falling—except for a very few, far out to sea. The storm was over.'

'And Talus?'

'I saw his hand. It was the only part of him left above the water. If I hadn't seen it, I think I'd have just waded out into the sea and kept walking until the waves closed over my head. Without Keyli, what reason did I have to live? Instead I grabbed Talus's hand and pulled him ashore and beat his chest to pump the water out of him. I thought he was dead, but eventually he sat up. We clambered back up the shore together, helped each other to safety. Then we just lay back and watched the dawn light come through the last of the clouds. It was a beautiful dawn. I never went home again.'

Lethriel bent and kissed Bran once on the lips. It was like being touched by a lightning bolt.

'I'm so sorry,' she said. She caressed his ruined left hand. 'I think that, in another life, I must have loved you, Bran, because my heart is breaking for you, and for what you've suffered and lost. But you've found a good friend in Talus. I think the two of you were meant to find each other.'

She was so like Keyli, yet so different. Her kiss was the first Bran had experienced since Keyli's death.

'It must have been hard,' he said, 'keeping your love for Tharn a secret.'

'It was. I'm sorry Hashath is dead, but I'm pleased Creyak is no longer crippled by the old bastard's will. Now Tharn is king, and his word will be the law. If that means we can be together at last, I'm glad of it.'

She spoke with a quiet authority that, Bran supposed, was entirely appropriate for a queen.

'I'm glad you have a chance to be happy,' he said. He took her hand and kissed its palm.

'Thank you.'

Bran tried to sit up again. This time he made it all the way. He rubbed the back of his head. The pain was fading.

He looked past Lethriel to the painting on the cave wall. The fire was dying, its meagre light coming and going in random spurts. Each little flash of orange picked out a different figure in the painted hunt, a different pose of the doomed mammut.

Before Bran's eyes, the ancient hunt came alive.

'So,' said Lethriel, 'what about you?'

'What do you mean?'

'Is there happiness somewhere for you too? You're searching for it, I think.'

'I... I hope there might be,' said Bran. 'Talus says...'

'What? What does he say?'

A distant roar sounded somewhere beyond the cave. It didn't sound like the sea.

Lethriel jumped to her feet, suddenly alert. Bran stood too. His head swam a little, but otherwise he felt all right. Better than he could have hoped for, in fact.

'It can wait,' he said. 'I feel better. We should go.'

'Well, if you feel up to it. But we must hurry. Do you think you're well enough to climb?'

'I feel well enough to face an army.' Bran stopped short. 'What do you mean: "climb"?'

CHAPTER TWENTY-SEVEN

NIGHT HAD FALLEN. As they climbed the cliff, Bran kept his attention fully on Lethriel's heels scrambling above his head, and the dark icy rock before his eyes. He tried not to think about how far it was to the beach below.

The sound of the sea flattened steadily to a distant murmur and, as the air cleared, they found themselves ascending into the silver glare of the moon. The fog lay beneath them, a billowing grey meadow. The sky was an upturned bowl, vast and black and flecked with countless stars. The moon blazed.

They still had some distance to climb, but at least now they could see where they were. Narrow, snow-clogged ledges meandered along the broken cliff face. Hanging off the ledges were scruffy nests of dry weed and twigs, glued in place by years of gull droppings. The gulls themselves were absent; Bran supposed they wintered elsewhere. The entire precipitous wall was deserted but for the two of them, creeping their way up it like tiny insects.

'Are you sure you know what you're doing?' Bran said. A bulbous overhang loomed over him. It looked insurmountable. Lethriel was already halfway up it.

'I used to climb here with Caltie,' she said. 'It's not as bad as it looks.'

Cursing his useless left hand, Bran followed her up and over the overhang. She was right: cracks in the rock, deep enough to be free of ice, made it easier to negotiate than he'd anticipated.

Above this obstacle the terrain levelled out. Bran's climb became first a scramble, then a crawl, until finally he was standing on his feet again.

He looked around, but Lethriel was already off and running towards a distant snow-covered ridge.

Bran took a last look down past his aching feet to where the cliff fell away and vanished into the ocean of fog. Somewhere down there was the cave, the beach, the cairn, the rest of Creyak. He felt remote from it all, as if he'd climbed into another world altogether.

Wind gusted in from the west, disturbing the fog. Bran relished the feel of the breeze on his face. He hadn't realised what a suffocating environment Creyak had become.

The wind grew stronger and near the northern tip of the island, a great tear opened in the fog bank. A jumble of gigantic boulders rose from the sea: the remains of a collapsed rock stack. Half-hidden among them was a smooth, pale form: Farrum's boat.

The fog closed in again. Lethriel was waving to him from the top of the ridge. He hurried to meet her.

'I saw the boat,' he said when he reached her. 'Farrum hasn't left after all.'

Lethriel forced him into a crouch and pressed her fingers to his lips.

'Keep quiet,' she hissed. 'Look there.'

Beyond the ridge rose the twisted wooden pillars of the henge. Rimed with ice, they twinkled in the moonlight.

Their shadows were long and blue on the snow. Bran shuddered. They looked like deformed giants, gathered for some unimaginable ritual.

Farrum's boatmen were ranged around the great boulder dominating the middle of the henge. At their head was Farrum himself. A man lay sprawled on the boulder, Farrum's obsidian swathe at his throat.

Mishina.

'What's going on?' said Bran.

'Farrum's been busy,' Lethriel replied. 'He must have repaired the boat and moved it to keep it safe, then brought his men back here.'

'So much for not having any boatbuilders on his crew. How did Mishina get here?'

'I don't know. Maybe Farrum sent men back to fetch him, or left them behind in the first place.'

'It explains why you didn't see him by the totem pit.'

'It doesn't matter. What matters is *that*.'

She pointed beyond the henge's far perimeter, where a second ridge rose in a row of jagged stone teeth. More men stood there: a long line of them, their white faces floating like pale flames before the starry sky. They carried wooden spears tipped with sharp flint heads. As Bran watched, the line grew longer and deeper. This was Creyak unleashed and ready for battle.

A man forced his way through to the front of the line: Tharn. Across his shoulders he wore a huge, black fleece that made him look twice his normal size. He carried an axe so big he needed both hands to hold it. The moon's light sculpted the furious look on his face. Unlike his warriors, he wore no paint at all.

A breath or two later, Tharn was joined by Arak. He held an axe much smaller than Tharn's, and looked ready to topple under its weight. His furs were caked in Sigathon's blood. He looked terrified.

'A lot happened while I was knocked out,' said Bran. 'I think things have just started to move fast.'

Tharn took a step forward. Now he was balanced on the very edge of the ridge overlooking the henge.

'Let Mishina go!' he boomed. His voice echoed around the guardian wooden pillars. 'Your lives will be spared.'

'You're a worse liar than your father was,' Farrum called back. 'I know you mean to kill me.'

'Tell me why I should not!'

'Because I'm the one who's going to give the commands, and you're the one who's going to obey. If not... your shaman is dead.'

As far as Bran could determine, Tharn's men outnumbered Farrum's by at least five to one. They also held the high ground. If Tharn chose to attack now, the battle would be over in a few bloody breaths.

And Mishina would be the first to die.

'Tharn won't risk Mishina's life,' whispered Lethriel. 'Not if he wants to stay king.'

She was right, of course. The shaman was the spiritual heart of the island village. If Mishina died, Creyak would instantly lose its link to the afterdream. A new shaman would be found eventually, but—with everything that had happened over recent days—Creyak needed Mishina *now*. Continuity was everything. If Tharn's first act as king was to sacrifice Mishina to a rival king, his reign would be over before it had begun.

'What do you want?' said Tharn. His voice was unwavering. The head of his axe was a lethal crescent of light.

'I want you to admit the truth about your father's death,' said Farrum. 'Then I want you to step back and let your people decide what happens next.'

A ripple went through the line of Creyak warriors. Through the unnaturally clear air, Bran heard their feet crunching in the snow.

'You are a spider, Farrum,' said Tharn. 'You spin lies and treachery and deceit. Now you try to cast your web, as a fisherman casts his net.'

'Clever words. But you're not so clever.'

'Let the shaman go and then go yourself, Farrum. Or I swear my axe will take off your head.'

'Killing talk from a killing son. Better be careful, boy.'

'You speak in riddles.'

'I speak truth. Killing comes naturally to you, Tharn. That's why it was so easy for you to kill your father.'

A gasp went up from Tharn's men. Some brandished their weapons at Farrum; others stared unbelieving at their king. Tharn glared at them, his gaze sweeping from one end of the line to the other. His axe shook in his hand. A few heads lowered in shame, but most remained high and resolute.

'More lies!' Tharn sounded uneasy.

'No!' said Farrum. 'Just the truth.'

'What does Farrum think he's doing?' said Bran. 'What does he really want?'

'Farrum wants what he's always wanted,' said Lethriel.

'Which is?'

'Everything.'

Opposite Tharn and his warriors, not far from where Bran and Lethriel were crouched, was a prominent outcrop of rock. The rock's strange curves, and its dusting of snow, made it seem to glow with its own internal light. To Bran's eyes it looked a little like a wolf's head, reminding him of the prow of Farrum's boat.

Two figures had climbed up onto the rock; if it really had been a wolf, they would have been standing on the tip of its snout. One was Talus, the other was Alayin. Noosed around Alayin's neck was a short length of rope. The other end of the rope was in Talus's left hand. In his right hand he held something long and slender: a bonespike. Talus twisted the weapon, allowing a small engraved mark shaped like a gull to flash in the moonlight. This was Gantor's bonespike: the very weapon that had killed the king.

Bran's heart lurched in his chest. 'What in Mir's name is he playing at?' He surged forward, but Lethriel held him back.

'Wait,' she said. 'We have to wait.'

'But what's he doing? Do *you* know what he's doing?'

'No. But we have to trust him.'

They weren't the only ones looking at Talus. Farrum had turned his head towards the wolf-rock, as had Tharn. Both men looked both furious and confused. Talus, however, looked entirely at peace. For all she was his captive, Alayin too seemed composed, her hands clasped in front of her and her scarred face entirely without expression. Her hood was thrown back; under the moonlight, her close-cropped scalp looked as bald as Talus's.

'Bard!' shouted Tharn. It came out as a curse, a plea for help, a cry of anguish, all at the same time.

'I agree with Farrum,' said Talus. His voice filled the henge from one side to the other. Tharn's grip tightened on his axe until his knuckles turned white. 'But only when he says that we need to hear the truth,' Talus added.

'Let my daughter go,' growled Farrum. He buried his fingers deep in Mishina's hair and tipped back his head. The obsidian blade hovered over the shaman's exposed neck.

'I think I will keep Alayin here,' said Talus, 'for a little while, at least.'

'What do you want?' said Tharn.

Talus's eyebrows went up. 'Have I not already said? I want the truth. But first... Farrum, will you please summon the rest of your men, so that everyone can see what they are up against?'

Tharn's men looked at each other, clearly mystified. Farrum's face contracted into a grimace.

'What men?' said Bran. 'What's he talking about?'

'*Ssh*,' said Lethriel.

'If they do not come out, Farrum,' said Talus, waving the bonespike for all to see, 'your daughter will bleed from her throat until she dies.'

Bran couldn't believe what he was seeing. He'd never known Talus to even carry a weapon, let alone brandish one. Yet he saw no fear in Alayin's eyes, nor did she make any attempt to escape. Had Talus drugged her?

One of Farrum's boatmen muttered something. Farrum elbowed him aside, pursed his lips and gave three clear whistles, two high-pitched, one low. There was a pause. Then, one by one, a troop of men wearing close-fitting sealskin appeared at the henge's northern perimeter. To Bran they appeared to condense out of the night. All bore scars on their faces; all carried clubs and knives.

'Where did they come from?' said Bran.

Tharn's men tightened their line. They, like Farrum's hidden warriors, looked grim and ready to fight. Between them, the two armies now encircled the henge almost completely. Bran was suddenly, acutely aware of how vulnerable he and Lethriel were here. And how exposed Talus had made both himself and Alayin.

'I'm going to put a stop to this,' said Bran, standing.

Once more, Lethriel pulled him down. 'No,' she said. 'The bard is about to speak again.'

'And what good will that do?'

Incredibly, she smiled. 'Isn't it what he does best?'

CHAPTER TWENTY-EIGHT

TALUS HAD ADDRESSED bigger crowds, but he'd never had an audience so divided, each so intent on killing the other. Whatever story he chose to tell them, it would have to be a good one.

Except this was more than just a story. It was the solution to the puzzle that had plagued him since his arrival on Creyak just two days before.

It was the truth.

'Once there was a king,' he began. 'This king—whose name was Hashath—loved his people very much. He feared for them too. His fear was so great that he decided that the only way to keep his people safe was to shut out the rest of the world. So he took the island where he and his people lived and he turned it inside-out. He set totems against the world outside, and set his back against their backs, and vowed never again to look beyond their gaze. He brought a kind of winter to his island home—a winter he hoped would never end. He froze Creyak, and its people, and himself at their head.

'He became the frozen king.'

The words came readily; Talus let them pour out. His mouth was the mouth of a river and the water gushing through it had come down from some high unknown peak, and he was only its channel.

'The king had six sons. Like everyone else in Creyak, they were forced to live by his rules. The strictest rule of all was that no son could take a woman, not until he himself was king. It was hard for them all, especially the younger ones, who grew up knowing that, as long as their brothers remained alive, they might neither marry nor take the crown.

'Hashath worked hard to maintain the peace he had created on this island of Creyak. But still he had his enemies. Greatest among these was a man he had played with as a child. This man's name was Farrum. Unlike Hashath, who looked inwards, Farrum looked out, out into the world. Hashath was a man interested only in protecting his borders; Farrum, on the other hand, was a conqueror. Long after he was driven from his home, he was driven by a burning desire to return.

'To return to Creyak, and to make it his own.'

Talus wondered how Farrum would react to his words. With this last part, he'd strayed from truth to speculation. Although Mishina had told him about the feud between the rival kings, Talus could only guess at Farrum's motivations.

The vivid scarlet flooding Farrum's scarred cheeks told him he'd guessed well.

'But Farrum needed to be clever,' Talus continued. 'He knew it is not enough simply to kill a king and take his kingdom. Invasions are brutal things. They breed resentment and fear. Sooner or later, those Farrum had conquered would fight back. No, victory did not mean defeating the people of Creyak. It meant winning them over. Farrum needed to do more than just kill a king. He needed to control one.'

Farrum had had enough. He brandished his obsidian swathe high over the subdued Mishina.

'Are you finished prattling, bard?' he shouted. 'I'll gladly save you the trouble of finishing your story and finish the shaman right here and now.'

'Stay your hand!' Talus roared. Every man in earshot flinched: Tharn and his men on the south side of the henge, Farrum's on the north, the boatmen clustered round the sacrificial boulder, Farrum himself. Bran and Lethriel too, hiding behind the ridge of rock to his right; Talus had already spotted them, and was glad to see them alive and well.

He caught Bran's eye and winked, hoping the gesture carried more confidence than he felt.

For a long breath, Farrum held his black blade aloft. Talus waited. Finally, Farrum lowered his weapon. Some of the onlookers sighed. If Mishina was going to escape, this was his chance. Talus saw Bran watching the shaman, saw the surprise on his companion's face as he realised Mishina wasn't moving.

Talus wasn't surprised at all.

'I sense impatience,' he said, 'so I will bring my story swiftly to an end. So far, I have told you only truths you might have worked out for yourselves—if you did not know them already. The truth about Hashath's murder is different. It is hard to see. But see, it I have.'

He paused. The snow shimmered and the stars revolved in the sky.

'There is a man among you,' he said. 'A man who, two nights ago, approached the king of Creyak from behind and drove a bonespike between his ribs, killing him within a breath or two. A man who then dragged the king's body out into the arena and fled the scene.'

Tharn stepped forward between two of the henge's wind-ravaged pillars. Each of the wooden posts stood twice his height, yet somehow he seemed to dwarf them and everything around him. Talus had never seen a man look more hungry.

'But'—Talus raised one finger—'the story is not quite as simple as that. No man commits murder without a reason. And no man kills a king unless he is insane, or unless something—or someone—gives him both the courage and the tools to do so.'

Talus tugged gently on the rope he was holding and Alayin stepped forward like a dutiful slave. To the watching crowd, she seemed tethered by the neck, unable to escape, but in truth the rope lay in loose loops over her shoulders. Talus needed no knots to keep Farrum's daughter at his side.

'Are you ready?' he murmured.

'Just finish your tale, bard,' said Alayin. 'I will do what I must.'

She too was watching Farrum. The hate in her eyes saddened Talus. Truth cut deeper than any blade he knew. Yet he had no choice but to wield it.

'Our killer had a goal, you see,' Talus said. 'Something he wanted more than anything in this world—or in any other. Murdering the king was his first step along the path to that goal. But, to reach the end, he would have to do more. He would have to kill each of five brothers, one after the other. Gantor, ever the loner, was easy. Sigathon's death, I suspect, happened more by fortune than planning. Because by now the whole plan was coming apart. Is that not right, Farrum?'

The old warlord glared at the bard. Wind ruffled his cloud of white hair. 'I don't know what you mean.'

'You do. Because you are the force that gave the killer the courage he needed to kill.'

Talus licked his lips. It was the bard's job to lead his audience down unknown paths. He'd done that well enough so far. But the sensation of control was just an illusion. At any moment the audience might look round and realise where they were.

'You, Farrum,' Talus repeated. Out of the corner of his eye, he saw Tharn take another step forward. 'But the courage you supplied was not enough. The killer also needed tools. They were supplied by another. By the man who lies in front of you, Farrum, and whom you have no intention of killing at all. Stand up, Mishina, and tell your new king what you know, and what you did. Put aside your so-called spirits and show us what is real.'

Tharn beckoned Arak to his side. The young man came dutifully forward. He looked like a miniature version of his brother and king but, where Tharn stood immobile, Arak's body snapped with tiny tremors he seemed unable to control.

There was no sign of Fethan.

Farrum's blade had lowered again. Moving like a snake, Mishina wriggled out from beneath it, dropped lightly from the boulder and shook himself down. His painted face cracked with an expression that might have been anger or amusement—Talus couldn't tell which.

Then the shaman punched Farrum clean on the point of his jaw. The old man staggered back, but made no attempt to retaliate.

'Spit out your words, Talus!' Mishina shouted. 'You have come this far. Let us see how far you dare to go!'

The buzzing in Talus's head—which during his speech had dulled to a gentle drone—went completely away. He had no desire to speak again. The silence both inside himself and across the henge was too blissful. The sensation of peace wouldn't last; it never did. But for now, briefly, he savoured it.

'Very well.' He forced the words out. 'If you will not speak, I must. However strong the killer's urges might have been, he still needed a way to overcome the taboo of killing the king. You, Mishina, gave him that. You supplied him with the intoxicating greycaps he needed to take away his fears.'

Mishina laughed. 'Your thoughts are muddled, bard. You have still not told us why this killer did what he did.'

'Two reasons, one of which leads to the other.'

Another laugh. 'As I said, you are a muddled man.'

Talus felt a prickle of irritation in the skin of his back. But he would not let this so-called magic-man goad him.

'The first reason,' he said, 'was simply to take the place of king. You see, the killer was one of Hashath's sons.'

This was a truth Talus had lived with for some time. Not so most of the watching crowd. Gasps and cries rose up on clouds of vapour. Flint weapons rang as their blades clashed together.

Talus raised his hand. 'The second reason was far stronger.'

'Stronger than the urge to become king?' said Mishina. 'What would a man desire more than that?'

Without prompting, Alayin took another step forward. Now, like Talus, she was poised right on the edge of the rocky crag. She spread her arms, and her bearskin shone in the moonlight.

'Me,' she said.

CHAPTER TWENTY-NINE

BRAN HAD BEEN listening hard to Talus's story. Much of what the bard said made sense—seemed obvious, actually. Bran wondered why he hadn't worked it out for himself. Right from the start he'd been suspicious of Mishina, but he'd put those feelings down to his general mistrust of shamans. Bran had never needed magic-men. His own relationship with the spirit world had always been a personal one: just him and the sea-guardian Mir, out on the waves together.

Until Keyli had died and he'd turned his back on Mir for good.

Yet, even though Talus had explained Mishina's role in what now appeared to be not just a single killing but a complex plot, Bran still didn't know who the killer was. Until the massacre at the totem pit, he'd been convinced it was Sigathon. But now...

'Tharn won't be able to hold himself back much longer,' said Lethriel. She'd risen to a crouch. 'I should go to him.'

Bran pulled her down. 'Are you crazy? Do you really want to throw yourself into the middle of all this?'

She looked at him with tears in her eyes. 'I'm already in the middle of it.' But she stayed all the same.

Up on the wolf's-head crag, Talus was speaking again:

'Alayin speaks the truth. With all his brothers dead, the killer would become king. More importantly, he would be free to take the hand of the woman who stands beside me: Alayin, daughter of Farrum, king of Sleeth. But Alayin was more than just a prize.'

'What are you saying, bard?' Tharn's voice exploded like thunder across the crater. Lethriel flinched.

Talus stared across the henge at Bran. Last time their eyes had met, the bard had winked. Now he just looked tired and sad.

'Alayin was a reward,' he said.

'Enough!' came a voice from somewhere to Bran's right, and Cabarrath stepped out of the shadows beside a henge-post that was more holes than wood. His long furs were wet with blood and the axe he carried dripped a red trail in the snow. His brow hung low over his eyes, which were lost in darkness.

'You say what you say, bard,' said Cabarrath, 'but how do we know your words are true? You are a teller-of-tales, after all. How do we know this is not just another of your stories?' He stopped, his body rigid but for the hand that held the axe, which was shaking. Blood dripped from the edge of its stone blade.

'Because I look with my eyes,' Talus replied. He seemed unperturbed by Cabarrath's arrival.

Cabarrath looked across the henge to where Tharn was standing. Arak stood close at the side of his brother and king. Like Cabarrath's, his axe was trembling.

Tharn nodded, once.

'What do your eyes see, bard?' said Cabarrath.

'When he was stabbed,' said Talus, 'Hashath managed to scratch his attacker's face.'

Tharn shouted in frustration. 'How can you know this? You were not there!'

'I found flakes of mud under the dead king's fingernails when I examined him in the cairn. Whoever killed the king did so with his face hidden under a coat of paint.'

'Mishina!' Tharn bellowed. He advanced between the wooden pillars and entered the clear ground inside the henge, swinging his axe.

After a breath, Arak scurried after him. Cabarrath held his ground, but his grip tightened on the handle of his axe. Bran raised his hand to touch the bump on the back of his head. Had Cabarrath noticed him hiding here with Lethriel? He hoped not.

Following their king, the Creyak warriors surged forward. Somewhere in the Creyak lines, a drum began to beat, then another. A low humming echoed across the henge, rising and falling in pitch as spears crashed on the snow-covered ground.

On the opposite side of the henge, Farrum's men raised their stone weapons in response. Unlike their enemy, they made no sound. Somehow their silence was more threatening.

Talus opened his arms. Wind gusted through his motley robes, opening them like wings.

'*Stop!*' he cried.

Incredibly, everyone stopped. If Bran hadn't seen it for himself, he wouldn't have believed it: this scrawny bald man in his tattered collection of skins holding sway over two armies that were ready to tear each other to pieces. How did he do it?

'Mishina is a man of many colours,' Talus went on. 'Enter his house and you will see them all, as I did. Blue, yellow, white, black... but nowhere in the home of the shaman did I see the colour of the paint I found under the fingernails of the king.'

Tharn and Cabarrath shared another inscrutable look. Between and around them, the entire henge was silent.

'What colour was it?' said Tharn.

'Red,' said Talus, and Bran knew instantly who the killer was. From the look in Tharn's eyes, it was obvious Creyak's new king did too. Cabarrath's expression was impossible to read, because already he'd turned his face away and started marching across the henge towards the spot where Tharn and Arak were standing.

Farrum moved his hands, sending a signal to his army. Six of his warriors broke from the horde to join him and Mishina at the sacrificial boulder.

'Explain!' Cabarrath roared at Talus as he walked towards his brothers. His long legs ate up the ground. He raised his axe, spraying more blood through the air. 'Do not start another of your games.'

'Oh,' said Talus, 'I'm afraid a game is exactly where this does start. A game for two opponents that uses coloured stones: some black, some red. The opponents wear the colour of whichever stones they take as their own.'

Cabarrath halted halfway across the henge. 'I know this game,' he said slowly. 'It is played by Sigathon and Arak. Sigathon always wears black. And Arak...'

Tharn had stepped back into the shadow of the nearest pillar. Now he was a dark, menacing shape looming over Arak. Only the tip of Tharn's stone axe showed in the moonlight, burning with cold blue fire.

Cabarrath started marching again, straight towards Arak, towards whom all eyes had now turned.

Arak started to edge backwards.

'Do not move, little brother!' Tharn roared. His face was lost in the shadows. Bran could only imagine the expression he wore: rage, grief, despair... perhaps all of them at once.

Arak halted. Bran thought he was crying, but it was hard to be sure. Cabarrath was almost upon him.

'Do you know this, bard?' said Tharn. 'Do you know this to be the truth?'

Talus bowed his head. 'Yes.'

Cabarrath covered the last few paces to youngest brother at a dead run. He swept up Arak in his long arms and held him tight. His face was a mask of misery.

Bran watched as Arak went limp. So that was it. It was all over. The truth was finally revealed, and the killer was caught. So why did he feel dissatisfied?

'Tell the rest of it, bard,' said Tharn from the shadows.

Talus spoke fast. 'Before he killed his father, Arak drugged himself with greycaps to take away his fear of the ancestors. Even now you can still see the effect of the drugs: the blacks of his eyes are large; his arms and legs are restless. He gave drugs to Sigathon too—an even bigger dose; did you not notice how quiet Sigathon had become? This was the only way for Arak to hide his plans from his twin, at least until the time came to kill Sigathon too.

'Arak killed his father with a bonespike he'd stolen from his brother Gantor—a clever way to move the blame if the weapon was ever found. But Fethan found him before he could drag the body away. I do not know what story Arak devised, but Fethan was loyal enough to keep quiet about what he had seen. And, later, to take the blame for it.'

'Arak was always Fethan's favourite,' said Tharn. He sounded broken.

'Well, then. Finally we come to Farrum. The night his boat arrived, I remarked to my companion, Bran, that it lay strangely low in the water. It was clearly heavily laden, yet there appeared to be only twelve men aboard. When he explored the boat later, Bran found a secret space under the deck. It was there that Alayin had hidden herself.'

Talus tugged gently on the rope he was using to hold Alayin captive... except Bran now saw that the rope wasn't knotted at all, but hung loose around her neck. Why wasn't she running? Unless...

'What Bran failed to notice,' Talus continued, 'was that the secret space ran the entire length of the boat. It was big enough not just for Alayin, but for the small army you now see before you.'

Tharn's voice floated out from the shadows. It might have been the voice of a ghost. The hairs on the back of Bran's neck prickled.

'Why?' he said. Who was he addressing? Talus or Arak? There was no way to tell.

It was the bard who offered the answer. 'If Arak killed both the king and his sons, Farrum would reward him.'

'How?'

'By giving him Alayin to marry. Arak would rule Creyak in name, but the real power would lie with his father-in-law. Creyak would be conquered not by force of arms but by love.'

Talus lowered the bonespike and dropped the rope, which slithered from where it had hung over Alayin's shoulders. She stood tall and proud, her neck long and her head high.

'One thing puzzles me,' said Talus. 'This was a difficult plan. It needed someone at the centre to make each thing happen at the right time. Someone to pass word between Creyak and Sleeth. Someone to supply Arak with the greycaps—and no doubt reassure him that the spirits would indeed be gentle with him when he finally entered the afterdream.'

Talus cocked his head like a heron assessing its next meal. 'I know it was you, Mishina. I know you helped Arak become a killer—likely even tempted him into it. I know you encouraged Farrum. When the men from Sleeth were trapped in the totem pit, I know it was you who helped them out—no doubt with Arak's help. Who struck you and prevented you from escaping with them then? Was it Sigathon, I wonder, come to his senses in time to stop you, but too late to save himself? These details do not matter. Here is the puzzle: *why* would you do all these things?'

A gust of wind blew through the henge. Tendrils of fog rose briefly over the distant cliff edge, then fell away. Mishina's long robes billowed around him. The shells on his staff jangled.

'The all-seeing bard is puzzled!' said Mishina. 'How charming. Do you *really* not know what drives a man like me, Talus?'

'I do not care for games, Mishina,' said Talus. Bran wondered if the bard really was puzzled by Mishina's motives, or whether he was playing an intricate game of his own.

'Ah, you see?' Mishina said. 'You do know after all.'

'Explain yourself.'

Mishina spread his arms in an expansive gesture that took in the entire henge and all the people in and around it. 'They do not understand people like you and me, Talus. They do not appreciate the *breadth* of us. They cannot imagine how deeply, desperately *dull* our lives must become.'

He spat on his hands and wiped them down his face. When he held up his palms, one was streaked blue, the other black.

'Who can blame men like us for having a little fun? You have your stories, Talus. As for me... yes, I have my games.'

It was clear to Bran that Mishina was trying to rouse the bard to anger. It didn't appear to be working.

'Is that all this is to you, Mishina?' Talus said. 'A game?'

Mishina continued to wipe the paint from his face. 'Games are all I have, bard,' he growled. 'Don't pretend you don't have your own.'

The shaman was prowling now, clearly angry— perhaps because of his failure to provoke Talus. Or perhaps, Bran thought, because he'd just been cornered into confessing his crimes before a line of the strongest warriors in Creyak. Not to mention his king.

Which, he suddenly realised, had been Talus's goal.

Lethriel tugged at Bran's arm. 'Fethan,' she said, pointing.

For a moment, Bran saw nothing. Then a clot of dark hair moved behind Tharn's ranks. Below it, mostly in shadow, was a blood-streaked face: Fethan. Bran had wondered where he'd got to.

The moonlight glanced off Fethan's upraised stone axe as he broke through the line of warriors; they spilled aside, taken completely unawares. Fethan covered the last few strides to where Cabarrath stood holding Arak and swung his weapon straight at Arak's head.

Cabarrath whirled round, taking Arak with him, his feet slithering on the ice. Arak dug in his heels and shoved backwards with all his strength, and Cabarrath went sprawling on his back, the younger man landing on top of him hard enough to drive the breath from his brother's lungs in a clean white cloud.

Fethan's axe sliced through the air precisely where Arak's head had been.

Arak sprang to his feet, landing square on Cabarrath's heaving chest. He fumbled at his brother's waist; when he stood upright he was holding a short spear tipped with grey flint. Fethan, still recoiling from his monumental axe-swing, shifted his weight frantically from one foot to the other in an effort to maintain his poise.

But his attempts were in vain. He'd poured all his weight into that single swing and now he was hopelessly off-balance. Like Cabarrath, he slipped on the treacherous ground.

He fell straight onto the tip of Arak's spear.

Arak cried out—whether in triumph or anguish, Bran couldn't tell. Fethan collapsed, the flint blade buried deep under his left collarbone. His weight carried him forward. Arak backtracked, fighting to stay upright on the slippery ground and simultaneously tugging at the spear. Finally he managed to yank it free, and Fethan collapsed on top of Cabarrath, his blood staining them both.

Holding the spear aloft, Arak turned a slow circle in the snow. His lips were drawn back from his teeth. He looked terrified.

Then, with a scream, he ran straight into the shadows of the henge-pillar where Tharn was standing. Black shapes flailed in the darkness. Bran strained to see what was going on. Beside him, Lethriel was on her feet.

A man stumbled out from the shadows and into the moonlight. His arms were loose; his face was a mask of shock. Dark blood stained the furs over his belly.

The man was Tharn.

The new king took three tottering steps into the henge and fell to the ground.

Lethriel shrieked and sprinted out over the snow-covered grass. Bran reached out his good hand too late to pull her back.

Arak was still screaming. He leaped over the fallen bodies of his three brothers and bounded into the henge. When he reached the middle, he sprang up onto the sacrificial boulder, raised the bloody spear over his head and howled. The howling went on and on, and the spear swung slowly in the moonlight, and the blood of the king dripped down, slowly turning the ice on the boulder's surface from white to red.

ChapTeR ThiRTY

WITH AN ALMIGHTY roar, Tharn's warriors surged into the henge. A scant breath later, Farrum's men followed suit. Leather boots kicked up snow; stone weapons sliced the air. The two armies met behind the great central boulder, breaking against each other like waves in a storm-tossed ocean.

Talus watched in dismay as the battle played out. Flint blades cut through fur and into flesh. Men bayed like wolves. Arms grappled, hands grabbed hair, gouged eyes. Compared with the war he'd witnessed in the desert, this was nothing but a skirmish, but already men lay dead on the icy ground, and many more would fall before this night was out.

A few of Tharn's men broke away from the main group. Axes raised, they made for Farrum, leader of the invaders from Sleeth. But Farrum's boatmen had formed a wall around the old man, and they deflected the Creyak marauders with ease.

Lethriel, meanwhile, had reached Tharn. She fell at his side, sobbing. Nearby lay Cabarrath, almost hidden beneath Fethan's bleeding body, just as Arak had been hidden by Sigathon's near the totem pit. Was either of them still alive? There was no way to tell.

As more men fell, Talus's horror grew. This was all his fault. If only he'd been quicker to solve the riddles Creyak had posed him, all this might have been avoided. Perhaps he could find a path across the battlefield to the stricken brothers. He was responsible for all this; perhaps there was a life he might still save.

Alayin's cries alerted him to trouble closer at hand: three of Farrum's men had crept up onto the rocky crag behind them. As Talus turned, one of them clamped his arms around Alayin's waist. She thrashed, trying to escape, but the second man grabbed her feet and lifted her completely into the air. Between them, they carried her swiftly down into the henge.

The third man stayed behind. He grinned through the scars on his face. In his right hand he held a flint knife; in his left was a vicious-looking bonespike, much like the one that had killed Hashath.

Talus—acutely aware of how close he was to the edge of the crag—picked up the rope he'd held draped around Alayin's neck. As the Sleeth man advanced, Talus drew back his arm and lashed the rope forward. At the last moment he flicked his wrist back. With a sound like a lightning strike, the rope cracked against the side of his attacker's face. Blood welled between the scars and the man took a stumbling step back, his mouth drawn down in surprise and pain.

Talus snapped the rope again. This time the Sleeth man dodged, avoiding the blow. The rope cracked in empty air. His grin returning, the man extracted a knotted-wood club from beneath his robes and swung it at the bard's middle. Talus sucked in his belly and felt the end of the club graze against his robes. The man swung again, this time aiming for Talus's head. Talus dropped low and wondered if this was the day he died. Already he was breathless, and this man was *fast*.

With an animal shout, Bran raced up the side of the crag, seeming not to climb the rock but to fly over it. The Sleeth man turned, wrong-footed. Bran lowered his head, dropping beneath his adversary's clumsy swing, and drove into his belly. Breath exploding from him, the man flew backwards over the edge of the rock, hit the snow and lay unmoving.

'Talus!' said Bran. 'Are you all right?'

'I am,' Talus replied. 'But there are many who are not.'

Down in the henge, the two armies were still locked in combat, hurling rocks, feinting and grappling and stabbing. The ground was littered with the fallen.

On the sacrificial boulder, his white face and wide eyes vivid under the glaring moon, stood Arak. Nearby, safe inside their cordon of boatmen, stood Farrum and Mishina. As Talus and Bran watched, the men who'd captured Alayin finally delivered their prize, throwing her unceremoniously at Farrum's feet. She sprawled with her hands planted wide in the snow, her chest convulsing.

'Thank you for coming to my rescue, Bran,' said Talus.

'You're welcome. How did you work it all out? How did you know it was Arak?'

'I did what I am cursed to do, Bran: I saw with my eyes.'

'Yes, but where everyone else sees questions, you see answers. Why was Alayin with you? You wanted it to look like you were holding her captive, but you weren't, were you?'

'Sometimes, Bran, you see things clearly too.'

'Just tell me you hadn't really lost your mind and decided to hold her prisoner.'

'My mind was my own, and Alayin was a willing participant. We thought our pretence would keep Farrum submissive while I told Tharn the truth about his father's murder. It is a shame the ruse did not work for a little longer.'

'Where did you find her?'

'It was Alayin who found me. She caught up with me as we ran from the totem pit to the beach. By that time, I had lost Tharn. The trick with the rope was Alayin's idea.'

'Seems like Alayin sees a lot too.'

'She is a strong daughter dominated by an even stronger father. Farrum had convinced her that to be queen alongside Arak would bring her the freedom she craves. So she went along with his scheme. She allowed herself to be hidden on the boat along with Farrum's fighting men, both to be brought out when the time was right.'

'So what changed?'

'When you stumbled over her hiding place, Alayin was in the process of doing what every woman has a reputation for doing well.'

'And what's that?'

'Changing her mind.'

Talus broke off. Long shadows were flowing over

the henge pillars to the south. Gradually, the sound of battle was drowned by a low chanting. One by one, white-painted faces appeared against the star-filled sky. It was the rest of the villagers—the entire community, by the look of it. The parade of the king, come at last.

'Creyak has thawed,' Talus said.

In the Sleeth ranks, raised weapons were lowered. Farrum's men bunched together, trading axe-swings for shouted insults, and slowly began to retreat.

For a moment, Talus thought the men of Creyak would press home the advantage; with so many reinforcements, how could they fail? Instead they fell back, while behind them the newly-arrived villagers made a silent wall around the henge's perimeter.

'What are they waiting for?' said Bran.

'These people are the product of Hashath's peace,' said Talus. 'They have come not to influence events but to witness them... and to honour their new king, whoever he may be.'

Down in the crater, Mishina had limped from behind the cordon of boatmen and out into open space. He carried himself with all his former pride. Despite the smeared paint on his face and the blood on his robes, he was shaman still.

He thumped his staff three times in the snow. The shells hanging from it made a ringing noise that seemed to merge with the moonlight, making it shimmer. On both sides, weapons hung slack at the sides of their owners. Mishina began to chant. One by one, the watching Creyak villagers sank to their knees.

Talus shot a glance across the henge to where Lethriel

was kneeling at the side of the fallen Tharn. Neither he, nor Cabarrath, nor Fethan had moved.

'So now it's just Arak,' Bran said. 'He's won after all. Mishina will pronounce him king of Creyak. We can't do anything to stop it.'

'No. But there is someone who can.'

Mishina's chanting rose in pitch. Farrum too was in the open now, striding across the snow towards Tharn and Lethriel. In his gnarled right hand he held his obsidian swathe.

Farrum had covered barely half the distance to the king's body when Lethriel stood. A gust of wind billowed her red hair out into a fan.

'Come no further, Farrum!' she shouted. 'The king is dead. I'll suffer no man to disturb his peace!'

Farrum kept walking, the swathe swinging at his side.

A few of the Creyak men who'd backed away from the fighting gathered behind Lethriel. Several more clustered around the motionless bodies of Cabarrath and Fethan. They all brandished chert weapons smeared with Sleeth blood.

Farrum faltered; his old, scarred face was etched with uncertainty. 'You're lying.'

'I'm telling you the truth. Tharn is dead. His brothers, too. You've done what you came to do. Now just go.'

The wind was gusting harder. Grey tendrils of fog curled up behind the watching villagers, as if the weather too wanted to bear witness to the proceedings.

Farrum regarded the glowering Creyak warriors, his lips pressed hard together. 'It's of no consequence,' he growled and made his way back to the middle of the henge.

Mishina stopped chanting. With a crooked finger, he summoned Arak. The boy jumped down from the boulder and made his way through the snow to the shaman's side. At another gesture from Mishina, the two Sleeth warriors hauled Alayin over. She hung limp in their grasp, head lolling, feet dragging in the snow. They forced her upright; when they let go, she remained standing, although she swayed from side to side, clearly dazed.

'We have to do something,' said Bran.

'Yes,' said Talus. 'We have to wait.'

'No, I mean we've got to stop this.'

'Events will run their course, Bran.'

'Oh. So you're happy that Tharn's dead and the scheming shaman is going to hand over the kingship to a murdering drug-addled boy and the vicious foreign king is going to win back the island he's coveted all his life?'

Talus was impressed by Bran's summary of the situation. It was almost enough to spur him to action. Almost.

'That is not what will happen,' he said.

'So you can see the future now?'

'I cannot see the future, Bran. But I can see the truth. At the heart of all this turmoil, Bran—amidst all these murders—there exists a single calm centre: a still point about which all else turns. When I speak of truth, this is what I mean. It is something you will see for yourself, Bran, one day.'

Talus sensed rather than saw the shiver that passed down Bran's spine. He listened to the buzzing in his own head and placed his hand on that of his companion.

'You must trust me, Bran,' he said. 'This is what I do, and it is all that I do. Every day I see something different. Today, I see a young woman torn by uncertainty, yet strong enough to know her own mind when it finally speaks to her.'

'Alayin,' said Bran. 'She's what this is all about, isn't she? That's what you meant about the calm centre. It's all about Alayin.'

'It always has been.' The thought came from nowhere, swiftly followed by another. 'And always will be.'

If these last words struck Bran as odd, the former fisherman didn't show it.

By now, Farrum had reached Arak and his daughter. His air of uncertainty had intensified. Slowly he held up the swathe. The moonlight lanced off the strange glass blade; a shiver travelled down Talus's spine.

Arak took the weapon, Farrum stepped aside and Mishina's voice echoed again across the crater.

'Arak is king,' said the shaman. Three words, a minimal proclamation, yet all that was needed. The words hung in the night.

Mishina took Arak's hand—the one that wasn't holding the swathe—and placed it on Alayin's. The queen-to-be was considerably taller than her king. She gazed down on him with blank eyes.

Mishina murmured something Talus couldn't hear. The shaman looked first at Arak, then at Alayin. Then he stepped away from the couple, ushering the old warlord and his retinue of boatmen with him. They retreated all the way to the henge's northern edge, where Farrum's bruised and bloodied army awaited them.

Arak and Alayin stood alone under the moonlight, hands clasped together, each looking deep into the other's eyes.

'You know what's going to happen next,' said Bran. 'Don't you?'

Talus said nothing.

chapter thirty-one

ARAK RAISED HIS free hand to stroke Alayin's cheek. His other hand was tight on the haft of Farrum's swathe. The muscles in his legs tensed as he stretched himself up, bringing his lips close to those of his new bride. The thought of them kissing revolted Bran.

Alayin spat in Arak's face.

Arak reacted instantly, swinging the swathe round so that its blunt wooden edge smacked hard against Alayin's ribs. She staggered, crying out. Arak struck again, but already Alayin was running. Her stupor had just been an act. The ice-bear furs blew like a blizzard behind her.

Arak gave chase. Everyone else—Farrum and Mishina included—looked on dumbfounded. Alayin was making straight for the wolf's-head crag, where he and Talus were watching.

'What's she doing?' Bran said.

'Go to her,' Talus replied.

Bran started clambering down. Alayin had already covered most of the ground between the sacrificial boulder and the crag. As Bran had already observed, she was fast, but Arak was faster, and he reached Alayin long before either Farrum—who'd finally given chase— or Bran could get anywhere near.

Arak used the swathe to trip the fleeing Alayin, then grabbed the hood of her furs and started dragging her through the snow. Bran marvelled at the strength of this slight young man, then remembered that here was the murderer who'd stabbed his own father in cold blood and then hauled his corpse hundreds of paces to its final resting place.

Bran lowered himself gingerly over the slippery rock, his view of Arak and Alayin momentarily obscured. He dangled for a moment, took a deep breath and let go, bouncing twice off the rock before landing in a deep drift of snow. When he stood up, Arak and Alayin had vanished.

Bran whirled round. What magic was this? He waded through the snow, scooping it aside with his hands.

'Talus!' he called. 'Did you see where they...?'

The bard's finger shot out, pointing straight at the base of the crag. Bran pushed on through the snow, ducking his head as he passed under the jaw of the wolf's stone head. Darkness yawned: the narrow entrance to a cave.

Bran crawled inside. It turned out to be a narrow tunnel with a shattered, treacherous floor, sloping steeply down. Beyond the entrance there was just enough room to stand. All the same, Bran kept his head low as he hurried through the darkness; the last thing he wanted to do was crack his skull open on the ceiling. He stumbled twice before the tunnel walls finally peeled back and spat him onto a broad shelf of rock.

Sudden wind blasted into Bran's face, forcing him to blink back tears. Beyond the rocky shelf was a sheer drop. Thick fog obscured its depths, but already the wind was beginning to tear it apart.

Just short of the edge stood Arak, his wiry arm tight around Alayin's neck, the swathe's obsidian blade brushing her skin. She was trembling, her nostrils flaring, panting softly.

Someone crashed into Bran from behind, and Bran turned to face Farrum. The old warlord looked haggard and lost. Bran hated the king of Sleeth for the part he'd played in this debacle, yet at the same time he knew Farrum was afraid for his daughter's life. Still, he found it hard to feel sympathy.

'Happy now, old man?' he growled.

Farrum said nothing, just extended his hands towards Arak in a mute plea.

Bran took a cautious step forward. 'Let her go, Arak,' he said. 'There's nowhere left for you to run.'

'Stay back!' said Arak. He touched the lethal swathe to Alayin's neck, and she flinched. Her eyes locked on Bran's, pleading.

'It's all over, son,' said Farrum. 'I've given you everything I promised. Everything you wanted. You're king now.'

'I don't want to be king,' said Arak. 'I never wanted to be king. I just wanted her.' He shook Alayin, as if there could be any doubt about who he meant.

'Arak,' said Bran. He took another step. He could feel the slippery ground trying to trick him towards the precipice. 'Arak, I'm sorry, but it doesn't matter how much you want Alayin. She doesn't want you.'

Something swam briefly behind Arak's eyes.

Understanding? It was there and gone so fast that Bran couldn't be sure. What replaced it was pure wrath.

'I'll kill her,' Arak yelled. 'I'll kill us both, I swear it!'

'You will not,' came a voice from the tunnel.

TALUS STEPPED OUT into the moonlight, slipping first past Farrum, then past Bran. In just two breaths he'd halved the gap between himself and Arak, moving confidently despite the icy ledge.

'Don't you start spinning one of your clever stories,' said Arak. He edged backwards. Now his heels were on the very brink of the drop. Bran could hear Alayin's breath hissing in and out through her tortured throat. Still she was looking at him. 'There's no way back for me now, bard.'

'If a path leads in, Arak, it must also lead out,' said Talus. He stopped and stood motionless, his palms pressed together.

'I've made my place in the afterdream. They're waiting for me there now, all of them. At least this way I take my queen with me.'

'Alayin does not wish to accompany you.'

'You think I don't know that?'

'There is another way.'

'Yes? And what's that?'

'Take your place at the side of the true king of Creyak. Tell him how sorry you are and pay for what you have done, not in the next life but in this. Pay by giving your service to the king, Arak. Help him light a fire to thaw the ice that has kept Creyak frozen for so long. Work hard, and you may yet gain the respect you have lost. Life is long, Arak, long enough for a man to do such things and more. Other worlds await, and you may yet enter them on your own terms. Admit the truth both to others and to yourself, and earn the right to walk tall, with your head high, at the side of the true king.'

'The... true king?' Throughout Talus's speech, Arak's pupils had grown wider and wider. 'I don't know what you mean.'

'The bard means me,' said Tharn, staggering out of the tunnel. He was leaning on Lethriel, who appeared to be bearing almost all his weight. His legs were clotted with blood from the wound on his back and his voice was thick with pain.

Arak's pupils snapped down to tiny points of darkness. His lip curled, exposing small white teeth.

'It's a trick,' he said. 'Shaman magic. You're the same, both of you.' He removed the swathe from Alayin's neck and swung it first at Talus, then at Mishina, who'd appeared from nowhere to stand beside the bard. Arak rose on the balls of his feet, poised as if ready to spring.

Bran was watching Alayin closely. The instant the swathe had left her throat, she too had tensed.

'Jump,' Bran said under his breath. 'For your life, woman, jump.'

'Arak,' said Tharn. He shrugged himself free of Lethriel's support and stumbled forward. 'Brother, let this end here.'

Tears sprang into Arak's eyes.

'Yes, Tharn,' he said.

He stepped backwards into space, his arm still locked

around Alayin's neck. He said nothing as they fell. Alayin screamed. Just as her feet kicked into empty air, she managed to wrench herself free. Her arms flailed, seeking solid ground, but she'd left it too late, and the fog sucked them both down.

Bran was first to reach the edge. His moccasins slipped on the slick rock, and for a moment he thought he was going over too. He plunged his good hand into a crack and just stopped himself from plummeting into the abyss.

Gasping for breath, he peered down.

Circular ripples were expanding through the sea of fog, their centre marking the spot where Arak and Alayin had fallen. The freshening wind snagged the ripples and tore them apart, opening a funnel in the mist, and suddenly Bran was staring all the way down the sheer cliff face to a narrow ledge on which two bodies lay sprawled. One was skinny and disarrayed, just a boy lying broken on the rock. The other was a sinuous curve of ivory fur.

A coil of rope landed beside Bran's head.

'Hold the end,' said Talus, 'while I climb down.'

He seemed very tall, looking down on Bran as he was. The moon framed his head, a perfect circle.

'You hold the rope,' said Bran. 'I'll climb.'

Men gathered behind Talus. Bran didn't know whether they were Tharn's or Farrum's. Nor did he care. All he wanted was to stop the endless cycle of death that had consumed this forsaken place.

'Get as much weight behind the rope as you can,' he said.

Talus passed the rope back through the throng. Bran took the free end and started to ease himself over the edge. Suddenly Lethriel was beside him.

'Let me go,' she said. 'You can't climb with just one hand.'

'It's enough.'

'I'm good on the cliffs, you know that. Caltie taught me.'

'You showed me the way up. I'm sure I can find the way down.'

'But...'

'There's no time. Go to Tharn. He needs you.'

Bran descended slowly, planting his feet with care and using his good right hand to feed the rope round his left shoulder, clamping its coils tight under his left arm whenever he needed to transfer his grip. Shards of ice and flakes of stone broke loose under his toes and fell pattering around the two bodies lying prone on the ledge below.

The falling debris roused Arak. He rose to a crouch, crawled stiffly across the ledge to where Alayin lay.

'Stay where you are,' Bran shouted down. 'Don't move.'

Arak was shaking Alayin. He didn't seem to have heard Bran. At first, Alayin didn't respond; then her head twitched. The instant she stirred, she started to slide towards the drop.

'No!' Bran cried. He let the rope slither through his fingers, ignoring the burning in his hand and in the pit of his arm. But he fell too slowly: Alayin was slipping inexorably over smooth ice towards the waiting precipice. The movement restored her senses and she flailed her arms, but there was nothing to hold on to. She teetered on the brink.

Arak scuttled towards her like a spider. His feet flew sideways, kicking away the swathe, which had landed on the ledge next to him. The strange weapon spun out into space and disappeared into the sea below.

At the last moment, Arak's thrashing feet found some hidden purchase, and he threw all his weight into Alayin's path. Alayin's ivory furs blossomed around him and, like the swathe, he vanished.

Bran came to a bone-wrenching halt an arm's length above Alayin.

'More rope!' he shouted. But there was no more.

'Alayin,' he said, 'Look at me.'

Her scarred face lifted to his. She looked serene.

'I came so close,' she said. 'I just wanted to be free.'

'You will be,' said Bran.

He held out his left hand, the crippled one with its livid starfish skin and twisted bones. The hand that had been struck by a star.

Alayin extended her long, perfect fingers. Instead of taking Bran's hand, she stroked it.

'Why would you do this for me?' she said.

'Just take my hand!' Bran could feel his grip slipping on the rope. If she didn't take hold now...

'Why?'

'You skinned the bear,' he said. 'You didn't run. You faced the monster and took its skin and made it your own. Whatever was in you that day, don't give it up now. Not for this. Not for him.'

A moment of silence, broken only by the steady tinkle of ice crystals raining down into the invisible sea.

Alayin's right hand clamped on Bran's burn-scarred wrist, then her left found his forearm. With a great bellow, he scooped her up and held her. She was lighter than he'd imagined she would be—too light to be real. Then the wind drew Alayin's furs up around her and they opened like wings, revealing Arak.

The boy was standing tall on the ledge's crumbling verge, supporting Alayin in his upstretched arms. He'd been taking her weight all this time. It was his strength alone that had supported her long enough for Bran to lift her to safety.

'She must live,' Arak said. His eyes, which had been so wild for so long, were calm at last.

'She will,' Bran replied.

Arak's feet lost their hold on the ice, and his arms lost their hold on the woman he loved and who could never be his. Bran was holding the full weight of her now and, though he heard his back creaking, he knew he could support it.

Arak fell.

The fog parted, opening the way for him, all the way down to the sea below and the rocks that crowded its edge like waiting teeth. Arak hit a sharp ridge, and the sound of his bones snapping reverberated up the cliff face just as if lightning had parted the air. The boy rolled with the foaming waves, his face peaceful.

As the men of Creyak lifted them to safety, Bran watched the sea wrap itself round Arak and bear him away. The boy floated briefly before he was sucked down into Mir's embrace. Some of the paths to the afterdream lay hidden in the deeps. Bran knew this well; Keyli had taken just such a path herself.

As for what would await Arak when he reached the other side, Bran could only imagine. He hoped it wasn't the hell they all said it would be.

'He killed the king,' said Bran.

'He saved my life,' said Alayin. 'That will save him, in the end.'

'How do you know?'

'Everything must be repaid, sooner or later.'

'Everything?'

She kissed his cheek. The scars on her face were coarse on his skin. 'I owe you a debt, fisherman, and you have my thanks. That will have to be enough, for now.'

Chapter Thirty-Two

TALUS HELPED BRAN up over the edge of the cliff and back to solid ground. Anonymous arms found Alayin and spirited her away into the crowd. For now, Talus was concerned only with his companion.

'You were brave,' he said.

Bran sat with his head between his knees, clearly dizzy. When he tried to get up, Talus pressed him back down.

'Alayin...' said Bran.

'Is safe. You did well.'

'I wasn't going to let you risk your life down there. Sometimes you can be so stupid, Talus.'

'At least I have you to point it out to me when I am. Can you stand?'

'Yes, please, help me up.'

Two groups of men stood facing each other on the broad ledge. At the head of one was Farrum, bent and old. Fronting the other was Tharn, bent too, not from age but from injury. Lethriel was beside him, holding him up.

Most of the men carried their stone weapons in plain view, but their muscles were relaxed. Axes drooped; chert knives and bonespikes hung loose above the icy ground. All the anger had gone out of the night.

Tharn and Farrum eyed each other for a long time. Finally Tharn spoke.

'There is a new king in Creyak,' he said.

'I see him,' said Farrum. The wind ruffled his white hair.

'This new king is different from the old. He brings with him a new season. A thaw is coming, Farrum. If you stay, you may be washed away by the meltwater.'

'I have no plans to stay.'

'That is good.'

A pale phantom drifted into the empty space between the two ranks of men. For the briefest moment, fantasy and reality merged and Talus found himself staring directly into one of his own tales. The phantom was an ice-bear, come to claim its prey.

Talus shook himself, and saw that inside the cloud of ivory fur was a woman.

'Tharn,' said Alayin, 'I'm sorry. I know it's not enough, but it's the only thing I've got left to say. And it's the truth. I'm sorry for the evil we've brought.'

'I believe you are,' Tharn replied. He faltered, coughing. Red sputum stained his lips. 'But if you stay I will kill you with my own hands.'

Alayin's eyes flickered. 'I understand.' She turned to her father. 'What will you do with me?'

Farrum glared at her, a scarred and ancient warlord shamed into retreat. His hand dropped to his waist, but he was no longer in possession of the obsidian blade.

'Father?' said Alayin.

Farrum extended his hand. 'You will come home, daughter,' he said. 'You will come with me to the place where you belong.'

Without waiting for her, Farrum led his men towards a narrow cleft at the far end of the ledge, where a narrow path led down the side of the cliff to the beach. The ground to the left of the path was a slick, steep chute of ice.

'Watch your step, old man,' Tharn called, 'or you will reach the bottom sooner than you expect.'

Alayin followed her father without speaking. She stepped onto the path without looking back. Already Farrum and his men were out of sight. Soon Alayin was too.

Tharn turned his attention to Mishina. The shaman stood a little apart from the Creyak warriors, motionless even in the rising wind, like a totem. A small smile played on his mud-daubed face. The paint had smeared, allowing the medicine man's true features to show through at last.

'You have brought misery to my people, shaman,' said Tharn. 'I advise you to run, before the spirits of our ancestors find you and take their revenge.'

'I have no need to run, little king,' said Mishina. 'But I will walk. It is something I have grown very good at over the years.'

There was something in Mishina's tone, the way the moonlight cut across his half-seen face, that brought Talus up short.

'Walk then,' said Tharn. 'You have no place among us.'

'On that point,' said Mishina, 'I have to agree.'

Yet the shaman lingered, eyeing the bard. Talus returned his gaze. What lay behind Mishina's mask? He was curious to know. Curious, too, to understand why it was suddenly so important to him.

As if he could read Talus's thoughts, Mishina stooped, picked up a handful of snow and rubbed it against his face. The white snow turned blue and black, coloured flakes falling to the ground. Slowly the shaman scoured away the mask he'd been hiding behind since the day Talus and Bran had arrived in Creyak.

At last Mishina brought his hands down. His face was hardly clean: stray streaks of paint still adhered to his chin, his cheeks, the long line of his nose. But he was revealed.

Talus looked long and hard at the mastermind responsible for Hashath's death, and for all the trials Creyak had suffered since. He felt cold and hot, both at the same time. His limbs wanted to move, yet he was frozen to the spot. He could feel his eyes opening wide, and could only imagine what expression the shaman had coaxed from him.

'You,' Talus said. The words did not seem his own. 'It is you.'

The shaman bowed. As he straightened again, he looked triumphant. Talus had seen that look before, long ago in a hot, sandy realm. The look of a warrior-priest who, alongside his cruel king, had attacked a desert temple and driven a queen into exile. A man at the head of an army that carried blades made of black glass.

How could Talus not have known?

'You,' Talus repeated. He lunged.

Mishina sprang aside, brandishing his staff. As Talus stumbled past him he swung it, narrowly missing the bard's head. The shells on the staff jangled; several broke free from their thongs and bounced across the ice and over the cliff edge.

'Talus!' cried Bran. 'What's going on?'

Regaining his balance on the slippery ground, Talus made another grab for Mishina. This time his bony fingers caught on the shaman's robe. They curled and clung and, for an agonising breath, they were face to face.

'I swore I would find you,' said Talus. 'Yet I never believed I would.'

'That is the difference between us, bard,' said Mishina. 'It is why I succeed and you fail. I believe. You do not.'

'I will make you pay for what you did.'

'I think not.'

Mishina ducked and wriggled, twisting himself entirely free of his robe. Naked, he sprinted towards the path at the end of the ledge, all trace of his limp gone.

'You think your prize lies north?' he called over his shoulder as he ran. 'I have been there, bard, all the way, and that place is not what you think. You will fail, Talus. The bone hunter will bring your story to an end.'

Approaching the path, Mishina dropped to his knees. Momentum carried him forward; he wasn't running now but sliding over the ice. He steered himself into the steep-sided chute and, with a ululating howl, slithered over the edge and plummeted out of sight.

Talus stood dumbfounded, his narrow chest heaving. The shaman's empty robe dangled from his hand. He couldn't believe what he'd just seen—more to the point, what he'd failed to see until now.

'Talus?' said Bran. 'What was all that about? Should we go after him?'

'He was here,' said Talus slowly. 'All this time he was here, right under my nose. I saw everything else, but I didn't see him.'

'Who? Who was he?'

Talus could say no more. His head wasn't just buzzing—it was screeching. A swollen hive of enraged bees. He wanted to chase Mishina, bring him back, subject the shaman to all the questions that had plagued him over the years.

But he couldn't move a single muscle in his body.

TALUS HAD FORGOTTEN the name Mishina had gone by in the desert. That bothered him: his memory was usually faultless with such things. Just another part of the man's strange guile.

Or, perhaps, his magic.

Was he magic? Who could say? Talus had met again the man who'd destroyed everything Tia had built—a true adversary of old—yet all he could think of was the story Tia had told him about the northlight, and which had set him on the path he now walked.

It was after the temple had fallen, when they were wandering lost and alone in the desert, that Tia had finally revealed the true identity of the travelling man from whom she'd heard the story in the first place.

'It was him,' she'd said, meaning the warrior-priest. 'He looked like a beggar then, but I know now it was the same man.'

'He must have been spying on you. Gathering information for his king.'

'I suppose so. It doesn't matter now. He told me that, when his work was done in the desert, he would go north himself, to see what he could see. I asked what work he meant, but he didn't answer. Now I know.'

She'd gripped Talus's hands. 'When you go north—no, don't deny it, I know you want to, have wanted to ever since I told you about the northlight—promise me this: if you ever meet him again, kill him.'

Talus had never killed a man in his life. Even looking into Tia's eyes, he didn't know if he was capable of it. All the same, he said:

'I will.'

Yet when the moment had come—when he'd faced the warrior-priest once more—Talus hadn't even recognised him.

'WILL YOU TAKE his place?'

Talus returned from his reverie. Tharn was before him. As he spoke, he tottered in the snow; several of his men rushed to catch him, but Tharn shooed them away.

'What? Whose place?' said Talus. Tharn's words had barely registered.

'You know who I mean. Will you be a wise man to us, now that Mishina is banished? For all his failings, he was strong.'

'Strong?' Bringing his attention round to Tharn was hard, but by degrees Talus managed it. After all, he was in the presence of a king.

'Yes,' said Tharn. 'I see the same strength in you, bard. But there is more: what I have just witnessed tells me you have walked under the same skies as our shaman-that-was. The two of you are connected. It is a sign. Just as Mishina was destined to leave us, so Talus was destined to stay.'

Talus shook his head. The pressure inside it was beginning to ease. 'I am no shaman. I am just a bard, a mere teller of tales. As for Mishina... do not ever imagine we are alike.'

'I did not say that. Will you stay?'

Talus gazed at the chute down which Mishina had fled. Perhaps there was still time to pursue him. Perhaps the shaman lay at the bottom of the slide with all his bones broken, his naked body slowly caking with salt from the sea and snow from the sky.

Somehow he knew it wasn't so.

'No,' he said. 'Bran and I must leave in the morning. Our work here is done.' The words echoed in his head, a bitter reminder of another man's work in a different land, a different time.

'Then I am sorry,' said Tharn. 'Will you at least stay long enough to tell us one last tale, bard? We go now to the cairn. I must say my last goodbyes to my father and brothers. I would have you with me when I do it.'

Talus bowed low. 'I will come when you call.'

Tharn rested his hand on Talus's shoulder. 'Thank you.'

The king departed then, hobbling away on Lethriel's arm, leading his men through the tunnel and back to the henge, and leaving Talus and Bran alone on the ledge.

Bran slumped in the snow. He was clearly exhausted. Talus sympathised. But he couldn't rid himself of the image of Mishina's naked face.

He must have known me all along!

The wind gusted. Bran shivered. Talus hardly felt it. He was more concerned with the storm blowing through his mind. In an effort to escape it, he tipped his head back and gazed up at the stars.

'We should get back under cover,' said Bran. 'The night is cold.'

'No.'

'Why do you always have to...?'

'Look up, my friend.'

'Talus, let's just... oh!'

Dazzling veils of pure green light had overwhelmed the black night sky. They rolled like ocean waves, shifting colour to turquoise and blue, orange and silver. They fluttered like the wings of a million butterflies. In their beauty and their silence they stilled the turmoil in Talus's cluttered mind.

'The northlight!' said Bran said. 'It's so beautiful.'

'Yes,' said Talus. 'That is the truth.'

As the northlight danced in the heavens, the last streamers of fog drifted out to sea. With the air finally clear again, the tops of the waves appeared, shimmering under the moon, under the many colours of the shifting sky.

A pale shape swooped low over their heads. Bran cried out; Talus might have done so too, had he not recognised it for what it was: a winter owl chasing its prey through the snow. The breath of the bird's wings was soundless on his face.

As if the owl's flight were a signal, the northlight began to dissolve. It faded fast, the myriad colours softening to a uniform glistening green before departing. As he always did when the northlight left them, Talus felt sad.

Looking west, he watched the last few remaining shards of light chase across the horizon, like shining leaves caught on a hidden breeze. Their glow played over the ocean, stretching all the way to Creyak's barren north shore where the cliffs rose high and wild.

A big grey shape emerged from between two rocks and ploughed towards the deep: Farrum's boat. Long oars pulled at the white-capped waves. At the boat's prow, a carved wolf's head scanned the distant horizon, seeking the way home.

'Well?' said Bran.

'Well what?' It was immensely peaceful standing here in the snow. Talus didn't want the moment to end.

'Are you going to tell me what that was all about?'

Talus rubbed his hand over the top of his bald head. Already he could feel his thoughts growing agitated again. But that was all right. A man could only stand still for so long.

'What what was all about?'

'Mishina, of course.'

'Of course I will tell you, Bran. The tale of my past is one I have never told you, and which you deserve to hear... and hear it you will, before we next make landfall. But first I must do the bidding of the new king of Creyak. I have no doubt he will ask a story of me too, and I am afraid the king's will comes before that of the fisherman.'

The eastern sky was beginning to brighten, not with the northlight but with the dawn. Another day already, with so much to be done. So far still to go.

Talus bounded away through the snow. The dawn intensified with every step he took. He felt filled with energy and entirely alive.

After all these years—Mishina! The name might have been different, but the man was the same. And so was his purpose—Talus was sure of this. Which could mean only one thing.

I have been given another chance!

Even better, there was a new puzzle to solve.

The bone hunter will bring your story to an end.

Who was the bone hunter? And had Mishina really travelled as far north as he'd claimed? The questions were delicious, and Talus savoured them. The answers were far from reach, lost in darkness and mist.

But he would seek them out.

'Talus?' said Bran as he trudged through the snow after the bard. 'What do you mean: "before we next make landfall"?'

CHAPTER THIRTY-THREE

LETHRIEL WAS WAITING for them at the henge. Behind her, the sky was a rich, gorgeous purple. The coarse grass rippled in the breeze. High overhead, a gull circled.

As Bran came up to her, Lethriel placed her hands on his shoulders.

'I thought you'd gone with Tharn,' he said.

'I wanted to see you.' She hesitated.

'We'll catch up with you, Talus,' said Bran.

'I can wait,' Talus replied, regarding them both with open curiosity.

'There's no need,' said Lethriel.

Talus didn't move. Bran waited. Smart as he was, sometimes the bard could be so slow.

'Oh,' Talus said at last. 'I'll... be on my way.' He paused. 'Thank you, Lethriel, for your help.'

'You're welcome. I'll see you at the cairn.'

'Yes, of course.'

The bard turned on his heels and loped away across the henge.

'What did you want?' said Bran when Talus had gone. It was good being close to Lethriel again. Difficult, too.

'Just to say goodbye.'

'Goodbye?'

'It's the only time we'll have, Bran. Soon you'll be gone and I'll be with the king.'

'It's where you want to be.'

Lethriel laughed. The sound fluttered out across the henge as if it had wings. Bran felt himself relax.

'Yes, Bran. It always was. But I had to make sure you'd be all right. That you'd find a place where you want to be too. And...'

'And what?'

'I wanted to hear the rest of *your* story.'

'My story?'

'In the cave you told me about your wife. About Keyli. I know she died, but I know, too, that somehow you're still searching for her. I don't understand how that can be, but I can see it clearly. It's like a light behind your eyes. Or a shadow. For some reason, you still have hope. I want to know where that hope comes from. I *need* to know.'

'Because of Caltie?'

'Yes. And Gantor. Because of all of those who died. I know... I know they've gone to be with the spirits in the afterdream. I know that if I wait I'll meet them again, when my turn comes. And I know in the meantime that Tharn will love me...'

'But?'

'But waiting is so very hard.'

The wind gusted, blowing scraps of snow through the henge. The dawn rushed towards them.

'Talus says...' Bran paused, began again. 'After Keyli died—right from the very moment she died—I lost all hope. I saw no reason to carry on living. I wanted to wade out into the water and follow her into the afterdream.'

'But Talus stopped you?'

Bran considered this. For a long time, the memories of that dreadful night had been trapped in his dreams. He'd been trapped too, unable to speak about them, unable to escape. Finally telling the story to someone— to Lethriel—had liberated him.

'He didn't exactly stop me. He... I suppose he gave me a choice. Talus told me that he was travelling. That he'd been travelling for a long, long time. He said there was an empty place on the path at his side, and asked me if I wanted to walk with him. I asked him where he was going. Can you guess how he answered me?'

'How?'

Bran grinned to think of it. 'He told me a story, of course. A short one. Do you want to hear it?'

'If you can remember it.'

'Every word. This is what Talus said: "A great queen once claimed that, in the far north of the world, lies a place where the northlight meets the ground. The place is called Amarach. It is a place where all the worlds meet: this world, the afterdream, and many others. If a man can only find his way to Amarach, he will be rewarded with a single moment in which he will see again all the people he has lost in his life. Inside that moment will come a single chance to go with them, or to bring them back home. Or to say goodbye forever. To find this place is hard, but if a man is both strong and true it may be done."'

Bran realised he was crying. Lethriel touched his tears.

'It sounds like a story told to comfort a child,' she said.

'I know,' Bran replied, 'and it comforted me for the longest time, all the time we journeyed north, even through the coldest depths of winter. But hope can only last so long. By the time we'd reached Creyak, I'd stopped believing Amarach even existed. I was tired of hoping, tired of dreaming. I'd decided to turn back.'

'And now?'

Bran dragged his good hand through his matted beard. 'I'm ready to go on again.' Saying it aloud was a revelation.

'What changed your mind?'

'A little of this place. A little of you.'

'And?'

Bran sighed. 'Mostly I think it's because the tale of Amarach is one of the tales of Talus.' He took her kind hand and squeezed it. 'And that can only mean one thing.'

'What?'

'That it's true.'

THE SUN ROSE. Strong men retrieved Arak's body and carried it up from the beach; others brought poor Sigathon from the totem pit. As he stood in the cairn, it seemed to Bran that Gantor, who'd been placed at his father's side the previous day, looked less lonely now in the presence of his brothers.

The whole of Creyak was there. Many of the villagers were crammed into the cairn, making its confines hot and cramped. Even more were gathered in a great crowd outside. Their faces—freshly painted with pure white mud—were turned up to the sky, and their singing was low and sad and filled with love.

Bran felt honoured to be one of those allowed inside. All his fear of the cairn had gone. Perhaps the press of living bodies made him feel safe. Or perhaps he'd changed.

Tharn took Mishina's place as speaker-for-the-dead during the funeral ceremony. Nobody questioned his right to do this. After all, he was the king. At his side was Cabarrath, whose injuries from his encounter with Arak at the henge had proven slight. Fethan had survived too, but his wounds were too severe for him to attend. Bran hoped he would live.

Tharn's words were halting; he was prompted frequently by Lethriel, who was familiar with shaman ways and able to direct all the small but essential rituals: the lighting of fragrant fires, the chanting of the names of the afterdream waykeepers and the drumming of the heartbeat-echoes of the newly dead.

It was the drumming that affected Bran the most— even more than the heady stench of burning grasses that filled the cairn's crowded interior, or the low murmuring of the foot-trampling throng that surrounded him. The drumming was like thunder in his head, and, just for a moment, he was back inside the storm.

A burst of flame illuminated the little door that led, so they said, to the afterdream. The door looked impossibly close. Bran wanted to touch it, wanted to see it slide open, wanted to see what—or who—lay beyond. But there were too many people in the way.

The drumming subsided, the moment passed.

'And now,' said Tharn, speaking over the dying echoes of the drums, 'the bard will tell us his final tale.'

Talus's story was about an old man who walked across a desert to fetch water for his family. He journeyed for many days over dunes of yellow sand and lakes of white salt. He did battle with venomous snakes and ravenous wolves. Finally he reached a deep hole filled with pure, clear water. He filled his watersacks and made the return trip, which was just as perilous as the journey out had been.

Eventually the old man came home. But when he went up to his wife and children he found they could not see him. When he spoke to them, he found they did not hear. When he tried to give them the water he had brought, he found it had turned to sand.

Then the old man saw his own body lying on a funeral pyre. As the flames carried his spirit away to the afterdream, the last thing he saw was the tears his family were shedding, and he understood that water had come to them after all.

Just as Talus concluded his tale, a dazzling beam of sunlight stabbed through the cairn entrance. The smoke filling the cairn turned orange in the new morning haze. The low chanting of the mourners subsided. The fires went out. The funeral was over.

The king and his sons had passed out of this world and into the next.

Slowly the cairn emptied. Bran let the crowd jostle him outside. Just as he emerged into the dawn light, Cabarrath found him and pulled him to one side. The tall man looked distraught.

'I am sorry I struck you, Bran,' he said. 'I saw you on the beach... the fog... I thought you were one of Farrum's men.'

'It was an easy mistake to make,' said Bran. 'But I have a hard head.'

'Then you forgive me?'

'There's nothing to forgive. Will Tharn be all right, do you think?'

'He will be a great king. A king-of-the-summer. And I will serve him. We all will. I see your friend over there. You should go to him.'

Talus's bald head was just visible over the crowd, bobbing like a float in the ocean. The bard waved, trying to attract Bran's attention.

'Look after your brothers, Cabarrath,' said Bran.

'I will.'

Talus continued to wave as Bran pushed his way through the mass of villagers. He looked like an excitable child.

'Tharn wishes to meet us at a sea-cave on the beach,' he said, as soon as Bran was at his side. 'He says he has something to show us.'

'What is it?'

'The king wishes it to be a surprise. What did you think of my tale?'

'It was a fine story. It made me feel... well, calm, I suppose. Even if I don't know what it meant.'

'Some tales do not mean anything at all, but that does not mean they are without power.'

'You know, this morning I might actually agree with you.' Bran watched the last of the mourners traipse out of the cairn and into the early light. 'This surprise of Tharn's—I suppose you know what it is already?'

With twinkling eyes, Talus led Bran towards the sea.

chapter thirty-four

It was the cave in which Bran and Lethriel had sheltered the previous night. In the daylight, the painted scenes on its sea-smoothed walls looked drab and still.

Just inside the cave entrance, the new king stood tall despite the pain he carried and his obvious exhaustion. On his head he wore a circlet of woven willow twigs: the crown of Creyak. Lethriel was at his side. Their hands were entwined.

'So, what's this surprise?' said Bran.

Without speaking, Tharn and Lethriel descended the sloping floor towards the back of the cave. Talus and Bran followed them round a polished knuckle of black rock to find themselves standing before a vast slab of flat stone that looked as if it had long ago fallen from the ceiling.

Lying on the slab, propped in place by angled wedges of driftwood, was a boat.

Bran, for no reason he could fathom, wanted to cry. To hide his emotion, he walked a slow circle around the vessel. It was a dugout, much cruder than Farrum's seal-skin ship, but undeniably beautiful. Its hull was carved from a single trunk of oak; Bran had seen no such trees growing locally and wondered where it had come from.

Four sturdy limbs splayed wide, two from each side of the hull, supporting a pair of outrigger pontoons woven from willow branches.

'Impressive,' he said as he returned to Talus's side. He didn't trust himself to say any more.

'It's yours,' said Lethriel.

'Do you mean it?'

'Take it,' said Tharn. 'May it carry you at least a little further on your way.'

Bran ran his good hand along the nearer of the two outriggers. 'Who made it?'

'Fethan,' said Tharn. 'My father forbade such things, but he built it all the same. Fethan always dreamed of leaving Creyak, even before a child started growing inside his favourite woman.'

'You knew about that?'

Tharn gave a sad smile. 'I am his first-brother. There is not much I do not know.'

'Will he be all right?'

'He has a lot to live for,' said Lethriel. 'When we've finished here, I'll go to him. I know remedies. And there are plenty of tender hands ready to soothe his hurts.'

Bran swallowed. He couldn't take his eyes off the boat. 'Then I suppose this is where we say goodbye.'

'That is your choice,' said Tharn. 'I would have you stay as long as you wish, but...' He looked at Talus.

The bard joined Bran beside the boat.

'The weather is fair,' said the bard. 'The lifting of the fog shows a change of weather to the south. Winds are rising that will help to carry us north. Our work here is finished. There is no reason for us to stay.'

'Well,' said Bran. 'I suppose that decides it.'

They kicked away the driftwood chocks and turned the boat to face the cave entrance.

'We might need some help,' said Bran as he uncoiled the ropes he'd found tucked under the bow.

'The boat is lightly made,' said Tharn. 'I believe you will manage.'

He was right. Big as it was, the boat was so artfully carved that it weighed barely half what Bran had expected. All the same, by the time he and Talus had dragged it to the water's edge, his bearskin was damp with sweat.

He was about to climb aboard when he remembered something.

'Our things,' he said. 'Our packs, water sacks—they're still in the house.'

'No, they're not,' said Lethriel.

She pulled back a tanned leather panel concealing a well in the centre of the boat's hull. There was Bran's pack, the little pouch containing Talus's firelighting kit... everything they'd been carrying with them when they'd first crossed the causeway to Creyak.

'These other pouches contain meat,' said Lethriel, pointing. 'And these are full of water. Enough for many days.'

'Are you trying to get rid of us?' said Bran.

Lethriel laughed. 'We just knew that, once you saw this boat, there'd be no stopping you. Mind you, Talus, we've made a liar out of you.'

Talus raised one eyebrow. 'Explain yourself.'

'When we first met, at the henge, you told me that when you left Creyak you would take nothing away.'

'Indeed I did. Nor shall we. As you said yourself, this boat belongs to my good friend Bran.'

Bran stroked both his hands—the good and the bad—along the hull of the boat. He smiled.

'All boats should have a name,' he said. 'What's this one called?'

'Its skin has not yet touched water,' said Tharn, 'so it does not yet have a name.'

'Why don't you give it one?' said Lethriel.

'What do you think, Talus?' said Bran.

The bard ran his finger over his chin. 'I believe the choice must be yours.'

Bran didn't have to think very hard.

'*Keyli*,' he said. 'The boat is called *Keyli*.'

MOMENTS LATER, THE boat was wallowing in the shallows; Talus climbed nimbly aboard and Bran followed. They picked up the broad paddles stowed in the hull and used them to shove the boat away from the shore. Tharn and Lethriel stood on the shingle with their hands raised in salute.

'I'm sorry we had to know you in such hard times,' said Bran as the boat's hull finally bounced clear of the stony sea bed.

'They were not of your making,' said Tharn. 'And I am glad you came with them. Especially you, Talus.'

'You honour me,' the bard replied.

The morning sun cleared the cliff, unleashing warm light onto the beach. The shingle turned gold beneath it.

'No winter lasts forever,' called Tharn. He was dwindling now, growing smaller as Bran's oar-strokes pulled them out towards the open sea. 'A thaw is coming.'

Lethriel shouted something, but the wind tore her words apart and they were lost. Soon it was too late even to wave. Creyak was a white-capped rock melting slowly into the larger coast. Ahead, the ocean was vast and welcoming.

'Well,' said Bran, 'you found your way to the truth in the end. There's still something that puzzles me though. Why did Arak collect all those things? The fur from Alayin's wrap I understand. But Lethriel said he'd stolen things from all his brothers.'

'A good question, my friend. Consider the bonespike Arak stole from Gantor—the weapon he used to murder his father. You found it in the cairn, hidden behind the door to the afterdream. How did it come to be there?'

'Arak didn't want anybody to find it, so he hid it.'

'A peculiar hiding place, do you not think? Would it not be simpler to throw it into the sea?'

'I don't know. I suppose so. So why did he put it there?'

'It was a gift.'

'A gift?'

'Yes. You must remember Mishina's role in all this. All the time he was urging Arak on, he was also reassuring him that he would be safe from the ancestors' wrath. I believe Mishina instructed Arak to take trophies from each of his victims and put them through the door. Not to hide them, but to send them on in advance to the afterdream. When Arak eventually died and entered the afterdream himself—no doubt after living a long and happy life as king of Creyak—he would retrieve the trophies and return them as gifts to their dead owners. In this way, he would appease the spirits of those he had killed and escape the tortures awaiting him.'

'I suppose you worked that out right away.' Feeling a little stupid, Bran resolved not to ask any more questions.

'Alas, no,' said Talus. 'Throughout this whole affair my heels have dragged in the dirt. The years have made me slow, Bran, so slow that I missed my own chance to make right the past.'

'Ah—this is about you and Mishina, isn't it?'

'Are you asking me to tell you my tale now, Bran?'

'You promised you would. "Before we next make landfall," you said.'

Talus put down his paddle and took up station in the prow. The dugout wallowed in the sea's heavy swell, but the outriggers kept it stable. The boat was fast and light, responsive to Bran's every move. He'd already fallen in love with it.

'Indeed I did. But, if I begin, will I be able to finish? It is a long story, Bran. I want to be sure you will still be here for the end.'

'What do you mean?'

'Think back to that night on the clifftop when we first looked down on Creyak. You told me you wanted to turn back. You told me you wanted to go home.'

'I suppose I did.'

'Is that how you feel now?'

'No.'

'Then I will ask you this.' He turned to face Bran. His face was the same gold as the shingle on the beach. 'Do you still wish to come with me to the top of the world, where the northlight touches the snow and many strange things may be possible?'

Bran tried to imagine this faraway place that Talus had described to him so many times before. But all he could conjure was the red glow of Lethriel's hair floating in the darkness of the cave. He thought about the story he'd told her there: a tale of lost love and falling stars. His story.

'More than ever before,' he whispered.

'Then ask me once again the question you asked on the cliff.'

Bran had to think hard. He remembered the dying fire, and the distant screams from the island. He remembered the northlight fading from the sky.

Finally he remembered what he'd said.

'Is it true that love survives death?'

Talus smoothed his scalp with the palm of his hand and gazed at the crisp northern horizon. 'Let us find out.'

AUTHOR'S NOTE

YOU MIGHT BE wondering exactly when and where this story takes place. The clues are there: tools and weapons are made from flint or bone, Creyak resembles the ancient settlement of Skara Brae in the Orkneys, and there's that passing mention of stepped tombs in a distant desert land. All these facts might lead you to deduce we're in the north of Scotland during the late Neolithic, and I'm not going to argue with that. Neither am I going to give you a precise date, because it's not as simple as that.

For one thing, I'm no historian. Sure, I've done my research, but you know how it is: one gust of wind and your carefully collated notes fly across the room. By the time you gather them up, they're all scrambled together. Then again, things look a whole lot more interesting that way. Then there's the simple truth that, when you're looking this far back in the historical record, the main currency is not fact but speculation. Relics made of stone and bone may feel hard to the touch, but the evidence they offer up is fragile and wide open to interpretation.

Today, there are clever people called *knappers* who keep alive the craft of sculpting raw flint to recreate the most beautiful Neolithic tools. Recreating the thoughts inside the Neolithic mind is a different thing altogether.

Thought is made not of stone, but of story. To really understand the humanity of the past, I think you have to put aside the facts and indulge in a little fiction.

It seems inevitable to me that the world's first detective would have been a storyteller. In order to explore motive and method, you need a strong sense of narrative and a keen eye for how people behave. Little wonder Talus has found himself walking this path: his head is full of stories. Some may seem familiar; for instance, if you've any interest in mythology, you might recognise aspects of Talus's tale about the feathered giant in the lake. Others were new even to me, untold until Talus related them to me. Once I'd heard them, I had no choice but to write them down, and wonder if they just might be true. That's what I do, you see. Like Talus, I'm just a teller of tales.

I'd like to thank Jon Oliver and David Moore at Solaris for helping me get this show on the road, in particular for their valuable feedback on the first draft. Thanks to Phil Edwards, Chloe Edwards and Andy Wicks for early readings and essential support, and to Anne Kearl for sorting out my right hand from my left. And thanks to Helen, for love, honesty and belief from start to finish and at all points between.

My final acknowledgement goes to my agent, Dot Lumley, who, to my great sorrow, is no longer with us. She believed in this project from the word go, and found it a home, but never got to hold a printed copy in her hands. Thanks for everything, Dot. We miss you.

Graham Edwards
January 2014

ABOUT THE AUTHOR

Graham Edwards is the author of novels including *Dragoncharm* and *Stone & Sky*. He's also written a number of novels under pseudonym. His short fiction includes the fantasy detective series *The String City Mysteries*. Graham writes regularly about movie visual effects for *Cinefex* magazine.

Find out more at his website and blog:
graham-edwards.com

'A breathtaking thriller set in the dark shadow of the everyday, *Plastic* is a razor sharp parable of modern life.' Jake Arnott

CHRISTOPHER FOWLER

PLASTIC

With a foreword by JOANNE HARRIS

June Cryer is a shopaholic suburban housewife trapped in a lousy marriage. After discovering her husband's infidelity with the flight attendant next door, she loses her home, her husband and her credit rating. But there's a solution: a friend needs a caretaker for a spectacular London high-rise apartment. It's just for the weekend, and there'll be money to spend in a city with every temptation on offer.

Seizing the opportunity to escape, June moves in only to find that there's no electricity and no phone. She must flat-sit until the security system comes back on. When a terrified girl breaks into the flat and June makes the mistake of asking the neighbours for help, she finds herself embroiled in an escalating nightmare, trying to prove that a murderer exists. For the next 24 hours she must survive on the streets without friends or money and solve an impossible crime.

 WWW.SOLARISBOOKS.COM

Follow us on Twitter! www.twitter.com/solarisbooks

IVO STOURTON THE

HAPPIER DEAD

**WHAT WOULD YOU DO FOR
THE CHANCE TO LIVE FOREVER?**

'Stourton is a name to watch' *Publisher's Weekly*

The Great Spa sits on the edge of London, a structure visible from space. The power of Britain on the world stage rests in its monopoly on "The Treatment," a medical procedure which transforms the richest and most powerful into a state of permanent physical youth. The Great Spa is the place where the newly young immortals go to revitalise their aged souls.

In this most secure of facilities, a murder of one of the guests threatens to destabilise the new order, and DCI Oates of the Metropolitan police is called in to investigate. In a single day, Oates must unravel the secrets behind the Treatment and the long-ago disappearance of its creator, passing through a London riven with disorder and corruption.

As a night of widespread rioting takes hold of the city, he moves towards a climax which could lead to the destruction of the Great Spa, his own ruin, and the loss of everything he holds most dear.